366 and more FAIRY TALES

**Retold by
Gianni Padoan**

**Illustrated by
Sandra Smith**

**Translation by
Colin Clark**

ℛℛ
Ravette London

The fairy tale of the month

Cinderella

Once upon a time there was a beautiful, sweet young girl, with blue eyes and long, blonde hair. She was the daughter of a rich merchant who loved her dearly. When her mother died, her father decided his daughter would need a good woman to bring her up and take care of her, and so he married again. Unfortunately, the stepmother turned out to be greedy and selfish, and her two daughters, the stepsisters of the beautiful young girl, were arrogant and envious. Since the merchant often had to travel, the stepmother and stepsisters began to rule the household. The young girl was forced always to dress in rags, dirty from dust and cinders, so much so that everyone soon began to call her 'Cinderella.'

One day, the son of the king, who wished to marry, invited all the young women in the kingdom to a great ball, so that he could meet them and choose a wife. In Cinderella's house, they began to make great preparations: expensive clothes were purchased, different hairstyles were tried, and a selection was made of jewels to wear. Nothing made Cinderella's stepmother and stepsisters happy and she, as usual, served them without a word of complaint. She, too, had been invited to the ball, but her stepmother had refused to take her.

At last, the long-awaited evening arrived: the stepsisters were transformed, each wearing a beautiful dress and covered in jewels. Cinderella felt so unhappy as she watched them depart. She too would have loved to go to the ball, she too would have loved to wear a silk dress! The poor girl couldn't hold back her sobs. She cried so much that the floor was bathed in her tears, but when she raised her eyes. . . . she was face to face with a beautiful lady. It was her fairy godmother.

'Why are you crying, little Cinderella? Do you, too, wish to go to the ball?' the lady asked her.

'The ball is no place for me,' replied Cinderella sadly.

'We'll see about that. Bring me a pumpkin,'

With one touch of her magic wand, the lady changed the pumpkin into a splendid carriage, she changed four mice into horses and a couple of lizards into coachmen in livery.

'Everything is ready,' said her fairy godmother, 'you may go to the ball.'

'But. . . . dressed like this?' said Cinderella, pointing to her rags.

The fairy godmother sighed. 'You're absolutely right.' With a wave of her wand, the rags disappeared and Cinderella found herself wearing a silk dress studded in gold, crystal slippers and precious jewels: only Cinderella's lovely face needed no change, for now she was happy and smiling.

'Now get in and go,' said the fairy godmother. 'But remember, at the first stroke of midnight, you must leave the ball. At that moment, my spell will cease to work: the carriage will again become a pumpkin, the horses will be mice again, and the coachmen will become lizards once more. And you will be the same Cinderella as before, dressed in rags.'

The ball was fabulous. Everyone admired the unknown princess and the prince insisted on dancing with her all evening. Cinderella's heart overflowed with joy.

Then the clock struck the first stroke of midnight. Cinderella did not lose a moment. Still smiling, she ran quickly away. The prince ran after her, but could not catch her. The only trace of her that he found was a little crystal slipper that Cinderella had lost while running down the palace stairs.

At the palace the prince was desolate. He had to find the beautiful girl who was at the ball, the one who had lost her slipper. There was a royal announcement: all the young maidens in the kingdom were to try on the slipper and the prince would marry the girl it fitted perfectly.

The morning after, the court officials began their search, but not one young maiden managed to fit into the extraordinary slipper. Finally, the prince arrived at the merchant's house and both of the stepsisters tried on the slipper. Absolutely useless! It was so small and so delicate that they could not even get their toes into it.

The prince, who was growing ever more sad and despondent, was about to leave when he noticed Cinderella, who was standing shyly in the background.

'And who are you?' he asked.

'Oh, she's only a servant. . . .' replied the stepmother. But the prince looked into Cinderella's eyes and, in great excitement, commanded her to sit down before the chamberlain. She extended her foot.

The slipper was a perfect fit. Immediately, Cinderella was dressed as she was at the ball. The prince asked her to be his wife and the marriage was celebrated that very day. It was a magnificent ceremony, worthy of their great love.

And as regards the stepmother and the stepsisters? The prince might have wanted to punish them for their wickedness, but Cinderella chose to forgive them. She invited them all to come and live with her at the royal palace and, soon after, the two stepsisters married two noble knights of the court. Her stepmother at last realised the error of her ways and became kind and gentle to everyone.

So the story finished with the most beautiful spell of all — they lived happily ever after.

1 The Twelve Passengers

A strange stagecoach drew up just as the bells were chiming midnight. Even though it was the New Year, the sentry rushed out to check on the passengers, twelve in number and all very strange.

The first was well dressed and must have been an important person because everyone else was watching him with an air of hopefulness. He said his name was January and then he darted off, saying that he had thousands of things to think of for the whole year. The second passenger said he knew that his life was short and his days were numbered, just twenty-eight in all, and so he wanted to enjoy himself while he could. His rowdy fun-making annoyed the sentries, but he replied haughtily: 'Don't you know me? I am February, the prince of the Carnival.'

Don March, the third passenger, was thin and moody. The fourth passenger pointed out the sliver of moon to March and told him it was a silver treasure, but this was obviously an April Fool's joke. To make up for it, Madam May sang one of her lovely blossom-time songs.

June and July were both dressed in summer wear and their only belongings were their swimming costumes. Mother August had a basket of fruit and she must have been very rich. She was overweight and perspiring, although she claimed that she loved to go for walks in the countryside.

The ninth passenger, Professor September, was an artist renowned for his method of painting leaves. The tenth, Count October, knew all about agriculture, but his words were constantly drowned out by the sneezes of his neighbour, November, a pallid type with a constant cold.

Grandad December, the last passenger, carried with him the fir tree which at Christmas he planned to decorate with lights and tinsel.

The sentry carefully checked all their passports and then saluted them.

'A very good year to all the Month family,' he said cordially.

---

2 The Queen of Riddles

The queen of Petersburg promised that she would marry anyone who could ask her three riddles she could not answer. Many young men tried to win her hand, but to no avail. Finally, along came Ivan the peasant and he said:

'I saw one good thing with another good thing in it. In order to do good, I took the second good thing out of the first good thing.'

The queen did not know what to say so pretended she had a headache to put off her answer. She got her maidservant to coax the answer out of Ivan. Next day the queen said to Ivan:

'Here is the answer: A horse was in a wheat field and I chased it out.'

Then Ivan put his second riddle:

'On the road I saw a bad thing. I took up a second bad thing and hit it. So one bad thing killed another bad thing.'

Once again, the queen got her maidservant to find out the answer from Ivan. Next day the queen said:

'Here is the answer. I saw a snake on the road and killed it with a stick.'

Then Ivan asked her the third riddle:

'How did you know the answers to the first two riddles?'

The queen did not want to admit that she had found out by cheating.

'I don't know,' she answered. That was how Ivan married the queen.

3 The Town Mouse and the Country Mouse

The town mouse was invited by his friend, a country mouse, to come for a visit. The fresh air was lovely and the hospitality very warm, but for the tastes of the town mouse life in the country was too simple and the food was too plain and not very appetising. The country mouse listened to what his friend had to say and decided to close up his own house and follow the town mouse to the city.

The town mouse's house was small and had no garden, but it was very luxurious; marble floors, mirrors, and paintings on the walls, and a large cupboard, not filled with wheat and hay, but dates, figs, and fruit, not to mention bread, cheese and delicious cakes.

The two friends sat down to dinner and for the country mouse it was a meal fit for a king. But it was also very stressful. From time to time, a cat would come along, or a woman would pass by, or a child, and the two mice would have to run and hide in a hole, with their hearts in their mouths.

After this had gone on for some time, the country mouse could not stand it any more. He was pale and trembling. 'Keep your luxury and your riches,' he said to his friend, packing his case. 'I prefer my own way of life. It may be dull, but it is so much more peaceful than yours.'

4 The Little Goldfish

One day a poor fisherman found in his net a little golden fish, which waved its fins about and moved its mouth, as if to beg him to let it go. The fisherman was so moved that he threw the fish back into the sea, even though, if he had sold it to a goldsmith, he would have earned a considerable sum of money.

'You will see how grateful I am,' called the fish from beside the boat, before disappearing back under the waves, 'but you must never tell anybody what has happened.'

When the fisherman arrived home, he found that his miserable hut had been transformed into a fabulous castle and his wife was wearing a dress fit for a queen.

'Where did all these riches come from?' was the first thing the w... asked, when she saw her husb...d again.

'Do not ask me, my wife, or ...ery-thing will disappear again.'

But the woman would not ...ve her husband a moment's peace, and in the end he told her about the little goldfish. At that very moment, the castle turned back into a hut, and everything was the way it had been before, and the woman remained what she had always been, nosey and dissatisfied.

5 The Fox and the Stork

In order to pay back a debt, the fox had to invite the stork over for dinner, even though he did not really want to. He made a tasty soup, but he served it up in a very shallow dish, and the stork's long beak could hardly manage to get hold of any of it.

Like a true lady, the stork did not complain, and even invited the fox to dinner with her. The stork in her turn cooked a delicious meal, but she served it in a tall narrow goblet that the fox could not even get his nose into. So he did not get anything to eat either. If you play dirty tricks on people, then you must expect to have them played on you as well.

6 The Gifts of the Three Kings

One night, a comet appeared in the sky. All who saw it were surprised and afraid. King Caspar consulted with two other kings who were, like himself, amongst the wisest men in the world, and asked them if they knew the meaning of this strange star. King Balthasaar, while studying old books, discovered an ancient prophecy: the comet was to announce the coming of the Messiah and showed the place where he was to be born. He invited the others to accompany him to pay tribute to the Messiah, and asked them to think of the most suitable gifts to take.

Melchior, who knew that the Messiah was going to be a man, decided to take a jar of myrrh as his offering, because with this he would be able to perfume his body. Caspar, on the other hand, said that the Messiah was Lord of heaven and earth, and he searched far and wide for a gift precious enough for such a powerful king. At last he chose a casket full of gold. Balthasaar believed that the Messiah ought to be worshipped as the Son of God, and he therefore decided to take him frankincense as his gift, the substance that people have always burnt to their gods as a sign of their devotion.

And in the stable at Bethlehem, the gifts of the three kings lay alongside those of the shepherds, whose riches lay in the love they showed.

7 A Happy Family

An old couple of snails lived happily in a wood where they reigned supreme, there being no other snails to dispute their sovereignty; but this was also their greatest heartache — they had absolutely no idea of where they might find a wife for their only son.

'Let us know if you see a beautiful little snail who might be suitable for our young one,' they instructed the flies, who buzzed everywhere in a frantic way, trying to give the impression that they were busy.

One day, at last, a butterfly told them, 'There's a pretty little snail ten minutes' flying time from here. She's a poor orphan but she has all the right qualities.'

'Tell her to come and visit us!'

The pretty little snail set out at once. It took her only eight days to complete the journey, which proved she was of excellent breeding. The marriage was celebrated at the earliest possible moment. The bees made the wedding-cake, and fireflies were in charge of the lighting arrangements; two ants acted as bridesmaids, and the wedding march was performed by the rain on the leaves. The new couple had many little snails and lived happily and long, as did the old couple who still ruled supreme in their wood.

8 The Greedy Dog

One day, a dog stole a big piece of meat and, proud of his own courage, ran off with it held tightly in his jaws. He reached the bank of the river where he looked down and spied another dog with a piece of meat in its mouth, every bit as big as his own. He did not realise that it was merely his own reflection in the water. Feeling full of himself already, he threw himself on the other dog to steal his meat as well. Unfortunately, when he found himself in the water, he had to let go of his own piece of meat to avoid drowning, and so was left with nothing.

9 The Indians of the Enchanted Valley

One autumn, in the valley, a great fire broke out and raged so violently that the Indians of the tribe could not extinguish it. In desperation, they sent a request for help to Man of Ice, a great man of magic who lived in the north. Man of Ice did not answer with a prayer. Instead, he simply removed his crown of feathers from his head, undid his long braids and shook his thick hair. The amazed messengers noticed an unexpected breeze blow across his face. He shook his hair again and it began to rain; then the rain changed to hailstones and then to snow.

The messengers returned to their valley where the fire was still burning. The Indians stared helplessly at the fearful sight from the surrounding hills. They knew what the messengers had seen but were afraid that their request had been made in vain.

A few days later, a strong wind blew up, but it served only to fan the flames still further. The rain which followed only caused damp clouds of vapour to form; but then the hail, which drove the Indians to find shelter far off, put out the flames and, finally, snow fell and covered even the ashes. Slowly the snow melted and when, at the start of spring, the Indians returned to their home, they discovered a beautiful lake where the fire had raged.

10 The Coachman Who Could Paint

John, even though he was in the service of the king himself, was only a coachman, but he loved to paint and had a great talent for art. His paintings seemed so alive that the people in them seemed almost to move. The one John liked most of all, however, was his portrait of Mary, his sister, of whom he was very fond. He kept this painting in his room in the palace stables, and when he felt sad he talked to the picture and sometimes he felt that his sister really did reply.

All this talking made the other servants so curious that they spied on him through the keyhole. The only thing they could see was the face on the painting, which they mistook for the face of a real young woman.

Very soon, people were talking about the indescribable beauty of the mysterious guest whom the young coachman kept hidden in his room. Finally, even the king learnt of this, and he too went to peer through the keyhole. When his eyes fell on Mary's enchanting face, he fell in love at once. When he learnt that this beautiful girl really did exist, John was asked to bring his sister to court, whereupon the king married her at once.

Thus his beloved sister became queen, and John was able to spend all his time painting instead of being a royal coachman.

11 The Man Who Came from the Sky

One day, a man who made his living by tricking people stopped a good woman on the road.

'Who are you?' asked the woman. 'Where do you come from?'

'I fell from the sky,' the man replied craftily.

'Oh really.' The woman's face lit up. 'Then maybe you have met my husband. He died last year.'

'Certainly I know him, but he's not doing too well. He hasn't found a job yet and he hasn't got enough to eat or enough clothes to wear!'

'The poor man!' cried the woman. 'If I give you some clothes, can you take them up to him?'

'No, I'm sorry but it's forbidden to take clothes into paradise,' replied the man. 'I might manage to smuggle some money to him. Nobody would find a little money bag hidden in a pocket.'

'Oh, thank you, then please take this. It's all my savings,' and the woman gave the man a little pile of money. She was so grateful to him for doing her such a kind service.

'Well, who would have thought,' she kept repeating, 'that in paradise my husband would be lacking even the bare necessities.'

12 The Musicians of Bremen

A donkey, who had always worked very hard, one day discovered that his owner was going to sell him to the butcher, so he ran away. He met up with a dog who had been kicked out of his home, because he was too old to flush out game for his master, and the two animals decided to travel together. However, if they hoped to eat, they would have to find a way to earn some money.

'I know how to bray,' said the donkey, 'and you can bark. We could sing in the choir.'

And that was what they decided to do, so they set off towards Bremen, the nearest city, where there was a famous choir. On the way, they were joined by a cat, and then by a cockerel, but when night fell they were still in the forest, a long way from the city. Looking for somewhere to stay, they came across a brightly lit hut.

It was the lair of four fearsome bandits who were preparing a delicious meal that made the animals' mouths water. Then they had a brainwave. The dog climbed on the donkey, the cat climbed on the dog, and the cockerel climbed on top. Then all together, they began to yell. The bandits were certain they were being attacked by a terrible monster, and they ran off as fast as their long legs could carry them, whereupon the four animal friends settled down to enjoy their feast. Then off they went to bed.

In the middle of the night, one of the bandits came back to investigate the monster who had taken over the hut. All of a sudden, two yellow lights appeared and something scratched at him. Something else began screeching up above him. It was the cockerel going 'cock-a-doodle-doo,' but the bandit thought it was the monster calling out. Then the dog bit him with razor sharp teeth, and finally the donkey sent him flying with a kick.

'Flee,' he yelled to his companions who were waiting outside for him. And the story goes that the robbers are still running to this very day.

13 Metabo and Camille

King Metabo was a famous javelin thrower. One day he went out hunting with his young daughter, Camille.

All of a sudden, the king was attacked by a band of enemies. He had to flee from them until he came to a fast flowing river, which he was unable to swim across because of his daughter on his back. It seemed he was lost until he thought of a way out.

Tying his daughter to his javelin, he hurled it with all his strength to the other side of the river; then he dived in himself and swam across to where Camille was. His enemies were so amazed that they gave up the chase.

14 The Stork in the Hen House

There was once a stork who was so tired from its long migratory flight that it crash-landed in a hen house. There the turkey began showing off to the stork and puffed himself up as much as he could. The hens, though, were jealous and made fun of the stork. 'What long legs you have! They really are so ungainly!'

The stork acted as if it had not heard. Instead, it began to tell them all about Africa, where it went often, about the heat of the desert, and the ostriches there. 'What a silly goose,' said the ducks, not understanding one word the stork was saying.

Soon the turkey also grew bored with the visitor and wandered off. Then the ducks and the hens jumped on the intruder, making a terrible noise. Along came the farmer to see what was happening: he opened the hen house door and away flew the stork.

The farmer was very sorry to see the bird go because all the other farmers would have envied him for having a stork. He turned on the hens and said: 'Do you think you are queens just because you are destined to end up in the stock pot?!'

15 The Hole in the Water

A young man who was alone in the world decided to get married. He was handsome and rich, but it seemed that in the whole land there was not the right wife for him: either they were too young, or too old, or already betrothed. There remained just one lovely young maiden, whom he had met at the well, but she seemed to be a bit mad. Not only did she say that her stepmother was a fairy, but she also insisted that her stepmother would only allow her to marry a man who could perform a certain very difficult task. 'What is that?' asked the young man.

'He has to make a hole in the water.'

'That's impossible,' exclaimed the young man. 'You will never find a husband.'

'Yes, I will find one,' replied the young girl. 'My stepmother says that when someone is truly in love, they can even work miracles.'

The young man was truly in love, but he had no idea how to solve the problem. He sighed and suffered for a long time but he did not give up. Then one day he found that the well had frozen over. Suddenly he understood. Seizing a stout stick, he made a hole in the frozen surface. . . . and so he was able to marry the beautiful maiden.

16 The Fly and the Ant

A fly and an ant got into an argument over a silly question as to who had right of way. The fly, which has always been one of the rudest insects, said all sorts of horrible things to the unassuming ant.

'You are such a tiny, insignificant creature,' it said. 'How dare you compare yourself to me, a daughter of the air? I go to the palaces of the greatest lords, and eat out of the plates of bishops. If I choose to, I can even walk about on the crown on the king's head!'

The ant waited patiently for the fly to finish, and then he answered carefully: 'Yes, I know that you can land on heads, but you are not even capable of distinguishing between the head of a king and the head of an ass. Furthermore, it is not as if you are welcomed in palaces. . . . But why am I wasting my time with you when I should be off gathering supplies for the winter? Although ants may be tiny, we are wise, and the cold doesn't kill us. You flies can fly up high. . . . but when the first cold comes, you fall to the ground, along with the dry leaves, and what good to you are your wings then!'

17 Little Henry Forelocks

Once upon a time, there was a queen who gave birth to a beautiful little daughter whom she named Curlylocks. However, her joy was dimmed by the words of a fairy, who appeared to her and said: 'Queen, Curlylocks will grow more and more beautiful and graceful as she grows up, but, I am sorry to say, she will have no spirit to speak of and she will be as dull as she is lovely. Nevertheless, she will have one other gift. She will be able to make the man she falls in love with very handsome.'

Now, in a nearby kingdom there was another queen who had been waiting for a son for many years. Finally, she had one, but he was very unpleasing to look at and he had a little tuft of hair on his head which earned him the nickname 'Little Henry Forelocks.' When his mother looked at him in her arms, she sighed with disappointment. A passing fairy took pity on her and said: 'Don't cry, beautiful queen. Although Little Henry Forelocks is plain, nonetheless he shall be wise and intelligent, and he will have the gift of transmitting his wisdom to the woman he falls in love with.'

Years went past. At the court of Curlylocks, all the young men were attracted by her beauty, but finding that she could not put two sensible words together, they went away again. Gradually Curlylocks became more and more lonely and sad. She would often walk in the woods so that she could weep without anyone seeing her. One day in the woods she met Little Henry Forelocks, who, upon seeing such a beautiful, sad, young woman, asked her to marry him. Henry also explained to her that by marrying him her troubles would be at an end, because he had the gift of transmitting wisdom to the woman he loved.

Curlylocks agreed to his proposal, but Henry gave her a year to consider her decision. The year went by very quickly for Curlylocks. She grew more intelligent by the day, and enchanted all the most handsome young men. As the day drew near for Henry Forelocks's return, she had very mixed feelings.

When Little Henry Forelocks arrived in the throne room, the trumpets blared and the royal guard presented arms. Henry fell to his knees before Curlylocks, who kept her eyes lowered. Imagine her surprise when she raised her head and saw before her a handsome young man.

'Thank you,' said Henry. 'Thank you, Curlylocks. The love that was born in your heart for me one year ago broke the spell which made me so plain, just like my love for you broke the spell which made you so dull. Come, Curlylocks, let us celebrate our wedding.'

18 The Frightened Cake

Once there was a mother who was always baking cakes for her children. One day she prepared a cake with so much love that when she took it out of the oven, even her spoilt children's mouths watered.

'Dear mother, kind mother,' her greedy and impatient children begged her, 'hurry up and give us a slice.'

'Wait until it cools down and you can eat it all,' was the reply.

But when the cake heard the fate that was in store for it, it was terrified. The cake jumped out of the dish, rolled off like a wheel, out of the door, and then disappeared down the road.

19 The Shoemaker Gnomes

A strange event once occurred to a very poor but good-hearted shoemaker. One evening he left his last piece of leather on his workbench, and the next morning he found a perfectly finished pair of shoes. He sold the shoes and bought some more leather which he cut immediately. He did not have time that evening to stitch the pieces and he left them on his workbench again. The next morning the shoes were finished and ready once more.

This went on for some time, until the shoemaker and his wife decided to get to the bottom of the mystery.

They stayed up all night, hidden in the workshop, and they saw two gnomes appear, take the leather, make the shoes and then go away. The shoemaker noticed that the gnomes had no clothes, so he asked his wife the next day to make them some clothes, while he himself made two small pairs of shoes. That night they left the gifts on the same workbench.

The gnomes were very pleased with this kind thought. They put their new clothes on and leapt about with joy. Then they went away and never came back. But the shoemaker never lacked anything after that, and he and his wife lived happily ever after.

20 The Spindle, the Spool and the Needle

All alone in the world, a young girl once lived in a small house in the middle of the woods. She was very poor, but she knew how to sew and, because she was very hard working and clever, she managed to earn her living by using her spindle, her spool and her needle.

One day, looking for a wife, a young prince came to the village asking who was the most beautiful and industrious young girl in the place. Many girls were pointed out to him, the richest and most elegant ones, but nobody thought of the poor young seamstress. Only the objects that she used in her daily work thought of her. The spindle jumped out of her hand and ran off through the woods, pulling a long golden thread behind it. The spool also jumped away, but it stopped outside the door and wove a lovely rug. The needle began to dance wildly in the amazed young girl's fingers, and made tablecloths, curtains and cushions, transforming the poor little house into a pretty and welcoming one.

When the spindle and the golden thread led the prince to her door later, the lovely little seamstress and her pretty house pleased him so much that he never left her side again.

21 The Flowers from the Moon

High in the mountains lived a prince whose great wish was to journey to the moon, because he loved its gentle glow. His dream finally came true. When he reached the moon he discovered its light came from the moon king's beautiful daughter.

The two young people soon fell in love, but the worlds they came from were just too different and soon they had to part. As a sign of her great love, the moon king's daughter gave the prince one of the smooth and lovely flowers that covered the moon like snow and this was how the first alpine flower was brought to earth.

22 The Fox and the Cockerel

A hungry fox was out looking for dinner one day when he came across a plump cockerel. The cockerel, however, was very quick in getting to the safety of a branch high in a tree. The fox pretended that he was hurt by such mistrustful actions.

'Why have you run away?' he complained. 'I only wanted to give you a brotherly embrace.'

'I'm not so stupid as to believe that,' replied the cockerel.

'Ah, so you still haven't heard the news?' said the fox.

'And what exactly should I have heard?' asked the cockerel.

'Peace throughout the world has been proclaimed between all animals,' announced the fox. 'And now that we're all brothers,' he went on, 'come down here so that we can show our love and goodwill.'

'Well, I would never have believed it' said the cockerel, pretending to be absolutely delighted. 'In that case it would, without a doubt, be best of all to wait for that pack of hounds that I can see over there. They'll certainly want to show you their affection.'

The fox looked very uncomfortable. He looked up at the cockerel and said: 'It's not that I'm not telling you the truth, it's just that I can't be sure they've heard the good news yet.' And he ran off as fast as he could.

23 The Little Piggy Bank

The little piggy bank was so full of coins that it did not even rattle when it was shaken. It stood on the highest shelf in the playroom, and it must be said that it looked very handsome indeed, being made of shiny porcelain and painted with little blue flowers.

Because of its great wealth, the piggy bank was much respected by all the other toys. Often, at night, the theatrical puppets would perform just for its pleasure, and the doll spent all her time singing or sighing in the hope that the piggy bank would notice her and ask her to marry it. The little tin soldiers marched endlessly to and fro

in front of the shelves to ensure that no thief ever tried to rob the piggy bank.

One day, however, one of the children of the house tried to push another coin in through the slot on the piggy bank's back, but it was so full already that it simply shattered into thousands of pieces.

Somebody gathered up the coins and swept up the pieces and a new piggy bank was bought to replace the old one. It was still empty and so it did not rattle either, and in this respect it was not so very different from the old one.

24 The Seven Wives of Bluebeard

In a distant town lived a very rich man with a sinister reputation. It was widely known that he had already been married six times and, on account of his beard, which was a fearful blue shade, it was whispered that he was really an ogre. He became known as 'Bluebeard'.

One day another maiden accepted his proposal of marriage, and at first everything seemed to go well. The husband gave every key he had to his new wife. What is more, he told her she could do anything she wished, forbidding her only to open one small room in the house.

This one strange order made the new wife very curious, and one day, as soon as Bluebeard had gone out, she ran to open the door to the little room. . . . She almost died of fright; in the room she found the bodies of the other six wives of Bluebeard. The seventh wife, still shaking with fear, had scarcely closed the door when Bluebeard stomped in.

'Now,' shrieked the ogre, 'you'll go back into that little room, and this time you'll stay there with the other six that you should never have seen.'

But, by good fortune, the seventh wife did not suffer the same fate as the others. At that very moment, her two brothers, who were valiant soldiers, arrived and slew her evil husband, to save her from a horrible end.

25 The Wedding of the Mice

The dream fairy woke up young Johnny. 'Hurry,' she urged, 'there are two mice about to be married underneath the floorboards and we've been invited. It'll be a splendid occasion.'

Even though he was really still asleep, Johnny rose from his bed in an instant. 'I'd love to go,' he said excitedly, 'but how will I ever get down that tiny hole?'

The dream fairy waved her magic wand and Johnny became so small that he was able to put on a uniform that a tin soldier was kind enough to lend him. A thimble was the perfect size for a carriage drawn by a small mouse. The banquet hall was crowded. All the guests were licking the walls, which were made of lard, and the tables were made of slabs of real cheese. The bride and bridegroom were sitting in a hollow dug in a large piece of cheese and were embracing happily. Every so often they threw pumpkin seeds over the guests.

Johnny had a wonderful time, until finally the dream fairy told him that it was time to go home and he was suddenly back in bed, sound asleep as before.

26 The Lazy Girl and the Three Spinning Women

There was once a young girl who was so lazy that one day, in sheer desperation, her mother began to beat her. At that very moment, the queen happened to pass by and, hearing the commotion, she went in to see what was the cause. The mother was so ashamed of the truth of the matter that what she finally said was the exact opposite: 'My daughter insists on working day and night on her spinning wheel, but I can't afford the flax.'

The queen had always been very impressed by people who worked hard, and so she took the young woman to the palace and left her with three huge chambers full of flax. 'When you have spun this flax,' said the queen, 'you shall marry my son.'

The young girl obviously did not even know where to begin. Luckily her three cousins came to her aid, and they were all highly skilled spinners. Unfortunately, as a result of acquiring this skill, one had an enormous foot from constantly working the pedal to make the wheel turn; the second had a thumb which was horribly swollen from twisting the flax, and the third, from constantly wetting the flax, had a grotesquely large bottom lip.

When the queen's son, the prince, saw the three cousins, he at once ordered his wife-to-be never to go near a spinning wheel again.

27 The Great Issumboshi

Issumboshi was a tiny Japanese man who was so small that he was really of no use at all at working in the fields. For this reason, his grandfather decided to send him to the city so that he might learn to become a valiant samurai warrior. As he was leaving, his grandfather gave him a wooden cup as a gift, to use as a boat, his mother gave him two long grains of rice, to use as oars, and his father gave him a pin, to use as a sword.

The journey was full of dangers, especially when you consider that a frog was the size of an elephant next to little Issumboshi. However, the young man soon learnt how to look after himself, and, because of his great courage and intelligence, he arrived at the city safe and sound.

He found the streets deserted; everybody was cowering indoors for fear of a fierce giant who was terrorising the city. Issumboshi did not hesitate for a moment, and strode straight out to face this terrible enemy. Small as he was, he found it easy to avoid the monster's clumsy blows. And he found it just as easy to sink his sword into the huge body, until the giant finally crashed to the ground, in agony from thousands of tiny wounds.

'What a mighty warrior,' shouted onlookers joyfully. Issumboshi felt taller than the giant.

28 The Cockerel and the Weathercock

Fixed to the roof of the farmhouse was one of those metal cocks which show which way the wind is blowing. This weathercock, so high above the other farmyard animals, was in a very good position to crow. Instead, he never made a sound.

The farmyard cockerel, on the other hand, was very proud of his red crest and his loud 'cock-a-doodle-doos'. In fact, he liked boasting so much to the hens and the little chickens that he sometimes told very big lies.

'Cockerels can lay eggs as well, you know,' he said one day to the hens.

'But they only ever lay one egg in their whole lives. Hah, but that one egg contains a dragon which is so terrifying that men die as soon as they set eyes on it. So you see, humans are very scared of us, and the real masters of the world are us cockerels, not men at all.'

Naturally the weathercock heard every word of this. He merely snorted. He had seen so many things and heard so many empty words in his long life that nothing surprised him anymore. He knew very well that the cockerel's boasts were nothing but hot air, but he felt so superior that he did not even bother to contradict him.

And, in the end, whether the cockerel or the weathercock was more important is a difficult question.

29 The Lute-Playing Queen

During the Crusades, the tsar was taken prisoner by the Turks. He wrote at once to his wife, asking her to pay the ransom demanded for his freedom, but he heard nothing.

One day, sometime later, a lute-player arrived at the sultan's palace. He played so brilliantly that the sultan insisted he stay at the palace as a guest, and finally offered him anything in his kingdom as payment. The lute-player asked to take away the tsar as his slave, and the sultan kept his promise.

They journeyed a long way, and when at last they were near the capital city of the whole of Russia, the lute-player suddenly freed his new slave and, without saying another word, disappeared.

At court, the unexpected return of the tsar caused great joy and excitement. The only unhappy aspect was that the tsar refused to see his wife. 'She didn't even bother to pay the ransom to free me from captivity,' he sighed.

The tsar was about to condemn his uncaring queen to death, when he heard the gentle strains of a lute and the mysterious musician reappeared. At last, the tsar recognised his queen in her disguise, and realised that her cunning had freed him. Thus it was a day of great rejoicing for everyone.

30 The Lucky Snowdrop

Somehow a ray of sunlight penetrated the snow on the ground and the flower, hidden underneath, thought that the spring had come. It stretched up, lengthening its stem as far as it could, and made a little hole in the icy roof, so that it could peek out at the world.

Oh dear! It had made a terrible mistake. It was still winter. Everyone laughed at the silly snowdrop, which would have died from the cold if a little boy had not picked it and taken it home. The snowdrop was put in a vase of water in a warm room, and it felt like a king.

Not long after, the little boy's big sister took the flower from the vase and put it in an envelope with a letter. The snowdrop could not read, but it somehow knew that the words in the letter were beautiful. After a long and uncomfortable journey in a bag with other letters and packages, the snowdrop found itself lifted gently out of the envelope by a young man who put the flower to his lips and gave it a loving kiss.

The young man became a great poet who remembered the lovely snowdrop in his poems, and it became famous. So, even though it might have been rather silly, it was still a lucky snowdrop.

31 The Wolf and the Shepherd

A certain wolf got into the habit of following a flock of sheep without ever attacking any of them. As a result, after some time the shepherd began to think of the wolf as more of a guardian than an enemy. One day the shepherd had to go to the city on business, and it seemed natural for him to leave his flock in the care of the wolf. When he returned that evening, every single one of his sheep had been killed. The shepherd thought long and hard over what had happened, and, in the end, realised that it was completely his own fault: whoever puts his faith in wicked friends should expect no better.

Contents

The fairy tale of the month: Cinderella
Charles Perrault

The fairy tale of the month

Snow White
and the Seven Dwarfs

The princess was a very pretty little girl: her hair was jet black, her cheeks pink and her skin was white as snow, and for this she had been named Snow White. Unfortunately the queen died and the little girl, who was growing more and more beautiful, became motherless. So the king decided to remarry, because every king needs a queen and every little girl needs a mother.

The king's second wife was the loveliest woman in all the kingdom, but she was also so vain that she could not bear the idea that there might be somebody more beautiful than she in all the world. She had studied the magical arts, and she had a bewitched mirror of which she always asked the same question:

'Mirror, mirror on the wall, who's the fairest of them all?'

And each time the mirror assured her that it was she, until one day the answer was different:

'Before, oh queen, it was you, but now Snow White is much more beautiful than you.'

The queen, whose name was Grimilda, shook with humiliation and hate for her stepdaughter, who had indeed, over the years, become a young woman of incredible beauty. Her hatred was so great that she ordered one of her servants to kill the princess: but the good man could not bring himself to commit such a crime, even to obey the orders of his queen. He told Snow White to run away and begged her to go so far that the queen would never discover that she was still alive.

The young girl was very afraid, and she ran and ran through the woods until she came across a pretty little cottage. Nobody was home. Inside, everything was small; the tables and chairs, the fireplace, everything. Even the beds were so small that Snow White, who was worn out from running through the forest, had to put them all together - and there were seven - to be able to lie down and go to sleep on them. When she awoke she found herself surrounded by seven friendly dwarfs, the owners of the little house. They listened with concern and amazement to the girl's story, and then told her she was welcome to stay with them forever. Every day they went off to work, and she stayed at home to tidy up the house, and every day they gave her stern words of advice, because they knew that sooner or later the evil queen Grimilda would find out where she was.

In fact, the witch found out from the mirror that Snow White was hiding in the woods. She dressed up as an old tinker woman and set off to find her. When she reached the little cottage, she offered Snow White a beautiful belt and put it on for her herself; but she pulled it so tight that the poor girl fainted. Luckily, the dwarfs came home just in time to save her.

Grimilda thought that she had killed her stepdaughter, but the mirror informed her that her wicked plan had failed. So she locked herself away in the highest tower of the castle, where she practised her witchcraft and studied her magic books until she found a spell that could not fail. She dressed up as a travelling tinker woman again, and made her way back to the little house in the woods. This time Snow White had been warned by the dwarfs, and so she did not let the woman into the house. She examined her wares through the window and she was tempted by a beautiful comb. As soon as she passed it through her hair, she fell senseless to the ground and the witch made off.

However, the dwarfs were concerned about Snow White, and so from time to time one of them ran home to make sure that everything was all right. And so Snow White was saved in time once more.

The magic mirror gave Snow White away again and Grimilda prepared an even more powerful spell. She returned to the little house dressed as an old peasant woman and offered the young girl one of the juicy red and yellow apples in her basket. Snow White did not trust her and refused to take even a bite from the apples. The witch had foreseen this and so she had put the powerful poison only in the yellow part of the apples. She took a bite from the red part to show that the fruit was not poisoned, and then she offered the young girl the yellow part through the window. Snow White took a bite from it and collapsed on the ground.

This time not even the dwarfs could do anything to help; the girl was dead, even if she only appeared to be sleeping.

They placed her in a crystal casket and took her to a clearing in the forest, so that they could come and look at their dear, dead friend every time they wanted to.

One day, when they went to see Snow White, they found, beside her coffin, a prince who was lost in the woods.

He was captivated by the beauty of the young girl, and when the dwarfs told him the sad story of Snow White he was so moved that he fainted.

He fell on the crystal casket which smashed into pieces; Snow White's body was so shaken about that the piece of poisoned apple fell out of her mouth. Immediately, the spell was broken and Snow White came back to life.

Imagine the happiness of the dwarfs when Snow White and the prince were married.

The queen Grimilda had to come to accept that she was not the most beautiful in the kingdom.

However, she smashed the magic mirror into a thousand pieces so that she would not have to hear it said every day.

1 The Magic Fish Bone

Once upon a time there was a man who had twelve children, but was not able to give them enough to eat. Alice, the obedient and hard working eldest daughter, became very thin, and it was, perhaps, for this reason that the Sea Fairy took pity on her and brought her a gift of a sardine, telling her to be sure to keep the bone after she had eaten the fish. 'It is a magic fish bone,' the Sea Fairy told Alice, 'and it will grant you one wish, but only one. So be sure to use it wisely.'

Alice was tempted on many occasions to use her magic fish bone; when one of her brothers was ill; when her sister was lost; but she always managed to put things right by herself, without resorting to the magic.

One day, however, Alice found her father in desperate poverty: he had no money left at all. 'Is there no way to find any money?' she asked, worriedly. 'No, I have already done everything possible!' her father replied, sadly. 'Well, then, if there really is no other answer. . . .,' and the young girl put her hand in her pocket and stroked the fish bone.

The Sea Fairy appeared and at once set about resolving all their problems: she even managed to find a handsome young man who married Alice, so that she never again felt the need to use the services of a magic fish bone!

2 The Lazy Threesome

An old king, with death approaching, remembered that he had not yet decided to which of his three sons he would leave his kingdom. As he thought about this, he realised that there was only one thing which they knew how to do well, and that was nothing! So he decided he would leave his throne to the son who was best of all at doing nothing. He called the three princes to him and began to question them.

'I am so lazy,' said the first, 'that if a grain of dust lands in my eye while I am falling asleep, rather than go to the effort of getting it out, I prefer to forget about sleeping and remain all night with my eyes open.'

'Ah, but if I,' said the second prince, 'should sit near the fire to warm myself, why, rather than tax myself by moving my feet, I let them get burnt by the flames.'

'I am so lazy,' boasted the third prince at this point, 'that if I were being hung and I was given a knife to cut the rope, I would let myself strangle to death, rather than make the effort of raising my hand.'

'That really is astonishing!' thought the old king. 'You couldn't get lazier than that! The throne is yours!' he said, turning to the third and laziest of the three princes.

3 The Boy Who Fell into the Water

A boy was playing on the riverbank, when he slipped and fell into the water. He succeeded in grabbing hold of a log and began to shout for help.

A man happened by. He was the kind of man who believes he has wisdom to share, and rather than helping the boy out of the water, he began to preach to him: 'You shouldn't play near water! You should have watched where you were putting your feet.'

This went on for a while, and the boy heard many wise and useful words, but he would have preferred to be saved without the lectures!

4 The Jumping Competition

A cricket, a frog, and a kangaroo challenged each other to see who could jump the highest.

The competition caused a great stir and excitement. From all over the world there arrived knights and ladies, dukes and duchesses, and counts and countesses. And, since such a grand occasion required a suitable prize, the king promised the hand of his daughter in marriage to the winner.

The court had never been so crowded. The competitors marched between two lines of drummers, trumpeters and flags. There were ceremonies and speeches, until, at last, it came to the moment for the three athletes to prove themselves.

To tell the truth, it was the cricket who jumped the highest; but he jumped so high that nobody could see him and the judges ruled that he never left the ground.

The frog jumped less than half as high, but he was bigger and at least everybody could see him.

The frog, however, had the serious misfortune to land on the king's head and was disqualified at once for disrespect.

The kangaroo jumped hardly any distance at all, but was intelligent enough to land in the arms of the princess, and thus the prize went to the competitor who had the best sense rather than to the highest jumper.

5 Birdchild and the Witch

One day, on his round of inspection, a wizard, who worked as a gamekeeper, came across a newborn child, which had been stolen from the cradle by an eagle. The wizard gamekeeper gathered the child in his arms and took it home, where he brought the baby up alongside his own daughter, Lena, who also knew a bit of magic.

The eagle, however, was really a witch and wanted to find the little boy again, because she planned to eat him. She searched high and low until she found him. Then she transformed herself into an old woman and persuaded the gamekeeper to employ her as a housekeeper.

Fortunately, Lena discovered the plan of the old witch, and fled with Birdchild (for this was what she called the baby her father had found). As soon as the witch realised what had happened, she flew off, disguised as an eagle, in pursuit. Lena then called on her own magic powers, and turned the little boy into a pool of water and herself into a duck.

The witch, however, still recognised Birdchild, and she bent down by the pool to gulp up the water. But Lena grabbed the eagle with her beak, and pulled the witch into the pool where she drowned. The two children returned home and were never again troubled.

6 The Pig and His Way of Life

The pig lived in the way that pigs always live and would never have worried about it at all, if it was not for the continuous taunts of the cow. 'What a lovely life you've got!' his companion would sneer. 'Leftovers for lunch and muck for a bed!' In the end, even the pig himself was convinced that he could not go on living this way and he went to see the judge.

'All the other animals on the farm get good food and they have clean stalls', he said. 'Why can't I enjoy a better standard of living as well?' 'You're right!' declared the judge.

'From now on, they must give you grain and peas for dinner, and you must have silk sheets on your bed.' The pig rushed home to his sty, impatient to give the good news to his wife. 'Grain, peas and silken sheets!' he repeated to himself happily all the way home.

But the cow, however, had taunted him so many times with 'leftovers and muck', that the words had become fixed in his mind. Thus, when his wife asked him what the judge had decided their way of life should be, he replied automatically: 'It went perfectly. From this day on we shall dine on leftovers and we shall sleep on muck!'

7 Beloved Orlando and the Magic Flower

Orlando was engaged to be married to a young girl. One day, this girl discovered that her stepmother, an evil witch, was planning to kill her. To save her life, she fled with her beloved Orlando. Firstly, however, Orlando stole the witch's magic wand.

When the wicked stepmother learnt of their escape, she put on her seven league boots and caught up with the two young people in no time at all. They heard her coming and Orlando waved the magic wand, transforming the girl into a flower, and himself into a violin.

But the witch realised that the beautiful flower was her stepdaughter and was about to pick it, when the violin began to play. Because it was a magic violin, the witch could not prevent herself from dancing faster and faster, until, at last, she fell down from exhaustion. Before she expired, however, she caused Orlando to lose his memory. So, when the effect of the magic wore off, and the violin became Orlando again, he no longer remembered that the flower was his love and he went away, leaving it where it was.

The red flower was later picked by a shepherd, who took it home and put it in a vase. From that day on, when the shepherd came home each evening from the pasture, he found the house in perfect order. He soon realised that there was magic at work, and so, one day, he pretended to leave as normal, but hid himself instead in the wardrobe. And so he discovered that it was the flower which was working the magic. Immediately, the shepherd recited a spell which he himself had learnt from a magician, and the flower changed back into the beautiful young maiden again.

Later, the young women in the country were invited to sing at a celebration for the new prince, who was none other than the maiden's beloved Orlando. The voice of his beloved brought back his memory, and Orlando recognised her at once and insisted on marrying her that very day, with the good shepherd as the best man.

8 The Hare Who Got Married

A young hare seemed unusually happy so the fox asked him why.

'I'm married,' replied the hare.

'Congratulations! What good luck,' said the fox.

'Not really good luck: she is old and as ugly as a witch!'

'Oh what bad luck!' cried the fox.

'Not really bad luck: for she gave me a beautiful house as a gift. . . .'

'What luck!'

'Not really luck,' the hare went on, 'the house has burnt down!'

'What bad luck!' said the fox.

'Not really bad luck, for my old and ugly wife was inside at the time!'

9 The Charlatan, the King and the Ass

A charlatan once boasted that he was able, thanks to certain magic potions that he had invented, to make even an ass as wise as any doctor. The king overheard him and, in order to teach him the lesson he deserved, he pretended to take him at his word.

'Take that man to the stables and give him an ass,' the king ordered. 'Pay him good money for the next ten years, but if, at the end of that time, the ass is not able to read and to count then the man will be hung!'

The sentence seemed just and wise and amused the courtiers. 'It will be something worth seeing,' one of them laughed at the charlatan, 'when you're swinging on the gallows.' 'Wait and see,' replied the charlatan, who was certainly not stupid. 'It is almost certain that somebody must die over a ten year period. Who knows if it will be me or you, the king, or the ass? And another thing – if things were to go badly for me, you will be amused on the day I hang; but I will have ten full years, in the meantime, enjoying myself watching you work every day to earn your money, whilst mine will be given to me for doing nothing!'

10 The Dragon and the Gypsy

A gypsy came upon a town deserted, save for a solitary peasant from whom the gypsy learnt what had happened. The town had been cursed with a dragon which came every day to eat someone. Since, the peasant said, there was now nobody else left, the dragon would come next day to eat him, and the day after, the gypsy.

The gypsy was not frightened and remained. The next morning, he heard a great rumble of thunder and the earth began to shake: the dragon was arriving. Despite the difference in size, the gypsy marched out to meet the dragon and challenged him. 'Eat me if you want, but you won't be able to chew me. You will have to swallow me whole, and when I'm down in your stomach, I will tear you apart and you will die.'

The dragon began to laugh. 'You really think you are that tough? Let's see how strong you are.' The dragon picked up a rock and squeezed it so hard that it crumbled to dust.

'Oh, that's nothing!' the gypsy shrugged. 'I'm so strong that I can squeeze water out of stones!' And the clever gypsy, instead of picking up a rock, lifted up a cheese he had hidden on the ground, and he squeezed out all of the whey. The dragon was so dismayed by the gypsy's strength that he ran off and never returned.

11 The Lion, the Wolf and the Fox

The lion was near to death and all the other animals tried to fawn on him, hoping to be named as his heir. The wolf tried to discredit the fox by telling the lion that the fox had not even been bothered to visit the king. The fox arrived at just the right moment to overhear this.

'Who could love you more than me?' the fox asked the lion. 'For I have been all around the world, in search of the miraculous cure I bring you!'

'And what is it?' asked the lion.

'If you want to get well again, skin a live wolf,' replied the fox, 'and wrap yourself in the fur while it is still warm!'

12 The Wandering Peas

The peas thought the whole world consisted of the pod which contained them. They were very surprised when their shell opened and they discovered so many new things.

'Now what will happen to us?' they asked each other worriedly.

It was their fate to become ammunition for a little boy's peashooter. They were fired a great distance, one after the other, and they never saw each other again.

One of the peas landed in a crack in a window frame, where it became covered by moss. Beyond the window, in the room, there was a very sick little girl, who, it seemed, did not have the strength to either live or die. Her family thought it was a miracle that she had actually survived the winter. . . . and, in the meantime, spring had arrived.

One lovely day, looking up from her bed, the little girl noticed a tiny plant growing on the windowsill. She gave an exclamation of pleasure and surprise. Her mother moved her bed right beneath the window, so that the sick child could see the plant more easily. A few days later, the sunshine caused the little pea to flower, and the little girl found she had enough strength to get out of bed and stroke the petals: she had begun to recover!

13 The Card Player

Once upon a time, there was a man who was always playing cards and, because he was clever, lucky and cheated just a little, he always won. The men, who had been reduced to poverty by him, denounced him when they got to heaven, and St Peter sent Death to take him. But St Peter waited and waited, and neither the card player nor any other soul arrived.

So St Peter sent down an Angel, who discovered that Death had been tempted into playing cards. Death kept losing but, in the hope of recouping his losses, remained at the card table, and thus not another soul had passed away. The card player tried to persuade the Angel to play, but, being an Angel, he could not be tempted. So the trickster had to resign himself at last to dying.

As soon as he had died, however, he began to play cards with Lucifer and won all his devils from him. The card player ordered all of his new servants to climb one on top of the other, and on this novel stairway he clambered up to paradise.

For a while, St Peter let the card player be; then, finally, when he won the haloes from a couple of saints, he threw him down. On landing, his soul flew into pieces and each tiny bit landed in the soul of another card player, taking him over for ever.

14 The Lover's Flower

The daughter of the king lost her power of speech when she was very young, and from then on she was always sad and silent. Her only pleasure lay in looking after the flowers in the royal garden.

One evening, a strange flower appeared amidst all the others. From its very first appearance, the young woman looked after it with care. She would stand in front of it for hours and hours, and, impossible as it may seem, it appeared that she was talking to the flower, and even making gestures as if she were astonished by what the flower was saying to her. At last, the king was sure that his daughter was bewitched, and he uprooted the flower and dashed it to the ground.

The shock returned to the princess the lost power of speech.

At the sound of her voice, the flower was changed back into a prince, who then explained to the king what had happened. In order to be always near the silent princess, the prince had asked a fairy to change him into a flower, with a voice that only the princess could hear, and which, in turn, was the only one to hear the silent voice of the princess.

That day was the 14th of February, and it is for this very reason that Saint Valentine's Day became the feast of all those who love each other.

15 The Pigkeeper

A prince, who desired the hand of a princess in marriage, sent her the most beautiful gifts he could find – a rose and a nightingale. Everyone, including the king, was enchanted by the gifts; only the princess turned her lovely nose up at them.

'This is a real rose, it is not even made of silver! And the nightingale is flesh and blood, not even mechanical!'

The prince was thus refused, but he did not give up. He disguised himself and took the job of pigkeeper at the palace. In his free time, he made strange little trinkets to attract the attention of the princess.

On one occasion, he made a pot with little bells which tinkled when the water boiled. The princess wanted to buy it at any price, and she was told she could have it only in exchange for a kiss. The princess accepted the pigkeeper's offer.

But the king came across the princess just as she was kissing the pigkeeper and there was a terrible scandal.

The pigkeeper then revealed that he was in fact a prince, at which the princess sought to make matters right by marrying him; but this time it was his turn to refuse her.

'For a rose and a nightingale, you refused a prince, but for a trinket you kissed a pigkeeper! So I now say that you can keep the pot and remain unmarried!'

16 Chichibio, the Cook, and the Crane

A wealthy hunter killed a crane and sent it to his cook to have it roasted. The bird was so plump and appetising that Chichibio, the cook, could not resist the temptation to cut off a leg and eat it.

When the roast came to be served at the duke's table, the duke noticed that the crane had only one leg and, in a severe voice, demanded an explanation from the cook.

'All cranes,' Chichibio had the nerve to say, 'have only one leg.'

'Really?' said his master. 'Then tomorrow we shall go together to the pond to see. If it turns out that you have tried to deceive me, you will be very sorry indeed.'

The next morning, the cranes in the pond, like all of their kind, were sleeping balanced on one leg only.

'What did I tell you?' said the cook with a sly smile.

The duke clapped his hands and the frightened cranes immediately dropped their other legs to the ground in order to flee.

'That's not fair!' protested Chichibio. 'You didn't clap your hands last night. If you had done that, then even the roast crane would have pulled out its other leg!'

17 The Fox and the Wolf

A wolf had taken a fox as his servant. The poor fox had had enough of her master, but since the wolf was so much stronger than she was, she had no choice other than to serve him.

'Go and get me something to eat,' the wolf kept saying. 'Otherwise I shall eat you.'

On one occasion, the fox went to steal a lamb from the nearby farm, and, on another, to steal the cakes from the kitchen window ledge, and she always managed this without being seen. Everything would have been fine, if the wolf, greedy and careless as he was, had not himself gone to steal the other lamb and the rest of the cakes. He ended up being beaten with a stick, coming home empty handed and getting angry with the fox.

One day, the wolf said yet again, 'Fox, go and get me something to eat or I will eat you!' 'I know of a farmer's storeroom which is full of goodies! Sausages, hams, cheeses! I will show you,' replied the fox.

'Fine,' said the wolf, 'but this time you're coming with me! I don't want any more nasty surprises.' Off they both went, and, slipping through a small hole, they got into the farmer's storeroom. The wolf threw himself greedily at the food. The fox, on the other hand, ran to the hole before every mouthful, to be certain that she could escape if danger threatened. 'Why are you wasting all this time instead of eating?' the wolf laughed at her. 'I'm not leaving here until I have eaten everything!'

At that moment, the farmer, who had been disturbed by the noises, came into the storeroom with a stick. The fox, who was as thin as before, slipped quickly out of the hole and escaped. The wolf, on the other hand, with his stomach bloated, could not squeeze through and had to suffer a beating yet again.

18 The Sun and the Moon

In the distant past, the moon used to be as bright as the sun.

This meant that mankind could not tell day from night, as it was always light.

There were all kinds of problems; people never knew when it was time to get up or when it was time to go to bed.

The Lord realised what was happening, and at once ordered the Archangel Gabriel to spread his wings and veil the light of the moon.

And thus, the marks, which we see on the surface of the moon, are scratches made by the angel's long wings.

19 Mavis and the Robin Redbreast

A blacksmith had two daughters: the older, who was proud and beautiful, was named Regina, and the younger, who loved singing more than anything, was named Mavis.

The father had a soft spot for his older daughter. He was in the habit of telling everybody that he would not give her in marriage to anyone less than a king, whilst he would give Mavis to the first man who asked for her hand.

Mavis was not upset by this. She had found a friend, a robin redbreast, and with him she sang beautiful duets.

'Mavis has found a husband!' her sister would taunt and laugh at her.

And it turned out to be true. One day, a young man came to the smithy and asked for Mavis as his wife. Her father gave his consent at once. Then it was Regina's turn. Her suitor was dressed as a peasant, but since everyone called him Prince, the father did not doubt for a moment that this was the son of the king in disguise, come from afar to marry his Regina.

But how great was his surprise, when he discovered that Prince was only the man's name, not his title, and that the husband of Mavis was really Prince Robin, the king's first cousin!

20 The Dragon with a Hundred Heads

A knight, on his way through a deep wood, suddenly spied a monstrous dragon in the thick of the forest. He was a very brave man and had often fought and defeated dozens of even bigger dragons. But this particular dragon had one hundred long necks, as many heads, and the same number of terrible, gaping jaws!

It would have been easy for the knight to have defeated a dragon with three heads, or even seven, but a hundred! He decided he had no choice but to flee. He was wrong in his judgement. It was because of its tangle of necks that the dragon would never have been able to get free from the thick undergrowth. It could, therefore, have been easily defeated.

A little later, the knight spied a second dragon in the thickets before him. This time the dragon had only one head, and thus the knight approached it fearlessly, sword in hand. But, although this dragon had only one head, it had one hundred legs, and in moments it rushed so quickly through the thicket, that it caught the reckless knight and made mincemeat of him.

This story shows that it is better to have a hundred legs that obey you, than a hundred heads to give orders.

21 Why the Bear Has a Stunted Tail

One day, when the bear still had a tail, he met with a fox carrying a load of fish.

The fox had stolen them, but he said he had caught them. 'It's easy,' he told the bear, 'all you have to do is make a hole in the ice and stick your tail in it. The fish come to bite it and they get stuck onto it.'

The bear decided to try it. In spite of the freezing cold he kept his tail in the hole for so long that the ice closed around it and imprisoned him. He had to pull so hard to free himself that his tail came clean away. . . . and it has never grown back again.

22 Adrian and the Magic Stone

Adrian was a painter, but he was also rather simple. His friends, Paul and Chris, who were also artists, always made him the target of their jokes.

One day they invited him to go along a riverbank with them and look for a magic stone which, they said, held the power to make whoever possessed it invisible.

'But how will we recognise it?' asked Adrian.

'It's a black stone,' replied Chris. 'We'll gather up all the black stones until one of us becomes invisible.'

Adrian wanted to be the one to find the magic stone, and so he gathered up as many black ones as he could find.

At a certain moment, his two friends pretended that they could not see him anymore:

'Where's Adrian gone?'
'He was here a minute ago.'
'He must have gone home.'

When Adrian heard his friends, he was sure he had found the magic stone and he happily began to run away, so as not to have to share his good luck with anyone else. . . . while his friends hurled rocks after him pretending they were just having a throwing competition.

23 The Little Bird That Cannot Sing

Once upon a time, there was a poor shoemaker who had a daughter he loved very much: it was enough for him to see her and he would burst into happy song. His daughter, however, was dumb, and so their friends called her 'the little bird that cannot sing'.

One day, the king's son became ill, and a fairy told him that he could only be cured by the little bird that cannot sing. Nobody knew what kind of bird this might be, but messengers were sent throughout the kingdom to find it. The news reached the shoemaker and he took his daughter to the palace. But when the king saw not a bird, but only a dumb girl, he had both the shoemaker and his daughter put into prison.

At this very time, in the prince's room, on his sick bed, he was heard to murmur: 'They have put the little bird that cannot sing in a cage.' While in prison, for the first time, the dumb girl burst into this song: 'Little bird that cannot sing, you will fly up on high. You'll make your nest at the top of the tallest tree, and you will never be silent anymore.' As soon as the king heard of this, he sent for the young girl and her father. The prince became well again and the couple were married and lived happily ever after.

24 Rapunzel and the Prince

A wicked ogre once kidnapped a young girl, but because he was very short-sighted and rather stupid, he thought she was an apricot and he put her up in the hayloft to ripen at the top of a tall tower. Every evening he would go up to see if his apricot was ready to eat, and each time he decided to wait for another day, so that it would be softer and more plump. In this way, the days turned into years and the girl, Rapunzel, turned into a beautiful young woman with long golden hair.

There were no stairs to the tower, and when the ogre wanted to come up, he would shout from below: 'Rapunzel, Rapunzel, let down your hair.'

Then the young woman would let fall her hair, and the ogre would climb up it as if it was a golden rope ladder.

This strange sight was brought to the attention of the king's son, who became curious to meet the owner of this beautiful pony tail. One evening, he too shouted: 'Rapunzel, Rapunzel, let down your hair.'

The prisoner thought it was the ogre and obeyed: but this time it was the prince who climbed into the tower. As soon as he saw the girl he fell in love: Rapunzel, who had never seen anyone but the ogre in her whole life, was also smitten with love for the handsome young prince. The couple planned to make their escape and get married; but Rapunzel could not climb down on her own hair, and thus had no way of getting to the ground.

'I'll come back every evening,' said the prince, 'and each time I'll bring you some silk with which you can weave a real ladder, and when it's long enough we'll escape.'

Unfortunately, the ogre discovered their plans. With a spell, he caused the prince to become blind. Then he took Rapunzel out into the middle of a desert, where he left her to her fate. And there, the young girl, convinced she had lost her loved one, sat down and wept.

Though unable to see, the prince would not give up Rapunzel. He began to wander through mountains and valleys. Each time he heard the sobs of a young woman in the distance, he would make his way towards the sound. At last, after a long period of suffering, the two lovers were reunited. As soon as Rapunzel's tears fell on the prince's eyes, his sight was magically restored: so the two lovers returned to the palace where they were married and lived happily ever after.

25 The Notebook Imp

The clock finished sounding midnight, and, as it did, all the things in the dark and silent playroom came to life. Even the notebooks in Andrew's satchel, ready for school the next morning, and the words which were written in them, began to move about.

The imp, who was in charge of the notebook, took one look at what had happened to the letters written on the lines and he clasped his hands in despair. The words would not keep still, and no two were similar any longer. Some of the letters had grown tall and thin, and some were so fat that they rolled all over the page. Some seemed to be standing on their tiptoes, and others appeared to be sitting down and having a rest. And then there were some that stretched to the left, and some that leaned way over to the right.

What a disaster! Andrew's handwriting was already a mess because he had made the mistake of writing too quickly; even without these goings on, he had a problem writing clearly!

The imp lost his temper. 'Halt!' he shouted. 'Now, on parade! I'll drill some discipline into you. Hup-two-three! Hup-two-three!'

And the imp made the poor letters do so many exercises, that they all became straight and strong, and clear and tidy, in spite of themselves.

26 The Crystal Ball

Once upon a time, a ship carrying a precious crystal ball as a gift to the emperor of Japan was caught in a terrible storm, and sank to the bottom of the sea. When the emperor heard of this, he sent his best divers to the place to try and find the crystal ball, but to no avail.

Then along came a small slender woman with her child in her arms, who asked if she could try as well. It seemed impossible that she could succeed where the bravest divers had failed, but she explained that if she managed to earn the reward, she could make her son, Kamatari, into a samurai. She was granted permission to make the attempt; so she tied a rope to herself and dived into the sea. She went down to the very bottom, where the dragon's palace is, and there, just as she had foreseen, was the crystal ball, stolen by the lords of the deep. The woman seized it and began to swim back up, when she was attacked by the most terrible sea monsters. With her dagger, she fought them all, refusing, despite many wounds, to let the crystal ball out of her hand, and there it was found when she was finally pulled onto the ship.

When the emperor received the crystal ball, he kept the promise he had made to the heroic mother, and that was how Kamatari became a brave samurai.

27 The Mountain of the Elves

That evening, on the Mountain of the Elves, there was a great feast in honour of the rich and powerful Gnome of the North. He had recently lost his own wife and had thus decided to find wives for his two sons, whom he had brought with him, so they could choose from the seven daughters of the King of the Elves.

The Gnome of the North, with his crown of icicles and pine needles, was kind and pleasant, but his sons were arrogant and rude. The seven daughters did not like them at all, but the Gnome of the North was too important for them to be able to refuse. In fact, the gnome didn't particularly care for the young girls either. Though they were beautiful and knew how to do many strange things, like becoming invisible or imitating the shadows, they knew nothing about how to keep a house and make it a happy and peaceful place.

But the youngest of the seven sisters had not yet learnt any special magic. All she knew how to do was to sing and tell endless wonderful stories. When the wise Gnome of the North heard her, his doubts were set aside; she was the ideal wife. But not for any of his sons. He asked for the daughter of the King of the Elves for himself.

28 The Magic Tinderbox

Once upon a time, as he returned from war, a brave soldier encountered a witch. 'Would you like to be rich?' she asked him. The soldier did not stop to think twice. He followed the instructions of the witch to the letter and soon found himself going down into a deep cavern, where there was a chest full of treasure. It was guarded by a horribly fierce dog, but the witch had taught the soldier the spell which allowed him to order the dog to do his will. The soldier filled his pockets and his knapsack with treasure, and before he left he also picked up the old tinderbox, which the witch's grand-mother had lost long before. The witch had promised the soldier that the only treasure she wanted was the old tinderbox.

Fortunately, the soldier was no fool, and before a wicked spell could be cast on him, he killed the evil witch. And so he kept the tinderbox as well, although he did not really know what to do with it. Now, however, that he was a rich man, he moved to the city and lived there like a lord.

One night, the streets of the city were so dark that the soldier could not see where he was going. He remembered his tinderbox, and struck it to see the way ahead. Immediately, the fierce dog from the cavern appeared, ready to obey the soldier's every order, and to satisfy his every desire. Whenever he wanted anything, the soldier simply had to strike the tinderbox and the dog appeared to fulfil his every wish.

One day, the soldier told the dog that he wanted more than all else to see the beautiful daughter of the king. She was held prisoner in the palace, and no man had ever set eyes upon her. The dog disappeared, but returned almost at once with the princess. The young couple fell in love and, after a very short time, the soldier and the princess were married.

The wedding feast lasted eight days and, in recognition of his services, the magic dog was fed from the same table as the king and the couple.

29 The Fox with the Stunted Tail

A fox lost her tail in a trap and was ashamed of her loss.

It seemed extremely unfair to her that she alone should lack a tail.

She seriously thought the world would be a much improved place if all the other foxes too were to have no tails.

And so she tried to convince them all to cut off their tails.

'The tail,' she said, 'is just an extra weight. And you could hardly call it elegant! Or pretty!'

'If that is so,' replied her friends, 'then why are you so unhappy without one?'

Contents

The fairy tale of the month: Snow White and the Seven Dwarfs
The Brothers Grimm

The fairy tale of the month

The Little Tin Soldier

He was made of tin, but so well finished, moulded and varnished, that he seemed real. He had a red jacket with golden buttons and a big white belt, black trousers, which looked as if they had just been ironed, and a shiny, sharp, pointed bayonet. His face was framed by a silver chin strap and he had red cheeks, blue eyes and a black moustache that twisted upwards at the ends.

Real soldiers like this were guards at the royal palace, but the tin soldier was only a souvenir brought back by a father, from a journey, for his son, so he guarded the other toys.

Right opposite him there was a castle built of little bricks, with its towers and its battlements and even a flag on the drawbridge.

There was a teddy bear which was all furry and an old spinning top that gave off a strange sound when it went round; there was a football which had been kicked so many times that it had lost all its brightness; and skittles, which were all marked, thanks to being hit so often by the ball.

But the toy the little tin soldier loved best was the ballerina. It was not really a toy, but one of those little porcelain dolls which used to be so fashionable. It stood balanced on the tip of its toe on top of a little box and when it was wound up it went round and round to the tune of a waltz played on a little carillon.

The little soldier fell in love with the ballerina at first sight. And who wouldn't have? The dancer was truly beautiful, in her graceful pose, with one leg stretched backwards and her arms slightly curved upwards; she was so elegant in her soft tulle outfit, just a little bit yellowed by time. . . .

Unfortunately, the lovely ballerina would not even deign to look at the tin soldier: she was facing the other way and, even at night when the toys came alive and moved about, she did not turn towards him.

The little soldier had once tried, with extreme politeness, to talk to her; but the lid had suddenly flown off a box next to the carillon, and a toy devil on a spring had popped out.

He was jealous and he made a great scene, threatening the soldier with all sorts of terrible things if he caught him addressing the ballerina again.

She was certainly not the devil's girlfriend, but with evil and very violent people it is always sensible to be careful.

On the other hand, though the soldier was not at all afraid, he did not know the ballerina's true feelings, so

he did nothing else from then on which might compromise her, even though deep in his heart he suffered greatly.

In fact, it was almost a relief when one day, through the carelessness of his young owner (or a plot by the springing devil), the little tin soldier fell out of the window and landed between two stones on the pavement.

There he lay for a considerable time and, bit by bit, he became covered in dust.

Then one day, there was a very heavy rainfall and the little soldier's red jacket shone brightly again amidst the stones of the pavement. He was found by two rough little boys who conceived the idea of making him into a sailor. They built a little paper ship and lowered it into one of the rivulets left behind by the storm, and on it they placed the little tin soldier.

From rivulet to rivulet the boat sailed on until it reached a small stream. What an adventure! There were waterfalls, gorges and dangerous fish. The soldier continued undaunted, as if he was a real ship's captain, but the boat became soaked through and finally sank. His last thought was of the lovely little porcelain ballerina.

A short time later, he was swallowed by a fish after which he no longer saw nor heard anything.

He had no idea how much time had passed when he saw light again and heard a cry: 'Oh, look what's in here. A little tin soldier.'

The cook, who was cleaning the fish before frying it, took the toy to her young master. The little boy played with it for a while, but he soon grew bored and went to put it in with the other toys.

And by sheer chance, the little soldier found himself once again before the brick castle and the spinning wheel. He moved his eyes and . . . . yes, there was the ballerina as well.

The little soldier's heart started beating so hard that she must have heard it, because she did a beautiful pirouette and turned towards him, with a graceful curtsey. The lid of the devil's box immediately flew up, but he did it too quickly. The spring broke and the ugly devil fell back into his box for good.

Since that time, the ballerina has learned how to be a sentry, while the little soldier has learned how to dance the waltz, following the tune from the carillon. And they are together and happy to this day.

1 The Imp's Saturday

It was Saturday night, but very few children had yet gone to sleep. They all relied on the sleep imp, whose job it was to sing the lullabies, but the imp had not passed by yet. So one mother decided to go and complain about him.

'I'm sorry,' the imp explained, 'but tomorrow is a holiday. It is Sunday, and we imps have to clean up the whole world so it looks prettier. You have no idea how many things I still have to do tonight.'

'What things?'

'I have to climb to the tops of the bell towers and polish up the bells, so that they will ring clear and true. I have to go into the fields and check if the wind has dusted clean the grass and the flowers. I have to go up into the sky and bring down the stars one by one and make them bright and shiny.'

'But the stars,' said the woman, 'are stuck up in the sky. You can't just take them down and clean them like light bulbs.'

'Are you suggesting I don't know what I'm doing?' asked the imp, a bit put out.

However, the little boy had fallen asleep in the meantime, so the mother decided there was no point in staying there any longer to argue about it: so whether or not the stars are really fixed in the sky, we never did find out.

2 The Legend of King Midas

A long, long time ago there was a king of Phrygia who was very greedy and stupid. One day Silenus, the god of the woods, who had been a guest of the king, offered, in return for his hospitality, to grant him a wish. After thinking for a long time about how he could become more rich and more powerful, Midas asked for a magic gift that would turn anything he touched to gold.

'So be it,' exclaimed Silenus.

Midas touched the seat he was sitting on and it immediately turned to solid gold. He touched his belt, his clothes, a vase, a statue. . . . every-thing turned to gold. He began to run about the palace, and everything he touched became gold: walls, furniture, ornaments. . . .

Midas was delighted, but all the excitement had made him hungry, so he sat down at the table and prepared to eat. Then he realised that every piece of food he brought to his mouth was turning to gold before he could eat it. Thanks to his greed, it looked as though he was going to die of hunger.

Fortunately, Silenus, who had foreseen what would happen, agreed to relieve Midas of his magic power. And so, for a bunch of grapes, Midas gave up all the gold in the world.

3 The Lion and the Grateful Mouse

A lion was preparing to eat a mouse it had just caught.

'Let me go,' the mouse begged him, 'sooner or later you may need my help.'

The king of the forest found this idea so ridiculous that he laughed aloud, but he let the little mouse go anyway. Some time later, the lion became trapped in a net which had been set down by hunters. But then along came the mouse, who chewed through the netting and freed him.

'As you can see,' said the mouse, 'even the mighty sometimes need the help of the weak.'

4 The Donkey's Skin

There was once a rich and powerful king who, though old and ugly, took it into his head to marry a young, beautiful girl at the court. The girl did not want to marry the king and asked her stepmother for help to escape from this marriage.

'You can never say no to the king,' said the woman, 'but you can lay down absurd conditions. Ask him for the skin of his donkey.'

Now this donkey was a magic donkey, on which all the king's power depended, so the two of them never dreamed for one moment that he would make such a sacrifice. But the king at once sent the girl what she had asked for.

The young girl decided to run away. She put on the donkey skin, so she would not be recognised, and fled to a nearby country. To earn herself a living there, she took the job of a serving girl in an inn: and indeed she was good at everything she did, especially baking cakes. She never took off her disguise and, though it made her look horrible, the donkey skin kept her safe. Only occasionally, when she was alone in her room, did she wash and comb her hair and put on the fine dress she had brought with her.

One day, the son of the king of that land happened to come to the inn. Looking around the place, he found a locked door. Out of curiosity he peeped through the keyhole, and saw such a beautiful young girl that he fell in love at first sight. When he asked who stayed in that room, he was told that it was only an ugly serving girl.

When Donkey Skin was shown to him, he was forced to admit that it was not the girl he had seen through the keyhole. The prince grew lovesick and lost his appetite. As he grew weaker, the court doctor decided that he could only be tempted to eat again by a piece from one of Donkey Skin's delicious cakes. So she was commanded to bake a cake, but when the prince took his first bite he found in it a ring, which had slipped from Donkey Skin's finger.

The prince remembered having seen the ring through the keyhole on the beautiful young girl's finger. He vowed he would marry only the girl on whose finger the ring fitted perfectly. To make him happy, the king and the queen agreed to this, especially since a finger small enough to fit that ring must surely belong to a grand lady.

The search began at once, and in the end even Donkey Skin was ordered to try the ring on. And then the 'ugly' serving girl had no trouble at all in proving that not only was the ring hers, but that she really was the beautiful young girl that the prince had seen at the inn. Everything was soon sorted out and a grand wedding took place that very same day.

5 The Tsar's Riddle

A tsar had taken prisoner a rebel leader. The rebel's daughter went to the tsar to beg him to spare her beloved father. She was a beautiful young girl, but the tsar looked on her with mixed feelings.

'I will free your father, and what is more I will marry you,' he said to her, 'if you are able to solve this riddle. If you fail, your father will die and you will be forced to marry my stable boy.'

'Agreed,' said the girl, 'what is the riddle?'

'You have to come back to me neither dressed nor naked,' said the tsar, 'neither on foot nor on horse- back, neither with gifts nor without gifts.'

The girl went away and thought hard. The next day she came before the tsar, wearing only a thick fishing net, so that she was neither dressed nor naked; she was riding on the back of a large dog, so that she was neither on foot nor on horseback; in her hands she had a quail, which she released in the tsar's presence, so that she had come neither with a gift nor without a gift.

The tsar, who admired clever people as much as he admired brave ones, kept his word. He freed the rebel leader and married his beautiful young daughter.

6 The King of the Forest Goes to War

King lion was getting ready to go to war and called to arms all the other animals.

But his ministers asked him to dismiss the donkey and the rabbit, because one was too stupid and the other too easily scared.

'Not at all,' refused the king. 'The donkey has a voice which is even more resonant than mine. He can be the trumpeter.'

'The rabbit, being so quick, will be invaluable for carrying messages,' added the king. To win a war you have to know how to get the best out of everyone.

7 The Two Bears in the Sky

Hans, the young giant, was kind and helpful. He was happy to do any kind of job and, because of his great strength, he was able to do the work of a dozen men.

One day, the village where Hans lived was attacked by two ferocious bears, one male, the other female. The mayor and all the people of the town rushed to find the giant to ask for his help. At once Hans went to where the bears were, only to find them frightening an old woman.

The giant leapt on the larger of the two animals, seized it by the arm and swung it round, hurling it into the sky.

He then did the same to the other bear, but the female bear, being much smaller, flew higher into the sky than the male did.

The male watched her fly past, but he could do nothing to stop her.

'Come over here,' he called out at the top of his voice.

'I can't. You come over here,' she replied.

Ever since then, the two bears have been roaming about the sky trying to get back together again and astronomers have referred to them as the 'Great Bear' and the 'Little Bear'.

8 Stupid Catherine and the Front Door

When Stupid Catherine went out, she often forgot to close the door behind her. One day, she had to go out of the house to take some lunch to her husband, Joseph, who was always telling her: 'Don't forget the door.'

This time, Catherine thought hard, until the answer came to her.

The best way not to forget the door was to take it with her. So she took it off its hinges and heaved it up onto her back. But then, what could she do with the heavy lunch basket?

'I know' she cried. 'I'll hang it on the door handle, so that the door has to carry it, not me.'

9 The Princess's Worn Out Shoes

It was a mystery. Every evening, the king's beautiful daughter was locked in her room, and every morning her shoes were worn out from dancing too much.

The king offered a great reward to whoever could solve this mystery. Many people tried, but in vain; then along came a young man who had a magic cloak that could make him invisible. He had been given this by his godmother, who was a good witch.

When evening came, the young man put on his magic cloak and hid beside the bed of the sleeping girl. In the night, he saw the princess rise from her bed like a sleep-walker and enter a secret passage which opened up in the wall. Without hesitation, the young man followed her.

They crossed a mysterious underground garden. At the end of a long avenue, there stood a castle, gleaming with lights, and there the princess was awaited by the Prince of the Night. A great ball began at once.

The invisible young man hurried back to the king and told him of all that he had seen. When the princess returned at dawn, she found her father waiting, together with the young man and his godmother. The good witch took away the spell that made the princess dance all night and cast another one on her, which caused her to fall in love with her brave godson.

10 The Swan and the Goose

A swan and a goose were both sold at the market on the same day to the same buyer. Then they were taken back to his villa and both put in the lake, the swan to please his eye, and his ears with its legendary song, and the goose to please his stomach eventually with its lovely, tasty meat.

For a long time, the two birds lived very happily together, becoming great friends. They swam about every day in the water and the master and his guests often came by to admire the two animals and feed them tasty morsels.

Nevertheless, the day came when the master ordered that the goose should be roasted for his dinner. The cook went down to the lake to fetch the unwilling guest to the banquet.

By chance that day, the cook was drunk, and instead of taking the goose he took the swan. When the swan saw the cook's knife coming for its throat, it began to sing its famous last song. The cook was so amazed that he refused to kill the bird.

Which goes to show that anyone who knows how to make good use of words can find a way out of even the most desperate situation.

11 The Fox and the Goat

A thirsty fox was wandering about the countryside looking for water. Eventually he found a well, but the only water was at the bottom. The fox studied the problem and realised that there was a pulley system to bring up the water, one bucket going down causing another bucket to come up. So the fox jumped into the bucket at the top and his weight immediately caused it to drop to the bottom, where he could drink all the water he desired.

However, now he could not get back up, but the fox had long ago realised that the world is full of fools, and a short time later along came a goat, looking for water in the well.

The fox explained the situation and said to the goat, 'Get into the bucket, then you can come down and I can go up.'

'Yes, but what about afterwards?' asked the goat.

'That's even simpler; then you can come up and I'll go down.'

So the goat got into the bucket, and in a moment he was at the bottom of the well, and the fox was at the top. But as soon as he was up, the fox bade farewell to the goat and made to leave.

'Wait a minute,' shouted the goat. 'You promised to get me back up.'

'Who promised?' asked the fox. 'All we did was to discuss the possibilities.'

12 George and Georgette

George and Georgette loved each other dearly and were soon to be married. One day they went for a walk in the woods and got lost. Wandering around, they came across a castle among the trees.

'Look,' said the young man.

'Tweet-tweet,' came the response.

He turned round and there, instead of his beloved Georgette, he found a thrush beside him. Over their heads flew an owl and as he watched, the bird flew behind a large tree. Then, from around the tree hobbled an old, wizened woman.

George realised at once that this must be a witch and he begged her to return Georgette to him. He cried and sighed and threatened, but it was all to no avail. The only thing left for him to do was to wait around the castle and hope that something would turn up. After a long time, a fairy came to him one night in a dream, carrying a red flower with a pearl at the heart of it. At sunrise, George went out to see if such a flower really existed. Finally, he found a rose with a dewdrop shining out from amongst its petals.

It was the Love Rose, a flower with magical powers. With the rose in his hand, he was able to enter the castle freely, and there he came across a large chamber absolutely filled with birds in cages. They were all young girls changed into birds by the evil witch. But how was George to know which one was Georgette? Why, there were hundreds of thrushes, let alone the other birds. As he moved from cage to cage, George caught sight of the witch herself, leaving the room with a cage in her hands. George sprang after her and seized the cage. The witch spat poison and bile at him, but she could not match the magic of the Love Rose. George touched her with the flower and her evil powers vanished.

The spells were broken; the birds turned into young maidens again. George and Georgette went away happily, leaving behind at the castle not a witch, but a harmless old woman.

13 The Eagle and the Woodcutter

Once, a woodcutter found an eagle which was caught in a trap. He was so taken with the beauty and the majesty of the bird that he let it go free.

Some time later, the woodcutter sat down on a rock on the very top of a steep hill. While he was having his lunch, the eagle dropped like lightning from the sky, and flew away with his hat. The man automatically ran down the hill after the bird, just as the rocks on which he had been sitting gave way with a loud crash.

The grateful eagle had repaid its benefactor.

14 The Wagon Driver's Patron

It had been raining and the track had turned into a muddy swamp. All of a sudden, the wagon that was on it got bogged down in a muddy hole, and it was so heavily laden that neither the efforts of the donkey that was pulling it, nor the curses of the man who was driving it, could get it out again.

The wagon driver was furious with the donkey. He shouted insults at it, he yanked it by the bit, he lashed it with his whip, but nothing did any good. So he called on his patron saint, and promised to light a candle to him.

'Before you go looking for a candle,' he seemed to hear a voice saying, 'why don't you stop beating the donkey, and go and get some stones to fill in the hole? Unload the wagon, and make it as light as you can. Pick up that broken branch and use it as a lever.'

Scarcely giving a thought to what he was doing, the astonished wagon driver did as he was told. When he had followed all the instructions, he said 'giddyup' to the donkey, and the wagon pulled easily out of the mud.

'A miracle,' shouted the man, covered in perspiration from all his efforts.

'Take notice,' warned the voice of his patron saint, 'this miracle was performed by you. The Lord helps those who help themselves.'

15 Doctor Knowall

There was once a peasant who envied the good life led by doctors, lawyers and notaries. So one fine day he bought himself a wig and a black suit, then he put up on his door a sign saying: 'Doctor Knowall'.

Shortly afterwards, a man went by, who had just been robbed of a large sum of money. 'If he knows all, then he also knows who stole my money,' he thought. So he invited Doctor Knowall to his house for dinner.

When dinner time came round, a servant approached the table with some dishes and the 'doctor' exclaimed, 'Oh good, here's the first.'

What Doctor Knowall meant was that the first course was being served, but the servant, who was in fact one of the robbers, thought that he had been found out. Terrified, he rushed back to the kitchen and said to another servant; 'You go and serve the meal.' The second servant was also the second robber, and when he went into the dining room Doctor Knowall said: 'Oh good, here's the second.' The robbers were frightened out of their wits. All they could think of doing was to give back the money. The master of the house rewarded Doctor Knowall handsomely for his skill . . . . but his greatest reward was the reputation he enjoyed from that day on as an infallible wise man.

16 Catherine and the Mirror

One day silly little Catherine went for a walk in the woods. When she reached the lake, she decided to eat, but then grew tired and slept till nighttime. When she woke up, it was so dark that she could not see her own reflection in the water.

'Am I really here or am I not?' she asked herself. She decided to go home and ask. When she got home she called out, 'Is Catherine there?'

'She must be in the bedroom,' replied a sleepy voice.

'If Catherine's at home,' thought Catherine, 'then I'm not Catherine.' So she went away and never returned.

17 The Donkey and the Crown

The rulers of a small kingdom desired one thing above all others, a son, but when finally a son was born to them, they were very disappointed. The little prince looked just like a donkey! All the same they loved him dearly, and he had such a lovable nature that his appearance came to be overlooked. But when he grew up and saw his own reflection in the lake, the prince was most upset. He was so ashamed that he fled from the palace at once and began to roam the world.

After many travels and adventures, he found himself in another kingdom where he was given employment as a court musician. The musical donkey was so kind and gentle that everybody grew fond of him, especially the king and queen, so much so that they asked him if he would care to marry their beautiful daughter. He accepted readily and the wedding was celebrated in great style; and, on that very evening, when the newly wed couple were alone in their room, the donkey skin, which had always covered the prince, fell away, revealing a handsome young man; the love of the princess for the donkey had broken the spell.

18 True, Very True!

A highly respectable hen was cleaning herself with her beak one day, when she broke off one of her feathers. 'Not another one,' she sighed. 'I'll never be beautiful at this rate.'

Her neighbour, overhearing, misunderstood the hen's words and went and told the mother hen, 'One of my sisters is pulling out all her feathers to make herself more beautiful. . . .'

Listening on the roof of the hen house, the owl remarked, 'What a shameless creature.'

'Be quiet,' warned his wife. 'Don't let the children hear you.'

But she flew off nonetheless to tell the pigeons. 'Have you heard? One of the hens has plucked out all her feathers for love of the cockerel. She'll catch a cold, if she isn't already dead!'

In the pigeons' retelling of the story the number of featherless hens had risen to two. From the swallows to the bats, the story grew more and more amazing. When finally it got back to the hen house, would you believe it, at least five or six hens were without feathers after a jealous fight over the cockerel!

Obviously the first respectable hen had no idea that she was a participant in a story of this kind.

'What a scandal,' she exclaimed. 'They should be ashamed of themselves!'

19 The Sun and the Wind

To see which was the stronger, the sun and the wind challenged each other to strip the clothes from the first passer-by.

The wind puffed with all the air in its lungs; but the more it blew the more the man drew his clothes tight around him and, feeling a bit cold, he even pulled on a cloak.

The sun didn't do anything so strenuous; all it did was shine. And gradually the man grew hotter and hotter until he took off all his clothes to go for a swim. Which just goes to show that gentle persuasion is more effective than violence.

20 The Wolf and the Seven Little Kids

Mother goat had to go out one day and leave her seven little kids alone in the house. But before leaving, she warned them sternly about the bad wolf and his great cunning. The little kids listened attentively, and so, when the wolf knocked on the door and said he was the mother goat, they were not fooled.

'No, you are the big bad wolf,' they answered. 'Our mother has a soft sweet voice.'

So the wolf tried again later, after eating some honey to make his voice sweeter; but the kids were still not fooled. This time the wolf was betrayed by his paws, which were black and hairy. Pretending to be their mother, he held presents for the kids in his paws.

The next time, the wolf went to the baker and ordered him to make a goat's paw out of bread dough, and when the little goats saw this they *were* fooled. They thought it really was their mother and they opened the front door. In a flash the wolf swallowed them all up – all, except one, who just in time hid in the cupboard.

When mother goat came home, the little kid told her what had happened to his brothers and sisters. Off went the mother goat to look for the rascally wolf. When she found the wolf, he was fast asleep under a tree, but in his full stomach the mother goat could see the shape of the little goats' heads. Then, with scissors the mother goat freed her young, and she put stones in their place. Afterwards she sewed up the wolf's stomach so neatly that he never even noticed. When he woke up and went to have a drink, however, the weight of the stones in his stomach made the wolf lose his balance, and he fell into the water and was drowned. So the seven little · goats were able to grow up strong and healthy, with big horns, so they could defend themselves against wicked wolves.

21 The Mystery of the Sphinx

A long, long time ago, the city of Thebes was guarded by a sphinx, a creature with the head of a woman, the body of a lion and the wings of an eagle.

She asked the same riddle of every passer-by, and when they could not answer, she consumed them.

'What being,' the sphinx asked Oedipus, when he came upon her, 'has four legs in the morning, two at midday and three in the evening?'

'Man,' answered Oedipus. 'As a child he crawls on all fours, in his prime he walks on two legs, and when he is old he leans on a stick.'

22 The Two Samurai and the Servant

A samurai was on his way to Kyoto, unhappy because he had not found a servant to carry his bags. A second samurai was also going to Kyoto, and he was unhappy because he had not found a servant to keep him company. The two samurai met up and decided to continue together. At least they could keep each other company.

Further on, they met a common man who was also going to Kyoto, and they asked him to enter their service. The man accepted willingly and the samurai gave him their long swords to carry; but they were unhappy with their servant.

'You can see a mile off that you are not a warrior!' they reproached him. 'You don't know how to carry the swords properly.'

After enduring this for a while, the man grew tired of being made fun of. He drew one of their long swords and pointed it at their throats.

'Hand over your short swords from your belts!' he commanded. Once the two samurai were disarmed, he made them hand over their money bags as well. Then he threw all the weapons into the river and off he went.

'Carry them by yourselves,' he said to the samurai. 'I already feel exalted enough carrying your gold!'

23 The Giant and the Miser

A good-hearted young giant heard tell of a blacksmith who was very miserly and treated his workers very unjustly, so he went along to the workshop and asked to be taken on as an apprentice.

The blacksmith thought that such a big strong lad could probably do the work of a dozen others. He was tempted to take him on, but he wanted to know how much money he would have to pay him.

'Just give me a little something for each hammer blow,' replied the giant.

Thinking of the money he would not have to pay the others, the mean blacksmith agreed. He put his new apprentice to work in the forge, but with the first hammer blow, the anvil sank so far into the ground that it could not be pulled back out. The blacksmith realised that he had not made a good bargain. He asked the giant to leave before he destroyed everything.

'How much do I owe you for that single blow?' he asked the giant.

'Not much,' answered the young giant. 'Just this. . . .' And he gave the blacksmith a kick that sent him flying over the rooftops.

24 Ali Baba and the Forty Thieves

Ali Baba had gone with his three donkeys to cut wood in the oasis. Suddenly he looked up and saw a dust cloud raised by many horses coming across the desert towards him. Immediately he hid himself, which was just as well, for it turned out that it was a band of robbers returning to the oasis, laden with treasure. The leader got down from his horse and went up to a large rock.

'Open Sesame,' he said.

Peering out in amazement, Ali Baba saw the rock open up and the whole band of robbers ride inside. The woodcutter remained hidden, and after a while the rock opened up again and out came the robbers, all forty of them.

'Close Sesame,' ordered the leader, and the rock closed.

Ali Baba waited until the horsemen had ridden away across the desert, before leaving his hiding place.

He went up to the great rock and said, 'Open Sesame.' When the rock obeyed, Ali Baba entered and found himself in a cavern full of treasure. He filled as many bags with gold coins as his donkeys could carry, and then he fled from the oasis.

From then on, Ali Baba lived happily, but he never returned to the oasis. He was a kind and generous man; he used the money from the forty thieves to help his friends.

25 The Lion and the Old Hare

In the jungle, there once was a fierce lion who killed many animals. The survivors decided that if they were not to suffer the same fate something must be done. The king of the jungle would have to make do with one meal a day. In return, to save him the effort of hunting, each day's victim would come to the lion of his own accord.

Things went on like this until it came to the turn of a cunning, old hare. Off he went to the lion, gasping as if he had just run a long way.

'On my way here,' he panted, 'I was attacked by a lion. But for my fast legs, I would never have escaped.'

'Another lion?' The king of the jungle roared with rage at the very idea of a rival. 'Where is he?'

'At the pool. He is big and young, stronger and braver than you.'

'We'll see about that. Take me to him.'

So the lion followed the hare to the pool and there, as he leaned over the edge, he saw another lion in the water below. He sprang at it immediately . . . . and that was how an old hare got the better of a cruel tyrant. And that is why there is a proverb which says: 'Cunning is more powerful than brute strength'.

26 The Deer-Witch and the Butterfly

One day a young hunter saw a magnificent deer and chased it through the woods. After a long pursuit, he arrived at a little house hidden in the middle of the forest, and there the deer was transformed into an old witch.

'You've fallen into my trap now,' cackled the witch, pointing a gnarled finger at him. 'Now I am going to change you into an animal as well.'

Terrified, the young hunter turned to escape, only to discover that the way was blocked by a toad, which suddenly changed into a bear. Then the witch changed again, this time into a black raven, which flew at the hunter to touch him and complete the evil spell.

But before the raven could reach him, a butterfly landed on the young man's shoulder and that was enough to break the witch's spell. The butterfly changed herself into a beautiful huntress with drawn bow and arrow pointing at the raven.

'Let us go, old witch, or else. . . .,' she cried.

And then, even the bear, who was actually the brother of the huntress, returned to normal. All three jumped onto the horse and escaped, followed by the uselessly croaking raven.

27 The Darning Needle

A large darning needle was very full of itself, almost as if it was a lacework needle, until one day, pushing through some tough cloth, its eye broke. But the seamstress did not want to throw it away, and used it instead to pin the scarf round her neck. The needle thought it had been promoted and became even more conceited.

One day, it slipped out of its high position, at the woman's neck, and landed in the kitchen sink. But it did not feel at all humiliated, rather it was convinced it had been made lord admiral of the seas, and was being sent out to discover new lands.

In truth, the only land it discovered was the drains, but all the dirt and waste that passed through only made it feel more important, because the needle remained slim and shiny. It even made a friend in its own social class – a bottle top, which, because it also shone, the needle thought worthy of its attention.

'I see that you are a diamond,' said the needle.

'And you are a sword,' replied the bottle top.

'Yes, you are right. I'm the king's sword.'

And the two of them are probably still there, telling each other about their exciting past lives.

28 The Bell on the Cat

Several centuries ago, the mice called a meeting to consider their sad situation.

All the speakers agreed on the fact that it was all the fault of the cats, and they debated ways in which they could avoid being hunted by them.

Finally, a solution was proposed and everyone approved. It was decided to attach a bell to every cat so that the mice would hear them coming.

This law is still in force, but unfortunately no mice have come forward to volunteer to put the bells on the cats.

29 Apollo and the Shepherd

Apollo, who was the Greek god of music, was very proud of how well he could play the lyre. Everyone agreed that no music was as good as Apollo's until one day he was told of a shepherd called Olander, whose melodies on the flute were just as sweet as his. So Apollo invited Olander to Delphos, his island home, and challenged him to a contest.

First the god, and then the shepherd, played before a great audience, and the most wonderful melodies came forth from their instruments. The Muses, who were acting as judges, found it impossible to decide which of the two was the better musician. Very put out at this, Apollo proposed a second trial.

'This time let us play our instruments the opposite way,' he said. Again Apollo played first, but even though his lyre was upside down, beautiful music still flowed from it. Then it was Olander's turn. He put the other end of the flute into his mouth, but though he puffed and puffed, he was quite unable to produce a sound.

Only at the end did Olander realise that he had been tricked, because a flute cannot be played from the opposite end to the mouthpiece. So Apollo won, but the Muses still refused to give him any prize because he had won by trickery.

30 The Bewitched Mill

The old mill was inhabited by ghosts and no-one knew what went on there, because each person who passed a night there was speechless with fear by morning.

The owner of the mill was in despair, because no-one wanted to work there. So he was delighted when a young man, too simple to be scared, came looking for a job.

That night, when the young man sat down on the bench, the door opened before him and a table moved forward, laden with all kinds of good things. Invisible guests then began to dine and the young man joined in, not at all put out by the fact that the cutlery was moving of its own accord. At a certain moment, all the lights went out and the young man was slapped in the face.

'Do that again,' he said, 'and you'll get a slap in return.' And when he did get another slap, he slapped right back at the invisible face. He went on all night, trading blow for blow. At dawn, all the strange happenings ceased, and after that nothing ever happened again, for ghosts are scared themselves of someone who is not scared of them, and in fact they prefer to run away.

31 The Hen with the Silver Eggs

One day, in an Arabian city, a woman went to the market and bought a beautiful hen.

You can imagine her surprise later, when the hen laid a silver egg. If the hen could only be persuaded to lay more than one egg each day, the woman was sure she would never have to work again.

So the woman decided that the hen must eat more, so that it could lay more eggs.

But the only result was that the hen died of indigestion, and did not lay any more eggs at all.

Contents

The fairy tale of the month: The Little Tin Soldier
Hans Christian Andersen

April

The fairy tale of the month

Peter and the Wolf

Peter had gone to his grandfather's house on holiday. It was a beautiful farmhouse on the very edge of the forest. He had lots of toys to play with, and the garden and the courtyard were full of friendly animals to keep him company. He was free to go wherever he wished; his grandfather had forbidden him to do one thing only – to go out of the gate which opened onto the forest, because in the forest there lived a wolf.

Needless to say, it was to the forest that Peter most wanted to go. One day his grandfather forgot to lock the gate, and when the boy realised this, he was quick to slip out. A duck followed him out of the gate, and took advantage of the opportunity to have a swim in the stream beneath the birch tree. A robin redbreast studied the duck and said:

'What sort of bird are you that doesn't even know how to fly?'

'And what sort of bird are you, that doesn't even know how to swim?' replied the duck crossly.

A quarrel broke out, and this attracted the attention of a cat, who was out looking for his lunch. Peter saw the cat creeping up and called out a warning. The robin redbreast flew to the top of the birch tree, and the duck sent the cat scurrying away by pecking it with its beak. All this fuss disturbed the grandfather, however, and he took

his grandson and carried him back inside the farmyard.

'What would you have done,' he scolded Peter, 'if the wolf had come by?'

'I'm not scared of a wolf!' boasted Peter.

And, in fact, the wolf did come on the scene, and while the robin redbreast was able to fly to safety at the top of the birch tree, the poor duck was gulped down in a single mouthful and ended up in the stomach of the wolf. As for the cat, it had had just enough time to jump to safety in another tree, but it was still in danger from the wolf.

Peter watched all this through the farmyard gate and bravely decided to go to the rescue. He ran to fetch a long rope, tied a loop in it and then threw it over the wall, catching the loop firmly onto a branch of the birch tree. Then by swinging across on this rope, he was able to reach the robin redbreast.

'Try and distract the wolf,' Peter told the robin.

The little bird began to fly round and round the fierce wolf, which spun round like a top in an effort to pluck the little bird out of the air. Peter, up in the tree, waited for just the right moment to throw his lasso.

He caught the wolf perfectly by the tail and lifted it up off the ground and hung it from a branch of the birch tree.

Just then four hunters emerged from the wood, with their rifles on their shoulders. As soon as they saw the wolf, they reached for their guns and began to fire like men possessed. But Peter was worried for his little friends, and shouted to the hunters at the top of his voice: 'Don't shoot! My friend, the little bird, and I have already captured the wolf. I wish you'd just come and help me to tie him up and take him to the zoo!'

While Peter and the four hunters were tying the wolf upside down to a long pole, so that they could carry it safely, his grandfather arrived. He could hardly believe that his little grandson, Peter, could have done such a deed, worthy of a brave and experienced hunter. Even he, however, had to accept the evidence that was there for all to see, and it was grandfather himself, full of pride, who led off the little procession in triumph towards the nearby village.

Right behind his grandfather walked Peter, and round the boy's head flew the little robin redbreast, his feathery chest puffed out. The bird seemed truly proud of himself for the important part he had played in the capture of the wolf. The four hunters followed, carrying the pole to which they had tied the wolf. And last of all, but with her tail stuck proudly into the air, came the cat, who had reappeared the moment that the danger was past, for she too wanted her share in the glory.

The only absentee, unfortunately, was the poor duck who, because of an innocent urge to swim in the stream, had been both the unwilling cause and the victim of the little tragedy.

And yet, if you strained your ears, you might have thought that she was there somewhere after all. Every so often you would have sworn you heard her distinct 'quack-quack', but it was so weak and distant that nobody could decide where the noise came from. Once again, it was Peter who saved the day. He took out his pocket knife and opened up the stomach of the wolf. At once the duck leapt out, for since the wolf had swallowed her in a single mouthful, she was still safe and sound.

Peter quickly sewed up the belly of the wolf so that it too remained alive and well. Any visitor to the Zoological Gardens can recognise the wolf immediately by the long scar on its belly, and by its careful habit of keeping a great distance between itself and all robin redbreasts.

1 April Fool

Once upon a time, a woodsman discovered a hoard of golden coins. Knowing full well that his wife was a terrible chatterbox, he set to thinking about the best way to keep his secret. He made some careful preparations, and then went off to fetch his wife.

'Look! Look!' he shouted out suddenly, as they passed beneath a tree, 'there's a fish, a trout, my dear, growing on that branch.' To his wife's amazement, he took down the fish (which he had put there himself), and they went on to the river where he often went fishing. Here, the woodsman pulled in his nets, and drew out of them the hares which he had placed there earlier. They went on again, and he pretended to stumble upon the hoard of golden coins.

And so when his wife, despite all the woodsman's pleas to keep the matter quiet, began to boast to their friends of their find, the woodsman was ready:

'A hoard of treasure in the woods? When exactly did this happen, dear?'

'You can't have forgotten!' insisted his silly wife. 'It was the same day that we found the trout growing in a tree and caught the hares in the river!'

Naturally, her friends assumed that she was making it all up, and they did not believe one word about the treasure. And so she is considered to be the first April Fool!

2 The Cockerel and the Weasel

Once, while the cockerel was giving a long 'cock-a-doodle-doo', a weasel walked up behind him. 'You are a very good singer,' the weasel purred, 'but I know a cockerel that can sing perfectly while standing on one leg.'

'That's easy!' said the vain cockerel, doing the same.

'Ah, but he also shuts his eyes!'

'I can do that too!'

And while the cock was showing off in this fashion, the weasel carried him off into the woods to eat him. When mealtime arrived, the weasel held the cockerel still with his paws and . . . .

'Didn't anyone teach you to say grace before eating?' the cockerel interrupted.

'Of course they did!' said the weasel, lifting his paws to put them together. The cockerel didn't hesitate, but flew straight up to a high branch. The weasel was determined not to give up a meal, so he picked up a dry leaf and pretended to read it.

'It's a letter from the king!' he murmured and turned to the cockerel. 'I don't understand a single word of it. Why don't you read it to me?'

'Gladly,' replied the cockerel, 'but some other time would be better. I can see a group of hunters coming.'

The weasel ran off and the clever cockerel returned to the hen house.

3 The Spiteful Gnomes

Once upon a time a woman had a lovely baby, but gnomes stole the child and put in its place a baby gnome in the cradle. The mother begged them to return the child to her, but they just laughed unkindly. Sad and distracted without her baby, the woman put a raw egg on the fire instead of into the pot of water. The gnomes, who were always running around the kitchen, burst out laughing at this, because, as we all know, gnomes like to laugh more than anything else. So they returned her baby to the mother and took away the baby gnome.

4 The Golden Clog

The shouts of the shoeseller, going up and down the street with his donkey, laden with shoes and clogs for sale, had begun to annoy the townspeople. Wishing to be left in peace, they decided to buy all his goods. But once they had agreed a price per pair, the people noticed that the more clogs they bought and piled up in the street, the more full seemed to be the baskets of clogs on the wagon. There was no doubt that there was witchcraft at work. A great argument broke out.

At that very moment, the king passed by in his carriage. The townspeople asked for his judgement, but the shoemaker made a gift of a golden clog to the little prince, who was with his father, and the king decided that no crime had been committed. As he announced this, the mysterious shoeseller disappeared.

Very soon after it was discovered that the golden clog was bewitched. Not only could nobody get it off, but the clog also grew little by little along with the prince's foot. Therefore it never caused him any pain at all.

Years later, the king chose a girl to be a wife for his son. Hardly had the marriage been celebrated when the golden clog began to hurt the prince. It only ceased to hurt him when his marriage was annulled. The king went to the court magician for advice, and learnt that his son would only be able to make a happy marriage to the girl who was able to take the golden clog from his foot. The princesses of nearby kingdoms were the first to try, followed by all the duchesses, countesses, and common people in the land until there only remained a dirty scullery-maid, dressed in rags. She kissed the clog and removed it with ease. The king was furious: he could not allow his son to marry a scullery-maid! At that moment the shoeseller's cry was heard from the street and the girl, who was actually his daughter, was changed at once into the most gentle and lovable princess. So, the king was content and the young prince and princess lived happily ever after.

5 The White Cat and the Imps

Once upon a time, there was a man who had captured a polar bear which he intended to present to the tsar. On the way home, he found himself in the woods as night began to fall, and he asked a woodsman for refuge.

'Of course, you may stay the night,' said the woodsman, 'but you'll have to make do as best you can, because there won't be much space. This night is the feast of the trolls, the impish spirits of the forest, and unfortunately they have a tradition of celebrating with a banquet in my house!'

The man laid out his bed in the closet, and the bear crawled in under the covers and soon fell asleep.

That evening the trolls arrived, hundreds of every shape and size, noisy and cheeky like little boys. One of them spied the white fur under the covers, and thought a large cat was hiding there. The troll tugged spitefully at the fur, until the polar bear leapt out in fury. The terrified trolls fled.

The year after, before turning up at the house, the trolls asked the woodsman if he still had his 'big cat'.

'Oh yes!' confirmed the woodsman, 'and the seven kittens she has had in the last twelve months are all bigger than the mother!'

Needless to say, the trolls never returned to the woodsman's house for their banquet.

6 The Owl and the Nightingale

There was once a nightingale, in a cage by a window, that was in the habit of singing only at night. An owl was puzzled by this and went to ask the nightingale what the reason was.

'When I was captured,' explained the nightingale, 'it was day and I was singing. In this way I learnt to be more prudent and to sing only at night.'

'Are you afraid you might be captured a second time?' asked the baffled owl. 'It would have been better if you had been more careful the first time when your freedom was at risk. Now it doesn't really matter any more!'

7 The Faithful Friends

A young page so cared for his horse and fed it so well that even the fox would have liked to have had the young page as her master, in order to be so well treated. So she asked to be taken into the page's service and was accepted. She was also treated so well that she was followed by the bear, and the wolf, and, one by one, by all the other animals in the forest.

One day the friends of the young page decided it was time they found him a wife. They chose the daughter of the king himself for their master, and cleverly arranged that they should meet and fall in love. The king, however, did not approve of the choice his daughter had made and locked her in a tower.

Then all the animals in the page's employ planned to free her. The cat persuaded the princess to follow him out onto the terrace around the tower, and then the eagle picked her up and carried her away. The king, in a fury, declared war on all the animals, but there were so many of them and they made up such a massive army that the king had to make peace.

So the page was pardoned and the king reluctantly gave him his daughter's hand in marriage. The two of them lived happily ever after, surrounded by all their faithful animal friends.

8 How The Rabbit Became White

Eye of the Eagle, an Indian brave, was a great hunter. One summer the weather was so hot and dry that all the prairie animals moved away in search of water, and even Eye of the Eagle could find no game with which to feed his tribe. Things got so bad that one day he got into his canoe and decided that he would have to follow the wild animals into the Great North where they had fled.

He paddled and paddled and went so far, that one day he was surprised to find himself in a snowstorm. This, however, did not disturb him, because he knew he could follow more easily on the snow the tracks left by the wild animals. When he found the tracks of a deer, he began to follow them; but the snow fell so heavily that the hunter was blinded and became lost. Luckily he came across a brown rabbit and it offered to help him by guiding him back to his canoe. The rabbit's dark skin stood out clearly against the snow.

In this way, Eye of the Eagle was saved. He was so grateful to the brown rabbit that he chanted a magic spell which made its fur turn white. This meant that the rabbit could no longer be seen against the snow in winter, and so no-one could hunt it again.

9 Hanaca's Hat

Hanaca, the daughter of a samurai, was made to wear a strange, wide-brimmed hat which concealed her entire face. Her father had placed it on her head shortly before he died, and from that moment on no-one had been able to take it off.

Everyone in the town laughed at the maiden because of her hat, and eventually she wearied of being ridiculed and decided to go away. She walked for a long time, until she arrived at another city where Hanaca entered into the service of the king to earn her living. There, however, it was the other servants who began to laugh at her and treated her badly.

One day the king's son found Hanaca in tears. He listened to her story and was so moved by it, that he desired to marry her. To put an end to the affair, the king expelled Hanaca from the palace.

Tearfully, Hanaca turned towards the palace gates, when there came a great gust of wind which blew her wide-brimmed hat off her head. Everyone could now see the maiden's extraordinary beauty, and they could also see, sparkling in her hair, the many jewels which had been concealed for so long beneath the hat. One of the royal ministers recognised the girl as the daughter of the samurai, whereupon the king at once allowed the marriage to take place after all.

10 The Bees and the Hornets Go to Court

The bees and the hornets were in dispute, because both claimed that they were owners of the honey in a honeycomb. Since they simply could not come to an agreement, they all ended up in the court-room. There, the judge, a wasp, found it impossible to decide who was in the right.

There were witnesses who declared that they had seen black and yellow insects going in and out of the comb, but this testimony did nothing to clarify the situation, as both bees and hornets are black and yellow insects. The wasp was obliged to make further enquiries and ask many questions. It seemed

that the proceedings would go on for ever until the Queen Bee finally lost her patience.

'The longer this goes on,' she said to the judge, 'the more time and money is lost to us. We are not able to work, so meanwhile our honey is going bad in the comb. I propose a quick solution: both the bees and the hornets shall build another honey-comb. Whoever builds the best honeycomb in the shortest time shall be declared owners of the comb.'

Naturally, the hornets, who cannot build honeycombs, did not accept this proposal . . . . and from this the wasp deduced immediately that the honey-comb could belong only to the bees.

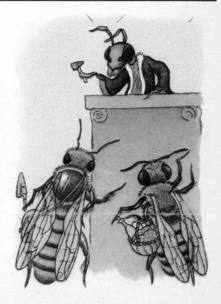

11 How Hans the Giant Became a Woodsman

Hans the giant decided to work as a woodcutter. On his first day, however, he was not even interested in trying to make a good impression. In the morning, when his colleagues came to wake him to start working in the woods, he just stayed in bed. When he finally did decide to get up, the first thing he did was to make chick-pea soup, and then he ate the entire potful. Chick-peas were the secret source of his enormous strength! Then off he went into the woods, pulled up the two biggest trees he could find, and loaded them onto his cart.

On the way back, Hans found the path blocked by a barrier of fallen trees. But it only took a moment for him to decide what to do: he simply lifted his cart, the two trees, and the horse, high above his head, and set them down on the other side.

The owner of the woodyard was delighted to see Hans back before anybody else, with two huge trees. Hans, however, did not spend any time chatting. He went back to bed.

When the rest of the woodsmen arrived back, they went at once to complain to the owner. 'Hans is still in bed!' they said. 'True,' said the owner, 'but while he's there he still manages to get a little work done.' And he pointed to the two enormous tree trunks in the woodyard.

12 The Shepherdess and the Chimney Sweep

The little shepherdess with the long floral skirt and the big straw hat was placed on the table beneath the mirror, and found herself beside the chimney sweep. Both of the little statues were of the finest porcelain and looked very attractive and delicate. The moment they saw each other they fell in love, and began to plan for their wedding. However, the old harlequin, with the clockwork head that always nodded 'yes', and who claimed to be the grandfather of the shepherdess, said her hand was promised in marriage to the mask of the Chinese dragon hanging on the wall nearby.

When the little shepherdess heard this, she was afraid that her little ceramic heart was going to break in two. The sad little chimney sweep suggested that she flee with him to escape marriage with the dragon, and she agreed.

So they climbed up the chimney (the sweep did not know any other way out) and found themselves up on the roof. Above them shone the stars and beneath them the lights of the city sparkled. The little shepherdess had never imagined that the world was so big and mysterious. She was so terrified that she asked the sweep to take her back at once. The patient and devoted chimney sweep was also frightened and, since he did not know how to say no to his beloved, the two little statues returned to their usual places on the table.

During their absence, the old harlequin had fallen off the table, when he attempted to pursue the shepherdess and had lost his head. The owners of the house had stuck his head back on with glue and a little iron hook, so now he had a stiff neck, and could no longer nod his consent to the dragon who wanted to marry his grand-daughter. And so the shepherdess and the chimney sweep were now free to marry, and the two little statues lived happily ever after.

13 Reynard the Fox and the Eels

A fisherman was returning home after a day by the river with his cart full of eels. Reynard the fox saw him and immediately thought of a way of getting himself a sumptuous dinner. He lay down in the middle of the road and pretended to be dead.

When the fisherman saw him, he fell for the trick. He picked up the fox, convinced that he had found himself a beautiful fox skin, and put it in the back of his cart. Once on the move, Reynard emptied all the eels out into the road, gathered them up and ran off. So the gullible fisherman lost both his fox fur skin and his fish.

14 How Men Came to Possess Fire

Many, many years ago, the American Indians did not know how to make fire, but they knew of its existence for they had seen smoke rising from an island inhabited by the tribe of weasels. On this island a lightning-bolt had struck, and set a tree on fire.

Unfortunately the Indians were unable to swim as far as the island, but the rabbit came to their aid. He offered to go and steal the fire.

'I can run and swim faster than them,' said the rabbit. 'I'll steal the fire and the weasels will never catch me.' Then he covered his head in pine resin and set off.

The weasels were having a party when he reached the island, and invited him to a sacred dance around the fire. This was just what the rabbit had been hoping for! As he was dancing, he drew closer and closer to the fire until eventually the pine resin on his head caught fire. Then he fled.

The weasels soon found they could not catch him, so they called upon the rain spirits to extinguish the fire on the thief's head. The spirits heard their prayer and answered, but the rabbit hid in a hollow tree, and did not come out again until the rain storm was over. He made his way back to the camp of his friends, the Indians, and handed over to them the fire which has burned there from that day to this.

15 The Viper, the Frogs and the Water Snake

A viper often went to drink at a pond which a water snake claimed as his own. The two snakes decided they would have to settle the matter by fighting. The frogs, eternal enemies of the water snake, supported the viper.

On the day of the contest, the frogs began to croak madly, for they could think of nothing else to do. The viper won the battle, and afterwards the frogs asked the victorious viper for their share of the spoils. The viper began to whistle and the frogs were baffled.

'I'm repaying you in the same way you helped me,' explained the viper.

16 The Fox and the Turtle

For want of a better meal, a starving fox captured a turtle, but then could not manage to break through the solid shell in order to eat it.

'You should try putting me in the water for a while to soften me up,' suggested the shrewd turtle.

This sounded like excellent advice to the fox. He carried his prey to the stream and immersed it in the current. The turtle, who was a superb swimmer, slid out of the fox's paws and re-emerged in mid-stream laughing, 'There are animals who are even more cunning than you. Now you'll stay hungry!'

17 The Frog Prince

A young and very beautiful princess lost her ball in the water, while she was playing by the side of a lake. She began to cry so sadly that the frog who sat beside the lake croaked to her, 'What will you give me if I get you your ball back?'

'All the gold you could wish for!' replied the princess. 'No, I ask only that I be allowed to stay with you and be your friend,' said the frog. The princess gave her word (what did such a promise cost her if it meant she could have her ball back?), but she had absolutely no intention of keeping her promise. In fact, the moment she had

her ball back she ran off so fast that the frog could not keep up with her. Nevertheless, after a while the frog arrived at the palace.

As soon as she saw the frog, the princess was frightened. She ran to ask for help from her father, but the king, who knew what had happened, ordered his daughter to keep her promise. So the princess picked the frog up gently in her hand, but, with a shiver of disgust, she let it drop to the ground again. But that one brief touch was enough to break the spell that bound the frog, and caused it to turn back into the young and handsome prince he had been before.

The story ends with the happiest of wedding ceremonies.

18 The Casket with Something Good Inside

A young boy found an old casket while he was wandering about the woods. He was very excited and tried to guess what it contained. 'Golden coins? Jewels? Maps to guide me to fantastic treasures?'

The casket, however, was locked and the boy had nothing with which to open it. Even more curious, he went out of his way to pass the hut of an old man who had a reputation as a fortune teller. The old man inspected the casket, felt it, smelt it, and finally said to the boy: 'There is something good inside.'

'What is it? Gold? Jewels?'

'Something good,' the old man repeated. 'More than this I cannot tell you.'

The young man was now sure that he had some great treasure in his possession and he felt more and more impatient. 'Something good,' he repeated again and again to himself. 'It must certainly be something of enormous value if the old man said that to me.'

Unable to control himself or to wait till he got home, the boy picked up a stone and began to bash at the lid until the casket finally broke open. Inside there was a liquorice root, but, unfortunately, because of the bashing he had given the casket, it too was broken.

19 The Singer and the Dolphin

Arion was one of the most famous singers in the ancient world. On one occasion he won an important festival in Sicily, and as his prize he received so many jewels and golden cups that he was obliged to hire a ship to carry them all home to Corinth.

Unfortunately, this huge treasure made the sailors very jealous, and in order to have it for themselves, they attacked the singer and were about to throw him overboard.

Arion did not put up a struggle; instead he asked only that he be allowed to sing one last song. His wish was granted and the sailors were so enchanted by his voice that they were hardly aware of what happened next. At the first notes of his song, a dolphin swam alongside, attracted by the beautiful music. Immediately Arion jumped overboard onto the dolphin's back and was carried back across the sea.

When the ship finally reached port in Corinth, the wicked sailors began to tell everyone that there had been a storm, during which the famous singer had been lost at sea. They were struck dumb with amazement, however, when Arion arrived with a company of soldiers to arrest them.

In memory of this event, a statue, of a young man on the back of a dolphin, was erected in the port of Corinth. This statue is still there today.

20 The Camel and the Jackal

There once was a jackal who hated water but needed to cross a river. He decided to come to an agreement with a camel.

'If you carry me to the other side of the river,' he proposed to the camel, 'I will show you a field full of sugar cane. Then, while you eat the sugar cane, I will dine on the fish and crabs I find on the river-bank.'

The camel agreed to this bargain and the jackal jumped up on his back. The crossing went perfectly, but afterwards the jackal, who had a much smaller stomach, satisfied his hunger long before the camel. Whilst the camel was still eating, the jackal began to howl. The noise brought the farmers running with big sticks. The little jackal managed to escape, but the camel could not avoid a beating.

'Why on earth did you do that?' asked the camel when he was carrying the jackal back across the river.

'Oh, it's just that I nearly always sing for a while after dinner,' replied the jackal.

'Well, I nearly always have a roll in the water when I've finished eating,' said the camel, and he splashed down in the river.

So with a ducking in the river, the camel repaid the jackal for the beating it had received.

21 The Nightingale and the Farmer

A nightingale, who had laid her eggs late in the season, was still hidden in the corn when it was almost ripe. She began to worry that the crop might be harvested before her young ones were able to fly away.

Whenever she left the nest, she always urged her chicks to keep their ears open and, upon her return, tell her every word that they had heard.

One evening, when she came back to the nest, she found her chicks in terror. The youngest spoke up: 'The owner of the field told his sons to go and get their friends to come tomorrow to help with the harvesting of our field.'

'Is that all,' smiled the nightingale. 'Don't be alarmed, my dears, because nothing will happen, you will see.'

And she was right. The next morning none of the friends turned up. The farmer sent them a second message, asking them to come and help the next day, and once again the nightingale was not worried in the slightest. . . . until the day she finally heard the farmer say to his sons: 'I've had enough. Tomorrow we shall bring in the harvest ourselves. When there is work to be done, we cannot count on our friends to do it for us.'

It was only then that the nightingale took her chicks, and flew swiftly away without further delay.

22 The Keeper of the Geese

A young man, who had gone out hunting in the woods, met an old woman who was bent over with age, and bent even further under the weight of an enormous bundle of firewood. The young man immediately offered to carry her load himself. He soon realised that it was much heavier than he had thought. He tried to slip the bundle off his back, but found that it was stuck to him as though it had taken root. The old woman was really a witch who had trapped him with a spell, so he had no choice but to follow her home. There also was the old woman's daughter, looking after the geese, and she too was very old and very ugly.

The young man was prepared for the worst, but the witch released him at once from the spell, and in thanks for having carried home her firewood, she gave him out of her jewel box an emerald with an inlaid pearl.

Sometime later, the queen noticed this unusual jewel and recognised the pearl as one of the teardrops of her daughter, who had been stolen away years before. She made the hunter recount his strange tale, and then begged him to take her to the old woman's house. They had almost reached the house, when they spied the old woman's daughter on the river bank. To their amazement, as they watched she took off her grey wig, and dirty old furs she was wearing, to emerge as a beautiful fair maiden! At once, the queen recognised her long lost daughter and cried out to her, which brought the witch onto the scene . . . . only the witch was not really a witch at all, but a good fairy in disguise who had freed the kidnapped princess from the evil ogre who had captured her. Afterwards the fairy had been obliged to disguise them to keep them from falling again into the clutches of the wicked ogre. The hunter and the princess fell in love at first sight. The fairy cast one more magic spell and conjured up an enchanted castle where the couple lived a long and happy life together.

23 The Crows' Challenge

Two crows challenged each other to see which of them could fly highest, whilst carrying a sack of an agreed size.

The first crow filled his sack with cotton and laughed at the other crow who had filled his, instead with salt, which was much heavier.

When, however, it began to rain, as the second crow had expected, the salt began to dissolve.

The cotton absorbed the rain water and became so heavy that the first crow did not even have the strength to get off the ground, and he had to admit defeat.

24 King Solomon's Vase

King Solomon was so wise and just that God gave him mastery over all spirits and demons, as well as the whole of the animal kingdom. Now the Queen of Sheba wanted to know if the tales of Solomon's extraordinary powers were true, so she sent him an envoy with a vase.

'Can you guess,' asked the envoy, 'what is inside this vase?' A spirit whispered the answer into King Solomon's ear and he replied, 'Two precious stones, a pearl and an emerald.'

'Look carefully,' said the envoy. 'There is a minute hole in each stone. Can you pass a thread through these holes?' A demon told the king the name of the best jewel cutter in the whole world, but even he could not perform such a feat, and it looked as though it was, in fact, impossible to pass a thread through such tiny holes.

Eventually there came a small voice from the ground. 'May I help your majesty?' It was a tiny worm, which took the thread in its mouth, entered the hole in the pearl, emerged from the other side, and then did the same with the emerald.

When she heard of this, the Queen of Sheba realised that no ruler could stand against a king who had not only demons and spirits, but even worms at his command. She went at once to pay homage to King Solomon.

25 Ivan the Archer and the Princess

Ivan was the tsar's valiant and courageous archer. He was always entrusted with the most difficult tasks.

One day, when Ivan was old, the tsar commanded him to journey to the furthest limits of the world and bring back the beautiful princess Vassilla to be the royal bride.

Ivan had to face a thousand perils in this quest, but eventually he succeeded in stealing Vassilla away.

But the princess wanted vengeance for her kidnapping and told the tsar she would never marry him, unless her kidnapper was first put to death in a pot of boiling oil.

The ungrateful tsar ordered that Ivan be executed. Even then the brave archer showed no fear, and stepped without hesitation into the steaming pot. But Ivan's extraordinary courage brought about a supernatural reaction, and he proved invulnerable to the boiling oil. When he was brought out of the pot, not only was he completely unharmed, but he had become young once more and astonishingly handsome!

On seeing this miracle, the populace denounced the tyrant and threw him into the pot of oil instead of Ivan, who was acclaimed as tsar in his place.

The Princess Vassilla, of course, could not refuse her hand in marriage to the new and handsome tsar.

26 The Caliph and the Clown

The Caliph of Baghdad hired an intelligent and high spirited man as his court jester, and was much amused by his clever, witty comments. The clown was so well loved by his master that everyone at court showed him great respect. And so the Caliph was much surprised one day when he heard his beloved clown crying out in distress from the throne room. The Caliph hurried there and was astonished to find the guards beating the clown badly.

'Leave him alone at once!' he ordered. 'Why are you beating him?'

'We found him sitting on your throne, O Majesty!' the captain of the guards explained.

'Out of my sight!' commanded the Caliph. 'For sure the jester did not do it with the intention of offending me.'

The clown, however, continued to weep and wail even after the guards had left.

'Stop it!' said the irritated Caliph. 'You're still in one piece, aren't you?'

'I'm not crying for myself, my lord; I weep for you,' the clown explained.

'For me?' exclaimed the Caliph in surprise.

'Certainly! If I get beaten so badly for having been only a few minutes on the throne, how many beatings must you have suffered in all the years that you have been there?'

27 The Soap Bubble

The king was suddenly afflicted by a very serious illness and was never the same from that day forth. Nothing amused him any more; everything bored him and he began to yawn so much that all his courtiers began to yawn as well. He knew there was something he wanted, but he could not say what it was, which meant that nobody could give it to him.

His ministers invited doctors and learned men from all over the world to solve the problem. They brought the king ever more games, puzzles and distractions. But it was all in vain.

One day, however, an old woman arrived at the palace. 'I have that which the king requires,' she said, 'but first I must have my weight in gold.'

A bargain was struck, but then nobody could believe their eyes. No matter how much gold was put on the scales it never seemed to equal the weight of the old woman. The treasurer was becoming desperate, when the old woman finally gave a happy laugh. Then she said, 'The king really wants to see the translucent beauty of a simple soap bubble. I can give him his desire.' And the old woman dipped a straw in soapy water and began to blow the most beautiful bubbles.

Immediately the king felt happy again and full of energy, and with that the whole court, indeed the whole kingdom, also felt a great deal better.

28 The Wolf and the Heron

The wolf had swallowed a fishbone and went to ask the heron to pull it out of his throat. 'I will reward you handsomely for your help,' he promised the heron.

The heron agreed and, in an instant, put his long beak down the throat of the wolf and pulled out the fishbone. At this, the wolf thanked the heron and began to walk away.

'What about the reward you promised?' the heron shouted after him.

'What?' the wolf replied. 'You put your head between my jaws and I didn't bite it off! Isn't that reward enough?'

29 Starcap the Elf

All elves, as you know, are very strange; there is one, however, who is even stranger than the others, and his name is Starcap. Suffice to say that he is no taller than your thumb, and always wears a silk jacket which changes hue constantly, now green, then red, now blue, then yellow. On his head he always wears an enormous top hat which is spattered with stars. He is always barefoot and walks right up on his tiptoes, so that no one ever hears him coming. In fact, there are very few people who can honestly boast that, before they fall asleep, they have caught a glimpse of him.

Starcap does a very important job: he is the elf who makes children go to sleep at night. He steals up to each child quietly, puts a drop of honey on each eye to seal it, and then blows on each child's head, making it heavier and heavier until the child falls asleep. Then Starcap opens out one of the two huge umbrellas he carries round with him, and he holds it over the sleeping child for a moment. If he has opened up the black umbrella the child will have a dreamless sleep; the other umbrella is covered in fantastic pictures and if Starcap opens that one, then the child will have beautiful dreams.

30 The Dragon of the Lake

Hidesato was a valiant samurai warrior. One day he set off in search of adventure and found that the bridge over the lake was blocked by a sleeping serpent, as large as a tree.

Fearless, Hidesato leapt over the serpent and made to go on his way, but the snake changed into a majestic looking man, the King of the Lake.

The king explained that he had transformed himself into a serpent to help him find the warrior who would be brave enough to confront the terrible dragon that was threatening his kingdom and his people. Hidesato was the warrior he had been looking for. So the two men journeyed to the King of the Lake's realm, making their way through a lake where the waters parted so that they did not get wet.

That night the monstrous dragon came down out of the mountains to the side of the lake. Its eyes were like pools of fire. Valiant Hidesato stood waiting ready for it with his bow. When the warrior's arrow struck the dragon, the fires in its eyes were extinguished. Then Hidesato's sword pierced the dragon's flaming tongue. With a howl of pain and humiliation, the dragon turned and fled, and was never seen again.

As a reward, the King of the Lake gave Hidesato treasure enough to last any man for a thousand years.

Contents

The fairy tale of the month: Peter and the Wolf
Russian Fable

The fairy tale of the month

The Sleeping Beauty

There was much rejoicing throughout the kingdom on the day that a beautiful baby daughter was born to the king and queen. At court, a magnificent banquet was held for the official presentation of the little princess to the people, and all the most important and powerful lords and ladies were invited, including the fairies, of which great numbers lived in that happy land.

On the set day, all the fairies came to the castle, with the exception of one, the Black Fairy, and no-one could understand why she had not accepted the invitation. They were later to learn that the invitation had unfortunately been lost, but the Black Fairy was convinced that she had been deliberately ignored. She was very offended, so she decided to take revenge.

The fairies all lined up by the new-born baby's cradle and, one by one, with a touch of their magic wands, they each gave her a virtue: one fairy gave her beauty, one kindness, one intelligence, another gentleness. There were so many good fairies that the last in the line hesitated for a moment, not being able to think of a virtue that had not already been donated by her friends.

While the last fairy was thinking about what present to give, the Black Fairy burst into the hall, stalked up to the cradle and pointed her wand threateningly at the baby girl.

'I cannot take away what my sisters have already given you,' she said in a voice that trembled with rage. 'But I can make sure that you only enjoy it for a few years. When you have grown into a beautiful young woman, you will be pricked by a spindle and will die!'

With this, the Black Fairy disappeared, leaving everyone shocked and dismayed.

'Please save my daughter from this terrible spell,' the queen begged the good fairies.

But they had already used up their magic powers to give their presents to the baby. Only the last fairy had not yet used her magic, but her power was not strong enough to undo entirely the spell of the Black Fairy.

'All I can do,' she explained, 'is to cast a spell which will mean that when she is pricked by the spindle she will not die, but instead will fall into a deep sleep for a hundred years.'

Although this was better than death for the princess, nonetheless the king was much distressed. In an attempt to keep the child safe, he issued a decree:

'All spindles in the entire kingdom must be destroyed. It is my command that the princess must never leave the royal castle and must be guarded day and night. Everything possible must be done to make sure that the evil spell does not come to pass!'

But no man, even if he is a king, can match the power and cunning of a cruel and wicked sorceress.

The king's orders were followed to the letter, and the princess became a lovely young girl of fifteen, full of all the extraordinary virtues that had been granted her. The only virtue that she did not possess – that which the last fairy did not have time to give her before the arrival of her wicked sister – was lack of curiosity, and to tell the truth the young girl was as inquisitive as a magpie.

She had passed all her years shut up in her rooms, so she was burning to find out what was in the rest of the castle. One day, her guards were distracted for a moment, and the princess immediately took advantage of the opportunity to escape.

She wandered round all the rooms of the castle, in the cellars and the attics, until she reached a high tower hidden amongst the trees.

Inside it was the Black Fairy. Now grown old, she was busy weaving on a loom. It was very easy for her to tempt the young girl in by showing her the golden spindle with which she was weaving, and then when the princess came close enough, the evil fairy pricked her with it. Immediately the spell took effect, but, thanks to the spell of the last good fairy, the young girl fell to the ground, not dead but deeply sleeping. But what took place then had not been foreseen by the good fairies. Along with the princess, all the other people and animals in the huge castle fell into a deep, deep sleep.

One hundred years later, an adventurous young prince was riding through the woods when he found his way blocked by a thick barrier of thorns. He took out his sword and cut himself a path until, to his great surprise, he found himself at the gates of a castle. When he entered, he found everyone fast asleep, sentries and courtiers, dogs and horses, even the king and queen side by side on their thrones.

From room to room the prince wandered, until he came to the tower where the sleeping princess lay. He was filled with grief at the terrible fate which had befallen such a beautiful young girl. He fell on his knees beside her and gave her a gentle kiss on her forehead.

That kiss broke the spell that bound the princess and she awoke, and the whole castle woke up. What a moment of joy it was when the king and queen were reunited with their daughter. The festivities, which included the wedding of the princess to her rescuer, lasted for three months. In fact it is not certain that they are over yet.

1 The Clever Violinist

One day a violinist decided to play some music as he was walking through the woods. But this attracted a large fierce bear.

'How well you play,' he said to the man, to gain his confidence. 'Could you teach me to play as well?'

'Of course,' answered the violinist, not fooled at all. 'As long as you do what I tell you. Put your paws in the crack in this tree.'

The bear did as he was told and the musician was quick to jam his paws in the crack with a large stone. The bear was stuck tight.

The next time the violinist played, he attracted a lion, and the same scene was repeated. This time the beast was caught in a trap and ended up hanging by its tail from a tree. Then it was the turn of a tiger, which was captured by a similar trick.

When the three wild beasts managed to free themselves, they chased after the violinist, seeking revenge; but they found him in the company of a new friend: a huge woodsman with a giant axe, who chased the animals away.

And so the clever violinist crossed the forest in safety.

2 Pandora's Box

A long, long time ago, almost at the beginning of time, the ancient gods met and decided to create a masterpiece.

They created an absolutely perfect young girl. Each of them gave to Pandora (which is what they called their marvellous creation) the most precious gift they could bestow; beauty, intelligence, wisdom and skill in all things.

Finally she was taken to Jupiter, the king of the gods, so that he too could give her a gift, before sending her down to earth. Jupiter, who did not approve of the gifts of the other gods, gave Pandora a very ordinary box with a lid. 'You must never open it under any circumstances,' he warned.

But Pandora could not resist the temptation of finding out what was in the box and one day she opened it.

To her horror, out came all the evils that have since afflicted mankind: old age, sickness, jealousy, selfishness, greed. . . . before Pandora could close the lid on them they had already spread all around the world.

But, luckily, hope remained in the box, and with hope mankind manages to survive all these ills.

3 The Two Mules and the Robbers

Two mules were on the same path. The first, who worked for a miller, was loaded with oats.

The other was owned by a banker and was carrying a chest full of golden coins.

Because of this it trotted along very proudly, full of itself.

But on hearing the clinking, some robbers realised that it was carrying a treasure.

As they stole it, they beat the mule badly with sticks.

'You see,' explained the first mule. 'Being rich and important has its drawbacks.'

4 The Husband Who Looked After the House

A farmer's wife became fed up with being criticised by her husband about how she ran the house, so one day she challenged him. 'Tomorrow I'll go out and work in the fields, and you can take care of the work in the house, if you think you can do it better than me!' The next day the husband did his best to do things right. He began to make the butter, but his efforts soon made him thirsty and he went down to the cellar to drink some wine. He opened the barrel, but then he heard the pig come into the house and knock over the butter dish. He rushed back upstairs to stop the animal from causing more trouble, but he forgot to put the cork in the wine barrel again.

He kept getting into trouble all morning long. At lunchtime, when he put the stew on to boil, he remembered that he had not taken the cow out to pasture yet; but there was no time anymore. He decided to take it onto the roof, so it could eat the grass that grew among the tiles. It was very difficult to get the cow onto the roof. In the end he succeeded, and, to make sure that the animal did not fall off, he tied it there with a rope.

Then he remembered the stew over the fire. To get back to the kitchen as fast as possible, so that the stew did not burn, he lowered himself down the chimney. For safety, he tied the other end of the rope to his foot. But the cow fell off the roof just then, and the man was yanked back up the chimney and got stuck there.

When his wife came home from the fields, the first thing she saw was the cow dangling from the rope, so she cut it loose. On the other end the man dropped down. . . . into the fireplace. When the woman entered the house, she found the floor covered in butter, the cellar flooded with wine, and her husband upside down with his head in the stew!

She returned to her housework. From then on, of course, he never grumbled at her again.

5 The Apple Tree and the Dandelion

It was spring and the apple tree put out its bright little flowers. They were so lovely that even the princess was much impressed.

She cut off some branches and arranged them in a valuable vase in the palace hallway.

The apple branch was very proud of this tribute to its beauty. Through the windows it could see the flowers in the garden and the meadow, and it pitied them greatly for their insignificance, especially the humble dandelion, because with one puff children could blow away their seeds, leaving them naked and defenceless.

He pitied them because their destiny was so different from his. At the same time, he was proud of his own shapeliness, his beauty, and his rich vase in the hall. It did not occur to him that the sun shone on the poor dandelion just as brightly as it did on him.

One day, however, the princess brought in a dandelion to paint, and put it in the same vase as the flowering apple branch. Beside the delicate beauty of the meadow flower, destined to be blown away by the wind, the white flowers of the apple grew a bit red, with shame.

6 The Princess and the Pea

One day a young stranger arrived at the palace, claiming she was a princess.

The queen had a room made ready for her, but, to put her to the test, she had a pea put in the bed and over it she put twenty mattresses and twenty featherdown covers.

In the morning, when the young girl woke up, she was aching all over and covered in bruises because of that pea. Such a delicate and sensitive skin confirmed her claim to be a princess, and the queen considered her to be a suitable bride for the young prince and heir.

7 The Pride of Icarus

Daedalus, one of the greatest inventors of ancient times, was asked by the king of Crete to build a maze where he could imprison the Minotaur, a monster half-man and half-bull, so that it could never get out again. The ingenious architect did as he was asked, but some time later he helped Theseus, a famous hero, to kill the monster. As a punishment, the king of Crete ordered Daedalus to be imprisoned himself in the labyrinth, with his young son, Icarus.

'Don't worry,' the father encouraged the boy. 'I know already how we can get out of this prison!'

Daedalus made a huge pair of wings and he stuck them with wax onto his son's shoulders. The wings could be moved up and down by moving the arms. Then Daedalus made another pair of wings for himself.

The wings worked wonderfully. The two men took off, and with a few armstrokes they managed to climb high enough to get over the walls of the labyrinth. But then the young boy, out of pride, wanted to fly higher and higher, until the heat from the sun melted the wax and his wings fell off. Then Icarus plunged to the ground and died. Daedalus, full of sadness, carried on flying until he reached safety.

8 The Wolf and the Lamb

A wolf spied a lamb who was drinking out of a stream, and began to look for an excuse to attack it and eat it.

'You are making my part of the stream dirty,' accused the wolf.

'How can that be?' said the lamb. 'You are further upstream than me, and the water flows down, not up.'

'Aren't you the lamb who insulted my father last year?' asked the wolf.

'I wasn't even born last year,' came the reply.

'Enough of all this talk,' snarled the wolf. 'I am not going to miss a chance of eating you just because you are good at excuses.'

9 The Three Little Pigs and the Big Bad Wolf

Three little pigs decided to go each their own way in search of their fortune.

The first thing each of them did, as soon as they found a suitable place, was to start building a house.

The first little pig was very lazy, so he quickly built himself a house of straw.

But then the big bad wolf came along and with a puff he blew it clean away.

The first little pig could only avoid being eaten by running away to the second little pig's house.

This one was a bit wiser and had built his house out of wood and twigs, but when the big bad wolf arrived, he blew it down also with just one puff.

The two little pigs fled as fast as they could to the third little pig's house.

The third little pig was hard working and clever, and he had built his house out of bricks.

Along came the wolf, and though he huffed and puffed he could not blow the house down.

So the angry wolf climbed onto the roof so that he could come down the chimney.

But the three little pigs put a huge pot of water on the fire to boil: and when the wolf came down the chimney, he got so badly burnt that he scampered straight back up and ran off as fast as his legs could carry him.

10 The Emperor's New Clothes

There was once a tailor who boasted that he could make wonderful clothes: only intelligent and sensitive people could see them, to all others they were invisible. The emperor heard of this and thought that such a suit would be very becoming. He called the tailor before him and ordered him to make a suit for him.

The tailor asked for thread and a great deal of money, and began his work; or rather he pretended to work, because there was nothing on the loom. However, each courtier, who was sent by the emperor to check on the work, returned full of enthusiasm.

'What wonderful cloth! What lovely work! What an original design!'

Actually they had seen nothing, but they were lying in case they were thought to be stupid or insensitive. In the end, the emperor also pretended to be enthusiastic about the suit, even though he could not see it either. He decided to wear it for a big parade, and as he passed through the crowd, all the people exclaimed: 'What a wonderful suit of clothes.'

Until a little boy shouted: 'Hey, look, the emperor's got no clothes on.'

And the crowd also shouted then, 'He's got no clothes on.' The only thing then for the embarassed emperor to do was to run back to the palace as fast as his legs would carry him.

11 Pen and Inkwell

On the desk of a famous poet there was an inkwell. During the night, when things come alive, it was very full of itself.

'It's incredible,' it said, 'how many beautiful things come out of me. A few drops of my ink are enough to fill an entire page, and then how many wonderful and moving things can be read in it.'

But its vanity began to annoy the pen. 'You don't understand, you fat fool, that you are just the supplier of the raw material. It is I who make use of your ink and write down on paper what I have in me. There is no doubt that it is the pen that does the writing.'

The poet came home from a concert and the music had inspired him.

'How stupid would the bow and violin be,' he wrote on a sheet of paper, 'if they boasted that they alone were making the music. So often men are just as stupid, when we boast of doing something, forgetting that we are all instruments in the hands of God.'

But still the inkwell and the pen, which had been used to write these words, learned no lesson from them.

12 The Three Sheiks and the Queen of Arabia

Maura, who liked to be thought of as the most beautiful and powerful queen of Arabia, had many suitors for her hand in marriage. One by one she discarded them, until her list was reduced to just three sheiks, all equally young and handsome, rich and strong. It was very hard to decide who was the best of them.

One evening, Maura disguised herself and went to the camp of the three sheiks, as they were about to have dinner, and asked them for something to eat.

The first gave her some left-over food; the second gave her some unappetising camel's tail; the third sheik, who was called Hakim, offered her some of the most tender and tasty meat. After dinner, the disguised queen left the sheiks' camp.

The following day the queen invited the three sheiks to dinner at her palace.

She ordered her servants to give each one exactly what they had given her the evening before.

Hakim, who received a plate of succulent meat, refused to eat it if the other two could not share it with him, and this act finally convinced Queen Maura that this was the man for her.

'Without question, Hakim is the most generous of you,' she announced to the sheiks. 'So it is Hakim I will marry.'

13 The Lovelorn Lion and the Peasant

A lion was unfortunate enough to fall in love with the beautiful daughter of a peasant, and he went to her father to ask for her hand in marriage. The peasant was worried about his daughter's future, but didn't have the courage to refuse the lion openly.

'My daughter,' he pretended, 'is allergic to teeth and claws. Come back after you have had them removed, and you can marry her.'

The lovelorn lion promptly had his teeth and claws removed, but when he came back, he was absolutely harmless and the peasant beat him with a stick and chased him away.

14 The Snake Princess

An intrepid cossack once saw some woods burning and tried to put out the fire, but there was nothing he could do. To his horror, amidst the flames he saw a young girl crying out to him to help her. He did not know what to do, as the flames were so fierce.

'Stretch your spear out to me through the flames,' she said. When he did this, the young girl suddenly changed into a snake, wrapped herself round the spear, and so the cossack was able to save her. The magical snake then ordered him to take it to a castle. As they arrived, the snake turned back into a woman.

'You must wait here for me for seven years,' she said to the cossack. Then she vanished instantly from before his eyes. Although there was nobody in the castle, it was bewitched. It was enough for the cossack to express a wish, and dinner, or anything else he wished for, would appear. For the faithful cossack the seven years passed quickly; eventually the snake returned to the castle. And then, transformed again into a beautiful princess, she explained to the cossack that she had been bewitched, but his courage and faithfulness had broken the evil spell on her. And so, of course, the cossack and the princess went off to her father, who gladly gave his daughter in marriage to our hero.

15 The Eagle and the Crow

A crow saw an eagle drop down from the sky on to a lamb, catch it with its claws, and fly straight back with it to its nest.

The crow thought he would like to do the same.

But the lamb was much too heavy for him, and what was worse, the crow's little claws got caught in the lamb's thick fur, so the bird was trapped there.

The shepherd saw the crow, caught it and put it in a cage.

So the one who thought to imitate an eagle ended up being laughed at by everyone.

16 The Never-Ending Story

There was a little flax plant which was very happy with its little blue flowers and the gentle caress of the rain; but one day the farmworkers pulled it out of the ground, and then it was put through a series of machines which twisted and pulled it in every possible way.

But the flax did not complain because it was grateful for all the good things there had been in its life. However, its life was not yet over: in fact, when it finally came off the end of a loom, it had become a magnificent cloth, and the praise of everyone who saw it gave the flax further cause for satisfaction.

Then the cloth was attacked by scissors and by a needle, which caused it great discomfort, but they transformed it into a most elegant blouse; and the flax kept on telling itself how lucky it had been in its life, in spite of everything it had been through.

But even yet, life with its pleasures and pain was not over; when the blouse became nothing more than a rag, it was thrown away and ended up being turned into paper. Then the paper was put through the cylinders of the printing machine and then turned into a book; and when at the very end the book was burned, it became smoke and rose up into the sky.

17 Blockhead and the Three Feathers

An old king, who had to choose one of his three sons to be his heir, invited them to take part in a competition.

'I will give the crown to whichever one brings me the most beautiful carpet.'

He then threw three feathers into the air and told his sons to look in the direction the wind took the feathers. The eldest son went to the east, the second to the west, the youngest, who was called Blockhead by the others because of his simple nature, saw his feather fall to the ground nearby, where he was not going to find any carpets, let alone beautiful ones.

He had begun to grow desperate when all of a sudden a hole opened up beneath his feet and he fell into a room, which turned out to be the Palace of the Frogs.

The queen frog was so moved by the young man's story that she made him a gift of a magnificent carpet, and with it the youngest son won the competition. But his brothers were jealous and asked for a second trial and the king agreed. 'The one who brings me the most beautiful ring will ascend the throne.'

The eldest son made do with the first beautiful ring he could find, as did the second son, but they were bested again by the youngest brother, who was once more helped by the queen of the frogs. And so a third test was agreed: the kingdom would go to the one who married the most beautiful bride.

This time it seemed that even the queen of the frogs could not help. All she told the youngest prince to do was to take a big carrot and hollow it out, then to attach six mice to it, and finally to put one of her frog maids into the carrot.

In his trusting simplicity, Blockhead did as he was told. As his reward, the carrot changed into a luxurious carriage, the mice into beautiful white horses, and the frog into a beautiful young princess, who then reigned happily alongside King Blockhead for many, many years.

18 Why the Sun and the Moon Live in the Sky

A long time ago, the Sun and the Moon were a married couple who lived on the Earth, and were great friends of the Sea. One day, they invited the Sea to visit them but the Sea hesitated, thinking that there might not be enough room in their house. But they reassured him.

So the Sea went along, with the fish and all the members of his family. Immediately the water began to rise, so that the Sun and the Moon, to avoid being drowned, had to climb up onto the roof, and then eventually into the sky, where they have remained ever since.

19 The Thirsty Ant

An ant was scurrying desperately around, looking for something to drink, but it could find nothing. It had become convinced that it was going to die of thirst when a drop of water fell from above and saved its life. In truth, it was a tear, and it was filled with all the magical virtues which are born from suffering; after that the ant discovered that it was able suddenly to understand and speak perfectly the language of men.

One day the ant went into a grain store and there, sitting on the floor, was a little girl, crying. 'Why are you so sad?' asked the ant.

'I've been imprisoned by an ogre. He will only set me free when I have made three heaps of grain, barley and rye, out of this huge mountain of seed where they are all mixed together.'

'That will take a month!' exclaimed the ant, looking at the huge pile of seed in the corner.

'If I haven't finished by tomorrow, the ogre will eat me for his supper,' the girl cried.

'Please do not weep. We'll help you.'

And the ant fetched all his companions and they set to work. The next morning the ogre found that the task was done.

Thus it was that a tear saved a little girl's life.

20 Aldebaran and the Celestial Camels

Aldebaran, the most luminous star in the constellation of Taurus, fell in love with Electra, the most beautiful star of the Pleiades, and he went to ask for her hand in marriage. He bore gifts of a herd of camels, but on the way he was attacked by another aspirant for her hand, Alcyon.

The fight between them is not yet over. Even now, on calm nights, it is possible to see pale blue Electra followed by red Alcyon and then by Aldebaran with his big herd of celestial camels, making up the constellation of the Hyades.

21 The Hunting Dog and the Guard Dog

A man had two dogs and he trained one as a hunter and one as a guard dog; but whenever the hunting dog caught some game, the tastiest morsels were always given to the guard dog.

One day the hunter protested to the guard dog: 'It's not fair. I work at hunting all day long and you get your food without doing anything.'

'That must be the way the master wants it,' replied the guard dog.

'Obviously it is more important for him to reward the dog who protects his home than the one who goes out hunting.'

22 The Oak Tree and the Spring

Poseidon, who according to the ancient Greeks was the god of the sea, was not satisfied with his immense kingdom and wished to extend his dominion onto dry land as well.

He decided first to attack Athens, which at that time was the most important city in the world. As a beginning to his campaign, he attacked the hill on which the city stood.

So powerful was the sea that the hill was pierced from one side to the other and out of this tunnel came a salt water spring.

But the city was under the protection of Athena, the famous goddess of wisdom. She thought long and hard about how to reconquer it. The sea god had placed a salt water spring beneath the city as a sign of his power. Athena wanted to place a sign there not only of strength but of immortality. She thought for a long time and then created a new tree and planted its seed next to the spring.

In this way there grew up the huge oak tree, which still stands on the highest part of Athens, while Poseidon's spring of water dried up a long, long time ago.

23 The Betrothed

The little spinning top fell madly in love with the ball which lived with him in the toy chest. He asked the ball to marry him.

'We are made for each other,' said the top, 'you can leap and I can dance. Together we are the perfect couple.'

But the ball was vain and thought that the spinning top was too unimportant to be her husband, so she turned him down.

'I fly so high up into the sky,' she explained, 'that I have become engaged to a swallow. He's the one I'll marry.'

One day the ball vanished and the spinning top thought she must have gone off to get married. He never forgot her and continued to yearn for her.

Some time later, the spinning top was pushed too hard and it spun off far away and got lost. Fate brought it to a little stream beside a country path, and there he found his old love again. The ball was very badly worn as it had been exposed to the elements for so long, but the spinning top recognised her at once and asked her to marry him again. The ball, who had not thought of the swallow for a long time, was happy to accept this time, even though the spinning top was also very scratched and marked by now.

24 The Magic Barrel and the Bewitched Sword

Ivan the cossack had saved the life of a sorceress. In reward, she gave him a magic barrel. If you twisted the lid one way, a castle appeared; if you twisted it the other way, the castle would disappear.

Now, Ivan did not really know what to do with the barrel and he looked forward to the day when he could trade it for something more useful.

One evening he was approached by an old man who asked him for a meal. Ivan caused the castle to appear, generously invited the old man in, and then let him eat his fill from the food-laden table they found ready. The old man was very taken with the castle and offered to exchange his own sword for it.

'Now what do I want with a sword?' refused Ivan, 'I have my sabre.'

'But this is a magic sword,' insisted the old man. 'Raise your arm and the sword will do everything by itself.'

To prove it, the old man raised his arm and the sword flew out of its scabbard and began hacking at some bushes nearby. Ivan was very impressed and agreed to the exchange. When Ivan returned home, he found his city besieged by enemies. He raised his arm and all by itself the sword destroyed the attackers. Ivan was put in command of the army and given his daughter in marriage – all because he saved the life of a sorceress.

25 The Artist and His Rival

A famous artist was commissioned by the ruler of a powerful city to paint frescoes on the walls of his palace. Scaffolding was put in place and the artist began to paint. The next morning he discovered that his painting had been scrawled on and covered with splashes of paint.

The artist was furious, thinking that one of his rivals had done it. To find the culprit, the prince ordered the guards to hide in the room, so they could surprise the vandal, if he returned, and teach him a lesson. The guilty party was caught in the act, and turned out to be the prince's pet monkey. It had watched the artist at work and tried to imitate him.

The monkey was put back in its cage until the painting was finished. When it was released and saw the painting, the monkey pulled a face, as if to say, 'I could have done it better.'

'Now you really are behaving like a true painter,' laughed the prince. 'It is well-known that artists do not have the gift of modesty, and they all think their own work is a masterpiece and other artists' work is rubbish.'

26 Ivan the Brave and the Water of Life

An old tsar heard tell of a princess from whose finger came drops of water with the power to restore youth. So the tsar sent his elder son to look for her.

The young man reached the edge of the world, but there learned that he still had to cross three bridges. The toll for the first bridge was one of his arms, for the second a leg, and for the third his head. The discouraged prince gave up the venture and returned home.

The younger son, Ivan, was then sent out on the quest, and he too went to the edge of the world. At the first bridge, instead of paying the toll of an arm, he used his arm to defeat the guards; at the second bridge, he made use of both his legs to run across before the guards could catch him; and at the third bridge, he used his head to find a way to sneak across.

He went on until he reached a golden castle. In it there was a beautiful, sleeping girl. From her finger dripped the water of life. Ivan began to collect it in his flask, when the maiden awoke and caused him to fall unconscious to the ground. But when she looked closely at Ivan and saw how handsome he was, she roused him again, and, together, the young couple returned to the tsar with the water of life. Naturally, then they were wed.

27 The Twelve Hunters

The prince of the kingdom of the East was called to his father's deathbed to hear his last words: 'Promise me that you will marry the queen of the Kingdom of the North.' The prince felt his heart freeze, for he was already in love with the princess of the Kingdom of the South, but he did not dare to go against his father, and he made the promise. When he failed to return to his true love, she decided to go and see for herself what had happened to him. She chose eleven handmaidens and bade them dress up as hunters. She, too, disguised herself and, with her companions, she went to the Kingdom of the East, where her loved one was now the ruler. The prince took the hunters into his service, not realising that they were maidens; nor did he recognise his beloved. But when the royal wedding was proclaimed, the princess of the Kingdom of the South was so pained that she swooned. The prince rushed to help her and then recognised on her finger the ring which he had given her as a token of his love.

Then the king realised that he loved her too much to be able to keep his promise to his father to marry the queen of the Kingdom of the North, and, when she saw how happy the two lovers were together, went back home and left them to their joy.

28 Figeater's Money Bag

They called him Figeater because he loved eating figs so much, but nobody knew his real name or where he had come from. The young man was a natural clown and his antics made everyone laugh, so everybody liked him and he considered himself happy.

One day, Figeater found an old money bag on which was embroidered the phrase: 'Ask and you shall receive.' It was a magic money bag and, indeed, it was enough to ask, for any wish to be granted. The young man tried out the bag by asking for small amounts of money, and then for a few golden coins. As his own needs were small, Figeater gave away to others everything he received; but his sudden wealth caused his fellow villagers to grow suspicious. They accused him of being a thief and chased him out of the village.

In his wanderings, Figeater came across an old beggarman. He looked very familiar, and as they spoke they realised that each was the one the other was looking for. The old man was a king in disguise, searching for his son who had been taken away by robbers and abandoned many years ago. The son, of course, was none other than Figeater, and he and his father went back rejoicing to their kingdom where they lived long and prosperously.

29 Hurashima and the Dragon

Hurashima was a young Japanese fisherman who was brave and generous. One day he came across some boys who had caught a turtle and were tormenting it. Feeling sorry for it, Hurashima used what little money he had to buy it from them and set it free in the sea.

Some time later, when he was out fishing, he heard his name being called. It was the turtle, who asked Hurashima to climb onto its back so that it might take him to meet the powerful dragon, the Lord of the Seas, who wished to show Hurashima its gratitude. So he climbed onto the turtle's back and was taken to a fantastic castle on the seabed.

The dragon received him with full ceremony and invited him to remain as its guest. Hurashima accepted, and for a while he was able to enjoy all the delights imaginable; but then he grew homesick and asked to return.

Back on dry land, Hurashima found everything changed. His house and loved ones were no longer there. He came to the realisation that he had been away for many years. Then, all of a sudden, Hurashima felt himself growing older and older. Only then did he understand that, by returning, he had given up the dragon's most precious gift, eternal youth.

30 The Sick Camel

A camel who lived all alone on the edge of an oasis fell ill and all his relatives and friends went to visit him there.

Because the journey was a long one, they each stayed for a while to rest up and eat the grass that was growing around the oasis.

The camel was pleased to be visited, but when he felt better and roused himself to go and look for something to eat, he discovered that his friends and relatives had eaten everything. What could he do? There was no choice but to set off. . . . and look for another oasis.

31 James the Simpleton

Although James was a complete simpleton, he was very willing and helpful. One day he went to a friend's house for lunch, which was very fortunate.

When he returned he found that his father, his mother and his two brothers had all eaten mushrooms and were now in so much pain that they feared that they had been poisoned.

'Run to the pharmacy,' said his father, who could not move for his stomach cramps, 'and get something very strong for stomach upsets, a dose for four people. Have you got that?'

'Yes, dad: I have to go and get something for upset stomachs, a dose for four people.'

'Good. Go on. Be quick!'

They waited and waited, but James did not return and his father began to worry; he knew his son was capable of doing anything. Luckily he began to feel better, and so he went out to look for the boy. He found James by the roadside doubled up and in great pain, holding his stomach.

'What have you done to yourself?' asked the father worriedly.

'Just what you told me to, dad,' James replied. 'I went to the pharmacy and got the four doses of medicine, and then I took them all.'

May

Contents

The fairy tale of the month: The Sleeping Beauty
Charles Perrault

1   The Clever Violinist   *The Brothers Grimm*
2   Pandora's Box   *Greek Legend*
3   The Two Mules and the Robbers   *Phaedrus*
4   The Husband Who Looked After the House   *Norwegian Fable*
5   The Apple Tree and the Dandelion   *Hans Christian Andersen*
6   The Princess and the Pea   *Hans Christian Andersen*
7   The Pride of Icarus   *Greek Legend*
8   The Wolf and the Lamb   *Aesop*
9   The Three Little Pigs and the Big Bad Wolf   *English Fable*
10   The Emperor's New Clothes   *Hans Christian Andersen*
11   Pen and Inkwell   *Hans Christian Andersen*
12   The Three Sheiks and the Queen of Arabia   *Arabian Fable*
13   The Lovelorn Lion and the Peasant   *Aesop*
14   The Snake Princess   *Russian Fable*
15   The Eagle and the Crow   *Aesop*
16   The Never-Ending Story   *Hans Christian Andersen*
17   Blockhead and the Three Feathers   *The Brothers Grimm*
18   Why the Sun and the Moon Live in the Sky   *African Fable*
19   The Thirsty Ant   *Russian Fable*
20   Aldebaran and the Celestial Camels   *Arabian Fable*
21   The Hunting Dog and the Guard Dog   *Aesop*
22   The Oak Tree and the Spring   *Greek Legend*
23   The Betrothed   *Hans Christian Andersen*
24   The Magic Barrel and the Bewitched Sword   *Russian Fable*
25   The Artist and His Rival   *Italian Fable*
26   Ivan the Brave and the Water of Life   *Russian Fable*
27   The Twelve Hunters   *The Brothers Grimm*
28   Figeater's Money Bag   *Luigi Capuana*
29   Hurashima and the Dragon   *Japanese Fable*
30   The Sick Camel   *Arabian Fable*
31   James the Simpleton   *Jerome K. Jerome*

June

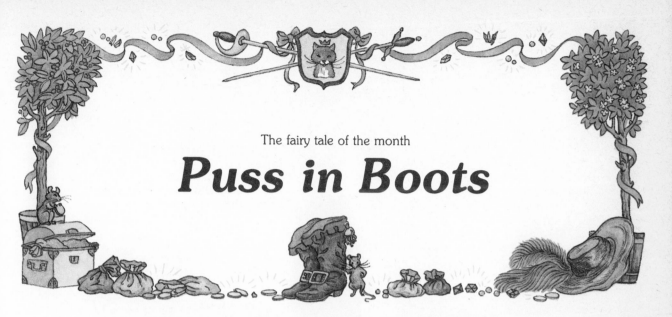

The fairy tale of the month
Puss in Boots

A windmill, a donkey and a cat were all that a poor farmer had left to his three sons when he died. The youngest son, who had inherited the cat, had no idea how he was to survive.

'Once I've eaten the cat and made a cloak from its skin, I will simply die of hunger!' He bemoaned his ill luck, with deep sighs. The cat understood that he himself was in the more immediate danger and his great fear of becoming a fur cloak gave him the ability to speak. 'Don't worry. I will provide for you!' promised the cat. 'You must simply obtain for me a pair of boots and elegant clothes which would be suitable for the personal servant of some great lord. And then just leave the rest to me.'

The young man was so astonished that the cat could talk that he did not think to ask any questions. He ran to the market and bought an excellent pair of boots and a very elegant feathered hat, such as is worn by cavaliers.

'Very good,' said the cat, examining himself critically in the mirror, 'but I really should have a cloak and a cane as well.'

'I have already spent every penny I have in the world!' the young man exclaimed.

'Then I am sure it will do splendidly the way it is,' conceded the cat.

As soon as it had finished its preparations, the cat went off hunting and, since he was expert and fast, after a few minutes he had caught a big,

appetising hare. The cat raced to the royal palace and asked, in a haughty tone, to be admitted to the king. The guards were awestruck and did not dare to try to stop a talking cat who spoke with such self-assurance. They let him pass freely.

Once before the throne, the cat bowed deeply and graciously and offered the hare to the king. 'My master,' he said, 'begs you to accept this gift.'

'Who is your master?' asked the king.

'The Marquis of Carabas,' replied the inventive cat.

'I don't know him,' said the king, 'but you must thank him on my behalf.'

On many other occasions, the king accepted gifts like this from the mysterious Marquis of Carabas.

One day, whilst engaged on a royal tour, in his carriage, with his beautiful daughter, the king saw the cat standing, waving in the middle of the road. He ordered his coachman to stop at once.

'Thieves have stolen my master's fine clothes,' said the clever cat. 'He had left them on the grass while he went swimming in the lake!'

The king looked out of the carriage window and, sure enough, he saw the young man in the water up to his neck. Having received so many gifts from him in the past, the king felt obliged to help the young man. 'Run at once

to the palace,' he ordered his servants, 'and bring some clothes which are suitable for the marquis.'

The farmer's son now found himself dressed in the rich attire of a nobleman at court, instead of his usual everyday clothes. He looked so handsome that, from her first glance, the princess began to fall in love with him. The king, of course, noticed this, but, he, too, when he thought about the matter, came to the conclusion that the rich and generous Marquis of Carabas might make a good son-in-law. He invited the young man to come to the palace. Completely bewildered by what was happening to him, the young man climbed into the coach with the king and the princess.

The well dressed cat went on ahead and came across some men working in an enormous field. 'Listen to me carefully, or you will regret it!' he threatened them. 'If anybody asks you whose fields these are, you must reply that they belong to the Marquis of Carabas. If you do not do as I say, then I give my word that I will claw you to pieces!' The poor men were so flabbergasted by a cat that wore boots and a feathered hat, and that spoke and uttered such threats, that they did not even dream of disobeying him. Thus, when the royal carriage did drive past and the king asked the peasants to whom the fields might belong, they replied in unison: 'They belong to the Marquis of Carabas.'

And the king got the same reply from everyone he asked along the road. It seemed indeed that his guest was the owner of most of the kingdom! Meanwhile the young man was struck dumb with amazement, while the king and the princess believed that he kept quiet out of polite embarrassment.

Further along the road stood the majestic castle of a terrible ogre, who had the magical power to transform himself into any animal he wished. The cat came to him and goaded him into giving proof of this ability, so the ogre turned himself into a huge and ferocious lion. The cat showed no fear: 'That is easy. It is much harder for somebody big and fat like you to change into a tiny animal like a mouse.'

This stung the ogre's pride and he immediately set about showing that he could do this just as easily. The cat leapt on the mouse at once and swallowed it in a mouthful, and that was the end of the ogre.

He then ran to the drawbridge of the castle just in time to welcome the king and the princess to the majestic home of the Marquis of Carabas.

At this, the king was so convinced of the wealth and power of the young man that he did not even wait until they returned to court to suggest that the Marquis should marry his daughter. Indeed, the wedding was celebrated that very night in what had previously been the ogre's castle.

1 The Magic Veil

A young farmer lived an impoverished existence in his little hut, but he never complained because the beauty of nature was more precious to his sensitive soul than any wealth.

One day his attention was caught by a lovely smell coming from the woods. He followed the sweet fragrance until he reached a pine tree and saw, caught in the branches, an unbelievably beautiful veil, woven from rays of sunshine, beams of moonlight, and studded all over with stars. The young man had just disentangled the veil from the tree, when there appeared a young maiden who asked for it back. At first the young man refused, at which the unknown girl burst into tears.

'I am a nymph,' she explained, 'and without my veil I will never again be able to rejoin my sisters.'

'If you really are a nymph, then you can prove it,' said the young man, 'by dancing for me as only nymphs know how to dance.' So the maiden began to dance in mid-air, her veil flying round and round the farmer, and from the veil there fell thousands and thousands of flowers.

Later, the farmer never could tell if he had dreamt it all, or if it had really happened, but from that day on the young man rejoiced even more in the beauty of nature.

2 The Story of King Prudence

There was once a king who was so cautious and diffident that he was known as Prudence. Since he did not trust horses, he went everywhere on foot, until, finally, his escorts grew tired of the long walks and asked a magician to invent some kind of seat that moved by itself.

Two days later the new invention was ready. 'It is called a bicycle,' the magician informed them.

A minister was then required to demonstrate to the king how the bicycle worked, but, unfortunately, he fell off and broke his arm. When he had recovered a little he went back to the magician and said: 'We need something safer than a seat; an entire carriage would be better'.

A whole week was needed before the new invention was ready and it was called an automobile. During the first test drive, however, the unlucky minister crashed into a tree.

After this, King Prudence continued to travel everywhere on foot, until the day he tripped, fell and broke his leg. Then he understood that he had been wrong to blame the bicycle and the automobile for accidents that were really due solely to the imprudence of men. He himself then went at once to the magician and ordered carriages without horses for himself and everyone else at court.

3 The Fox and the Crow

One day a fox came across a crow who was perched on a branch with a piece of cheese in its beak. Immediately, the fox began to consider how he might obtain it for himself.

'You have everything; strength, beauty, wisdom!' he said flatteringly to the bird. 'If you only had a beautiful voice, then you would be perfect.'

Not wishing the fox to think that it did not have a fine voice, the crow began to sing. Of course the piece of cheese fell from its beak and the fox claimed it at once. 'Your most serious problem,' laughed the fox, 'is that you have more vanity than intelligence!'

4 The Dancing Teapot

Once upon a time, a ragman found a badger caught in a trap. He took pity on the animal and set it free. Now this badger had magic powers and thought for a long time about how to repay the man. Finally the badger turned itself into a beautiful teapot and slipped itself into the ragman's bag.

When the ragman found the teapot, he was very puzzled as to how it had got into his sack. He decided to take it at once to the priests in the temple as a gift, so that they might always remember him in their prayers.

When, however, one of the priests put the teapot on the fire to boil some water, he heard it cry out. He immediately began to shout in terror: 'The teapot is possessed!'

The other priests came running, but the teapot seemed to be boiling away in the normal fashion. However, the priest insisted on calling the ragman back and returning his teapot to him.

That night, the kindly ragman was awakened by a tiny voice. When he looked around, he saw that the teapot now had the head, the tail and the paws of a badger.

'Take me to the market,' the teapot said to him, 'and I will dance for you and make you a rich man.'

And thus it was. To see something that was half badger and half teapot, that danced by itself, was such an extraordinary sight, that people were willing to pay to witness it.

The ragman became so rich in this way that in a short while he had enough money to last him a lifetime. After this, instead of going on to make even more money, the ragman decided that the least he could do for the teapot, to whom he owed so much, was to allow it to rest.

So that the teapot might not fall into the hands of some more greedy person, he took it back to the temple where the priests again agreed to look after it.

From that day, a thousand years have passed, but the teapot is still in the temple where it basks in the rays of the sun through the windows.

5 The Mark of Wisdom

In the forests of Africa there once lived a very clever rabbit who wished to become even more wise. So he went to ask for help from a witch.

'Bring me a live python,' the witch told him, 'and then we shall see.'

So the rabbit cut a long branch from a tree and went to the python's lair, where the snake was curled up. The rabbit showed it the branch. 'You are always boasting about your size,' said the rabbit, 'but this branch is longer than you.' 'Don't talk rubbish,' said the python. 'Very well then, prove it, let me see which of you is longer.'

The python stretched itself out alongside the branch, whereupon the rabbit lost no time in tying the snake to it. 'Well done, indeed,' the witch praised him. 'Now you must bring me a swarm of bees.' So the rabbit emptied a pumpkin, put some honey inside, and hung it up near a beehive. When the bees had gone inside the pumpkin, the rabbit closed up the little hole he had made and carried the pumpkin full of bees to the witch. When the witch saw that the rabbit had succeeded in the second test as well, she rubbed a little magic ointment between his ears and a small white spot appeared. The rabbits of Africa still have this little spot and it is considered a mark of wisdom.

6 The Oak and the Sugar Cane

The oak, which was very proud of itself, showed a great deal of sympathy for the sugar cane. 'What a sad lot is yours! A breath of wind is sufficient to make you bow your head. On the other hand, I stand up straight and tall in the strongest gale!'

'Yes, but,' the sugar cane objected, 'although the wind can make me bend, it can never break me.'

A furious storm then broke out. When it had passed over, behold there was the oak lying on the ground with its roots in the air, while, little by little, the sugar cane straightened itself up, as strong as ever before.

7 Reynard the Fox and the Cockerel

Reynard, the famous red fox, was lucky one day. He found a hole in the fence and got through into the hen coop and caught a cockerel by surprise. He would have got clean away except that all the hens began to cluck with fear and the farmer's wife heard the racket and sounded the alarm.

The farmer set off in pursuit at once with his men and his dogs. And, while the men shouted the worst insults imaginable at the thief, what the dogs were barking was scarcely more complimentary.

'What kind of fox are you?' asked the clever cockerel. 'You let them call you all these names and you haven't even got the pride to answer them?'

Reynard, his self respect in question, turned to shout at his pursuers: 'You blockheads! You great snails! You'll never catch me!'

As he opened his mouth to shout the first word, the cockerel fled from his jaws and flew into a tall tree.

'You are the blockhead!' the cockerel crowed, raising its crest. 'Catch me now, if you can.'

Reynard, however, had enough on his plate without trying to recapture the cockerel. He forgot all about him and ran off at once; and he did not stop until he was safe in his den.

8 The Indians with Black Feet

A long, long time ago, an American Indian had a strange dream. He dreamt that he went to the edge of the great northern forest and there he found such abundant wildlife that not even a hundred generations of hunters would suffice to kill it all.

Following the message in his dream (for, like all Indians, he considered a dream to be a sign of divine guidance), he gathered his family together and set out. On the prairies, the Indians encountered immense hordes of bison, but these great beasts were so fast that not one of his family could get close enough to kill one.

Disappointed, the Indian prayed for a long time before falling asleep. In his dreams he had a new vision; he had to find a certain magic plant and rub it onto the feet of his first-born child. Again he obeyed this vision and, to his surprise, the feet of the little boy turned black; so much so that his father decided to call him 'Siksika', which means 'Black Feet'.

And the magic plant had a further effect: Siksika became such a fast runner that he was able to catch the bison.

From Siksika was born the great nation of the Blackfeet, who, from that moment to this time, tint their moccasins black and are known everywhere as great hunters.

9 The Two Brothers and the King's Turnip

There were once two brothers and, whilst one was very rich and powerful, the other was extremely poor and raised turnips. One of them grew so big that the poor brother did not know what to do with it. He couldn't eat it because he would have needed a hundred guests to help him finish it, and they would have wanted something else to eat as well as turnip; nor could he sell it at the market, because the price he would get for it would never compensate him for getting the turnip there.

So he thought and thought about the problem, and finally decided to make a gift of the turnip to the king, who was, in fact, highly delighted and was convinced that such a rarity must be valuable. The king wanted to make a gift of something exceptional to the poor brother, in return. So he presented him with enough gold to make him rich.

When the rich brother heard of this, he thought to himself, 'If the king makes such a generous recompense for a turnip, however large, what will he offer in exchange for a truly valuable gift?' Thus he filled a casket with the most precious jewels he possessed and presented it to the king who, of course, was most grateful. To repay him for this generosity he gave this brother his most precious possession: the turnip that the other brother had given him.

10 The Great Kotei and the Golden Eagle

Kotei was the greatest emperor in ancient Japan. He defeated all his enemies and conquered vast territories. Amongst other things, or so the legends tell us, it was Kotei who invented the compass and also sailing boats in order to achieve his amazing conquests.

Moreover, he also knew how to rule with wisdom and justice, and did so well that the Japanese people have never been so rich and happy as they were then.

One day, the emperor, who was by this time a very old man, was in the park, walking slowly with the aid of his walking stick. All of a sudden, an eagle flew down towards him. It shone as if it was made of gold, as it circled slowly to the ground and landed right at Kotei's feet.

'Messenger from the sky,' asked the wise emperor, 'have you come to tell me that my life is ended?'

The eagle nodded its great head in assent, so the emperor said farewell to his family, who wept many tears and hugged his knees. Then Kotei climbed onto the back of the eagle, which spread its wings and flew off into the sky, where it soon dwindled to a tiny speck in the brilliant rays of the sun.

11 The Faithful Horse and the Fox

An Arab once had a horse that had served him faithfully for years, but was now very old and thus no longer wanted. 'Go away!' the master told the horse. 'When you return as strong as a lion, you'll find the stable door open for you again!'

So the poor horse had to leave. On the road he met a fox, to whom the horse told his story. The fox consoled him at once: 'Have courage, dear horse! Lie down here on the road and pretend to be dead. Then just leave everything to me!'

The fox then ran off to the den of a large lion. 'There's a dead horse on the road!' he exclaimed. 'You should go and get it!' 'Fine,' said the lion, 'but how will I drag it back here? It will weigh too much!'

'Don't worry, my friend,' replied the fox. 'I will tie the horse to your tail!'

The lion agreed to this plan, and when they reached the horse the fox tied it tightly to the lion's tail. As soon as the last knot was tied, the fox shouted, 'Hup! Home!' to the horse.

The horse leapt to his feet and ran home to his master, dragging the enraged and struggling lion behind him. When the Arab saw the two animals, he said, 'Well, my old friend, you really are stronger than a lion. From now on, I'll look after you until the day you die!'

12 Tremble and the Miller's Daughter

A miller, who liked to boast about his daughter's skill, was in the habit of telling people that she could weave gold from straw. Unfortunately, the king overheard him and took the miller at his word. 'Send me your daughter,' he ordered, 'and if what you say is true then I shall marry her. If not, then she will die.'

The young maiden was locked in a room full of straw, with orders to transform it into woven gold before dawn. Despairing, she sat down and burst into tears. The sound of her sobs was heard by a gnome, who offered to turn the straw into gold himself in return for the maiden's necklace.

The next morning, the delighted king found that all the straw had been transformed into woven gold and he immediately ordered that next night an even greater quantity of straw be brought to the room. This time, the gnome did the work in exchange for the girl's ring, but when he returned on the third evening the maiden had no more jewels left to give him. So that he might agree to weave the straw into gold yet again, the girl was forced to promise him her first-born child.

In this way, the king and the miller's daughter were married. But as soon as their first child, a little prince, was born, the gnome arrived to carry him away. The queen offered him every treasure she had, but it was useless.

'You may keep the child,' the gnome finally conceded, 'if you can discover my name in three days.'

How could she ever guess the name? She followed him to his little house in the wood. There she hid and heard him singing: 'Today I bottle wine, tomorrow bake the bread, then Tremble the gnome shall have a prince instead!' The queen hurried happily back to the palace. After three days, the gnome arrived and asked, 'What, then, is my name?' At once, the queen replied, 'You bake bread and you drink wine, the name Tremble seems to suit you fine!'

Tremble flew into a terrible rage. He ran out and disappeared for ever.

13 The Father and His Daughters

A man once had two daughters, one of whom had married a poor farmer, the other a potter. The father went to visit each of them and asked: 'How is business going?'

'Very well,' replied the first daughter, 'but we could use more water to irrigate the land. We pray every night that God will send us rain!' When he asked the second daughter, she replied: 'Business is going well, but we pray to God for dry weather to harden our pots!' 'And what should I pray for?' exclaimed the father, 'if one daughter wants one thing, and the other the opposite?'

14 The Fountain of Youth

On one of the islands of Japan there once lived an old woodsman with his equally elderly wife. Yoshida and Fumi, for these were their names, were happy with the long life they had lived together, but they knew that the day would come when death would separate even them, and this was the only thing that made them sad.

One day, Yoshida went off into the forest, but everything had changed with the passing of years and the old woodsman lost his way. He found a spring and drank a few drops of water. He realised then that he had become suddenly as young and healthy again as he had been when he was twenty years old! He had discovered the legendary fountain of youth.

He ran home and his wife almost failed to recognise him. When, however, Fumi learnt what had happened, she set off at once.

When a few hours had passed and still Fumi had not returned, Yoshida began to grow worried. He went back to the fountain and found there a baby girl who could not even walk! The old woman had drunk too much of the magic water! But Yoshida knew what to do; he took the baby in his arms, and, because of his great love for her, from that day on he acted as her father and they continued to live happily together for many more years.

15 The Ice-Cream Cart

There was once a little girl and her mother who were so poor that often they could not even afford to buy bread. When the ice-cream cart passed, the little girl would watch with yearning, not greed, in her eyes, the other children licking their huge cones. The ice-cream seller noticed this and felt so sorry for her that he gave her his entire cart as a present.

'What will happen when all the ice-cream is finished?' asked the little girl. 'This is a magic cart,' the ice-cream vendor reassured her, 'and it makes ice-cream all by itself. You only have to tell it what kind and then, when the containers are full, you must remember to say, "Enough now".'

From that day onwards, the little girl and her mother had as much ice-cream as they wanted. One day, however, while the little girl was away, her mother wanted something to eat. 'Chocolate and nut,' she ordered, and the cart immediately began to produce ice-cream. It made so much that floods of ice-cream began to pour out. The poor woman did not know how to make it stop. Soon the whole town was buried and, when the little girl returned, the ice-cream was already as high as the roof-tops and people coming into the town had to lick for themselves a path through it.

16 The Lion and His Partners

The goat, the sheep and the cow went into business with the lion and, just as in every company, it was agreed that costs and profits would be divided equally. It happened that they trapped a deer and held a shareholders' meeting in order to apportion it out. In fact, the lion was most meticulous about dividing the catch into four equal parts. 'I shall take the first share,' he said, 'because it is my right to do so. Being King of the Forest, I shall also take the second, and also the third, because I'm the strongest. Should you lay claim to the rest, then I shall make a meal of you as well!'

17 The Magicians' War

The Wizard of Ah had declared war on the Wizard of Oh. Oh changed himself into a wild horse and galloped away. Ah observed his escape and changed himself in his turn into a hare which ran off in pursuit. Just as Ah was about to catch up, Oh changed again into a wolf and threw himself on the hare. Ah would have been torn to pieces had he not changed into a bear, then Oh transformed himself into a lion.

To escape the wild fury of the lion, Ah became a swan and flew away. He realised that Oh was chasing him in the form of a falcon, and threw himself into the sea, where he took the form of a fish. Oh, who had now become a shark, was about to eat him in a single mouthful, when Ah succeeded in reaching shore just at the spot where the princess was doing her washing. Ah changed into a bar of soap which the princess was about to pick up, when Oh appeared beside her in the form of a gold ring. She had just placed the ring on her finger, when a merchant, who was really Ah, arrived and bought the ring from the princess. The ring shattered into grains of wheat which fell to the ground. The merchant became a hen which gobbled up the grains, but one grain remained hidden and it now changed into a handsome prince, who, of course, married the princess.

18 The Bags Full of Faults

According to a Greek legend, when men were created, the great god Zeus gave each one a gift of two bags. One bag was full of man's own faults, the other full of everybody else's faults. But when the moment came for Zeus to give man his two bags, each one hanging at the opposite end of a carrying pole, by mistake he put the bag with the defects of everybody else in the front, whilst the bag with each man's own defects finished up behind his back.

It is perhaps for this reason that it is so easy to see other people's faults and so difficult to see our own!

19 The Piper of Hamelin

Hamelin was a rich and beautiful city until it was invaded by rats. The people of the town tried everything, cats, traps, poisons, to free themselves from this plague, but all was in vain.

One day, a man, dressed as a wandering minstrel, arrived in the city. He claimed he knew how to free the city from the plague of rats, but his price was a million gold coins.

'Only one million? We'll give you a hundred million!' promised the mayor.

Then the minstrel pulled out a pipe and began to play. At once the rats ran to him from all sides, drawn by the magic of his music. As soon as the piper was sure all the rats were following him, he marched down to the sea and into the water. The rats followed him in, and, naturally, they all drowned. The job done, the piper went to the mayor to collect his pay.

'A million gold coins for a little tune on a pipe!' said the mayor, who, now the danger was passed, began to think that the price was too high. 'You're mad. We'll give you a hundred!'

The piper ignored his offer and went back to the middle of the city and began to play his pipe again. This time, however, all the children of the town followed him, enchanted by the music. He led them far off to a place where they lived happily and learnt to keep their promises, and the people of Hamelin never saw them again.

20 Rita's Chicken

Rita was a good cook. One day, her master ordered her to prepare a roast chicken, because he was having a guest to dinner. The girl did her best and roasted the chicken so well that your mouth watered just to look at it; and, in fact, her mouth really did water.

'I must just taste it and make sure that I've added enough salt,' she said to herself and broke off a wing and ate it. 'It's absolutely delicious!' she congratulated herself: 'But if I leave only one wing, then the master will be bound to notice that one is missing. It would be better if I ate the other wing as well.' By the time she had practised some more of this logic, there was nothing left of the chicken when the master returned. Rita, however, assured him: 'The chicken is ready. You can even begin to sharpen the carving knife.'

The guest arrived shortly after. 'Run away! Quickly!' Rita whispered to him. 'My master only invited you here in order to kill you. Can you not hear him sharpening his knife?' The guest did not wait to be told again but fled immediately as fast as he could.

'That was a strange person you invited for dinner!' she immediately went and complained to her master. 'Your guest came in, stole the chicken I had cooked, and then ran away!'

21 The Cossack and the Witch

A valiant cossack came across some splendid apples on a tree, but they were enchanted and had been placed there by a witch in order to capture men. In fact, the cossack had scarcely touched one of the apples when the witch appeared.

'I will give you a chance to save yourself,' she said. 'You must hide and I must try to find you. If you are clever enough to remain hidden for ten hours, then I shall marry you; if not, then you will be my slave!'

Now the cossack was very good friends with a fairy who changed herself into a great eagle and told the cossack to leap up onto its shoulders.

'I will carry you so high up that the witch will never be able to see you'.

Unfortunately, the witch had a magic book which told her everything. No sooner had she asked the book than she learnt exactly where the cossack was hiding. 'Come down out of the sky at once!' she screamed.

The friendly fairy then transformed the cossack into a needle, with which she sewed the pages of the witch's book together. The witch, thus, lost the challenge and had to keep her promise to marry the cossack. But she reformed completely and the two lived long and happily together.

22 How Simple Simon Became King

The king's own herald had ridden from city to city to make the announcement that the princess would marry whoever turned out to be the most amusing conversationalist. Immediately the most learned men in the land set out for the capital, determined to try to win the hand of the princess.

There were some who came by horse and some, seeking to arrive in an even more impressive manner, who came by carriage. There was one, however, who came on a goat and everyone called him Simple Simon.

Simple Simon noticed, on his journey, that all the other suitors were bearing rich gifts for the princess, whilst he was going to arrive empty handed. In an attempt to put this right, he gathered up the things which most impressed him on the way. He collected together a dead crow, a ruined wooden clog, and a lump of mud, and stuck them all in his pocket.

And at the palace, strange things were happening. No sooner had the suitors observed the fabulous luxury of the court and found themselves face to face with the stunningly beautiful princess than they were struck dumb with excitement, and thus, of course, rejected at once as unsuitable. Only Simon was not overwhelmed by the beauty he beheld.

'It is extremely hot in here!' he complained.

'The ovens are all burning,' the princess explained to him, 'because they are roasting so many chickens in the kitchens in preparation for the wedding celebrations.' 'Good!' exclaimed Simon. 'Then I can also roast my crow.' 'But what will you cook it in? All the pots and pans are already being used.' 'I will cook it in this,' Simon said, pulling out the clog. 'And the sauce to cook it in?' laughed the princess. Simple Simon pulled out the lump of mud that he had in his pocket. The princess had never been so amused by anyone's conversation so she decided that Simple Simon was the man for her.

23 The Stag and the Lion

A stag was immensely proud of his majestic set of antlers. Yet, on the other hand, he was extremely dissatisfied with his slender legs and hoofs.

One day a lion began to chase him. By virtue of his speed, the stag succeeded in fleeing from the lion, but then he ran into a thicket and his antlers caught in the branches and he was trapped. 'Alas and woe is me!' thought the stag. 'How wrong I was to complain about my slender legs and delicate hoofs which have served me so well. How wrong I was to be so proud of my large antlers which are now the cause of my ruin!'

24 How Hans the Giant Was Caught in the Well

Hans, the young giant, had worked hard for a certain farmer, but when it came to the time for payment, the farmer did not want to give him anything. The greedy farmer asked his wife, who was every bit as mean as he was, for her advice. She immediately suggested to him that they persuade the giant to go down their well. There they could easily kill him, by dropping the enormous grindstone from the mill down on top of him.

The first part of their plan presented no difficulty at all. Innocent as he was, the giant went down alone into the well without the slightest suspicion. It was much more difficult to roll the millstone to the edge of the well, for it was so heavy that the two cheats had to order more than a dozen servants to help them. Finally, however, the huge stone disc fell to the bottom of the well. There was a terrible crash.

The miserly farmer and his wife were delighted, certain that they were free of the giant forever, but instead they heard a voice: 'Hey, you people! Chase away those chickens that are scratching about up there; they are dropping specks of dirt into my eyes!'

A short while later, Hans appeared at the top of the well with the millstone sitting around his neck like a collar, and the farmer hurried at once to pay him what he was owed.

25 He Told No Lies

A farmer had a younger brother, who had the bad luck to be in love with the daughter of a duke. Her father was so mean that he would never agree to give her hand in marriage to anyone who was not rich. The elder brother therefore decided to do something to help the younger one.

First, he made his brother put on his oldest suit, which was patched with dozens of pieces of cloth. Then he got him to sit beside the fireplace, where the roof was sound. Then he put a bowl on his lap, and gave him two gold coins which he was to pass from one hand to the other, then into the bowl, then round again. Then he went to see the duke.

'How is your brother off for money?' the miserly father asked.

'I can honestly say that money is passing through his hands all the time.'

'What's the state of his house?'

'He has a sound roof over his head.'

'Ah! So he is rich and has his own house!' exclaimed the duke. 'And what about his wardrobe?'

Said the older brother: 'He has far more pieces of cloth to wear than I have.'

The miser was most impressed, not realising that he had not had a direct answer to any of his questions.

In this way, without telling a single lie, the wedding was quickly arranged.

26 The Unlucky Adventures of Mr. Bogeyman

The cockerel and the hen decided to pay a visit to Mr. Bogeyman, the very one that mothers threaten their children with if they behave badly. The cockerel and the hen also invited their friends along, and so they were accompanied by the cat, the goose, the egg, the vase of flowers, and the hatpin, who had brought as well its little cousin, the needle.

When they all arrived, Mr. Bogeyman was not at home (he always had so much to do!) and the visitors settled down to wait for him. The cock and the hen roosted up on a beam, the goose settled down on the water-pump, the cat curled up in the fireplace, the egg nestled on the towel, the hatpin stuck itself into the chair, the needle slipped into the pillow on the bed, and the vase waited on the ledge over the door.

When Mr. Bogeyman came home, he lit the fire and the cat leapt into his face; he went to wash and the goose bit him on the nose; he dried himself and the egg ran all over his face. He threw himself down into his chair and was stabbed by the hatpin; he went to bed and the needle pricked him. He ran away and the vase fell on him!

'He must have done something really bad,' commented the cockerel, awakened by the commotion, 'to deserve a punishment like that.'

27 The Miller and the Enchanted Ass

A miller set out to seek his fortune and, in effect, he found it, in the form of an enchanted ass. It was enough for him to say, 'Abracadabra', and the ass began to spit out silver coins. You can imagine how much the young man enjoyed himself, able to indulge his every whim! Whenever he was short of money, he would shut himself in the stable with his ass and come out with as much silver as he required.

One day the young man stopped at a hotel, and began to spend money like a king. The hotel keeper thought that such a rich guest deserved the best, and gave him a large bill.

The miller did not even bat an eyelid when he saw the size of the bill, but since he did not have enough money in his pockets he had to go out to the stable to see his ass. The hotel keeper followed, to spy on him, and thus discovered everything. Then he stole the ass that spat out the silver coins and replaced it with his own ass.

The young man did not notice the difference and left the next day. When he needed money, he did what he usually did and . . . . what a surprise! This time the ass began to spit out golden coins! The hotel keeper's ass was, in fact, even more precious than the one which had belonged to the miller. Its owner had simply never thought of saying the magic word!

28 The Sick Lion and the Prudent Fox

The lion was old and tired and realised that, if he still wanted to get enough to eat, he would have to resort more to cunning and less to force. So he pretended to be sick and retired to his den. Then, every time that one of his subjects came by, the lion would reach out with his paw, grab the visitor and eat him.

It came to the fox's turn, but the fox remained at the entrance.

'Do come in, fox!' said the lion cordially. 'Thank you, but I'd really rather not,' the fox replied. 'Although I can see so many footprints going in, I cannot see one which comes out!'

29 The Flying Trunk

A young man possessed a very unusual treasure; an old trunk into which he had only to step, then press the lock and it would begin to fly.

Thus it was that one day the young man landed in a city in the East, and learnt that the daughter of the king was being held prisoner in a high tower, to prevent her meeting any man who might make her suffer.

The young man was intensely curious about this princess and he got into his trunk and flew to the top of the high tower. The young man fell totally in love at first sight with the beautiful girl, and she too fell in love with him. Since they were of the opinion that the young man had fallen from the heavens, the king and queen had nothing to say against their marriage. The celebrations duly began and the young man decided to make his contribution to the joyous occasion by letting off a display of fireworks from his flying trunk.

Instead of returning at once to the tower, he landed afterwards in the crowd to find out if they had enjoyed his fireworks. When he went back to the place where he had left his magic trunk, he discovered that it had been burnt to a cinder by a spark. So the young man was no longer able to fly, and the princess is still awaiting the return from the heavens of her husband-to-be!

30 The Godmother of the Gnomes

A young girl, who worked as a chambermaid, one day found a letter attached to her broom. She had never learnt to read, so took the letter to her master, who read it to her. It was an invitation from the gnomes for her to be godmother to a newly-born little gnome. Since it would have been unthinkable to refuse, the maiden accepted the unusual invitation. Three gnomes arrived to fetch her and take her to a cave in a mountain, where she found that everything was tiny, but exquisitely precious and beautiful. There were ivory decorations, golden carpets, diamond glasses. . . .

The christening took place and the young girl acted as godmother, as she had been asked. She was then invited to remain for a few days. She accepted and was treated so well by her hosts that she felt like a queen.

She stayed for three days, but when she returned to her house in the city, she found everything had changed there, even her broom, and there was no sign of her master. The young woman then discovered that each day she had passed with the gnomes was equal to one hundred earthly years, and she had therefore been away for three centuries!

So she asked the gnomes to come back and take her to live with them. What else could she have done!

Contents

The fairy tale of the month: Puss in Boots
Charles Perrault

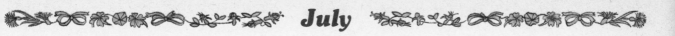

The fairy tale of the month

The Ugly Duckling

Mother Duck was aching all over from keeping still for so long. She could hardly wait for her eggs to hatch out. At last, one of the eggshells cracked open and a lovely little duckling came out; then the second broke open, and the third, and the happy mother found herself surrounded by lively chirping youngsters.

With a sigh of relief, she got up and prepared to return to the farm. Then she realised that one egg was still whole, and it was the biggest of all.

The turkey also noticed the strange egg, and came over to get a better look at it.

'That is not a duck's egg,' he assured her. 'It's a guinea fowl's egg.'

'Guinea fowl?' said the amazed duck. 'How did a guinea fowl's egg end up among mine?'

'Who knows,' said the turkey, shrugging. 'Perhaps some bad little boys wanted to play a dirty trick on you. Anyway, there's no point in you staying here to hatch it. Nothing good will come out of it. Take my word.'

In spite of this, the duck was not convinced: maybe the turkey was wrong, maybe another beautiful little duckling would be born. . . .

But when the last of the eggs hatched out, the duck's immediate thought was that it would have been better to have listened to the turkey's advice.

The last duckling was much bigger than he should have been, and he was also a different shape from the others. Worst of all, he was not even white.

But when she looked at her strange chick, the mother duck realised that she loved him just as much as all her other children, maybe even more, if that was possible, because, when she saw what an ugly little duckling he was, she knew he was going to have a hard life.

The ugly little duckling's problems began as soon as the mother took him out into the farmyard to meet the others: not only the hens, the cockerel, the turkeys, but even the other ducks, made it quite clear that they did not approve of his looks, and they all attacked him, and tried to chase him away. The worst thing of all was that even his own brothers pecked at him with their beaks, and made fun of him. Mother Duck did all that she could to defend him; but there were so many other animals against him, that in the end the ugly duckling had to run away, as this was the only way to get any peace.

So he wandered away to the lake on the far side of the farm. There he became used to living with the wild geese, even though they did not have a good reputation, and their life was very hard. But the geese accepted the

ugly duckling without any problems, and they were actually quite happy to have him with them. Then, one day, some hunters came down to the lake and began shooting at the geese. During all the confusion, the ugly duckling was jumped upon by a huge dog. He thought that his end had come, but, incredibly, the dog just moved on without even biting him. Afterwards, the poor little thing felt sadder rather than happier about this: 'I am so ugly,' he thought, 'that not even the dogs want to eat me.' From that day on, the duckling remained alone on the lake.

Actually, there were some other big birds on the lake; they were all white and very elegant, with lovely black and yellow masks on their faces. But these birds, which were called swans, lived in a far-off part of the lake, so that our ugly little duckling did not really get to know them.

One day he saw them flying overhead and he was fascinated.

'How I would love to be one of them,' he thought wistfully. 'If only I could go with them.'

He tried to stretch his wings to follow them, but fell back into the water; and when he lifted his head back up again, the big white birds had already disappeared.

Then the winter arrived, and, bit by bit, the surface of the lake began to freeze over. So as not to be trapped in the ice, the ugly little duckling had to keep continually moving the water around him. He had very little rest, fighting all the time for his survival, against fatigue and hunger.

For the duckling, that long winter was a time of one hardship after another, but then the spring returned, and the lake became, once again, green and blue, warm and peaceful.

During the winter, he had grown a lot and, naturally, his wings had grown a lot as well.

Then the ugly duckling stretched his neck and legs, tried stretching out his wings as well. . . . and discovered that he could fly.

With a few beats of his great wings, he lifted off from the water and rose up, until he was flying above the trees and over a magnificent park. Finally, he came to another lake, where the beautiful swans, that he had admired so much in the autumn, were swimming about.

And there, he was at last made to feel welcome. The ugly duckling, that all the others had made fun of because he looked different, was not really a duckling at all, but a swan.

After that, he was praised so much for his beauty by everyone who saw him, that he was more than repaid for everything he had had to put up with before then.

1 The Magic Table

A good-natured and industrious young man worked for a magician, who gave him a magic table as a payment. All he had to say was, 'Set yourself,' and everything he needed for a meal would appear on it. Thanks to this gift, the young man thought that he would not want for anything again for the rest of his life, and so he decided to return home, to his father.

On the way, he stopped in a tavern for a meal and a night's sleep. The owner had no food left because he already had a large number of guests, so he told the young man he would have to make do with a crust of bread.

'It doesn't matter,' the young man said, not at all worried. 'I'll take care of the rest myself.' Then the magic table provided so much food, that all the others there were able to eat their fill as well. After that, the landlord decided that he could make good use of a table like that. He stole it and replaced it with one that looked the same, so that the young man did not notice. But the magic turned out to be with the young man who owned the table, not with the table itself. So the new table continued to provide the young man with all the food he needed, and when the landlord of the tavern tried to give orders to the table he had stolen, a stick appeared and gave him a good thrashing!

2 Catherine and the Cheeses

Catherine the farm girl was so simple and naive that she was always getting into trouble. One day, she was taking the cheeses to market, when one fell out of her basket and rolled off down the hill.

'I really don't feel like chasing after it,' she thought. 'I'll send someone else to get it back.'

So she rolled another cheese off after the first. She waited and waited, but neither of the cheeses came back. 'Perhaps they want company,' thought Catherine, and sent off a third cheese. When none of them came back, she thought that perhaps the third cheese had gone the wrong way, and so she sent a fourth to look for it. She then sent off the fifth cheese, and the sixth, and the seventh, until eventually her basket was empty.

For a while, she waited patiently but then she grew annoyed. 'If you cheeses think I can be bothered wasting time waiting for you, you're wrong. I'm going ahead without you, and you can just run along behind me. That'll teach you to be so disobedient.'

So she arrived at the market empty-handed, and her husband shouted at her. 'Why are you getting angry?' said Catherine. 'In just a few minutes those cheeses will be along, you'll see!'

3 The Cat and the Hens

A cat had heard that all the hens in a chicken coop had fallen ill. He had been thinking for a long time of a way to get the coop door open, and at last this seemed like a very good opportunity.

He dressed up as a doctor, with a bag full of instruments and medicines, and off he went to the chicken coop.

'Good day, hens, how are you feeling? I've come to give you a check up. Please open the door.'

But the chickens all answered together: 'Thanks very much, but we'll all feel a lot better if you would just go away, thank you.'

4 Beauty and the Beast

Once upon a time, a man became lost in a snowstorm. He had wandered about for a long time, and had little hope left when, through the snow, he spied a castle. When he reached it, he found all the candles lit, and the table set for a meal, but no-one was there.

He ate a meal himself anyway, and then he fell asleep. When he awoke the storm had passed, and the man was just preparing to journey on, when he noticed a flowering rose tree. He decided to pick a rose and take it home to his daughter, Beauty. Suddenly, the owner of the castle appeared, so fearsome a sight that the man thought he was a beast.

'Have you not been given enough already?' Beast asked the traveller furiously. 'Why are you taking my flowers as well? As a punishment, now you will die.' The traveller begged Beast to relent, and at last it was agreed that his life would be spared, if he would send his daughter to the castle. So Beauty had to go to the castle, and, as had happened with her father, there was no-one there to meet her.

The Beast only showed himself to her after some days had passed. Little by little, the two of them got into the habit of eating together, despite the fact that the sight of him was always a shock to Beauty. But every day, she was more and more impressed by his kindness and his gentleness.

As for Beast, he had fallen in love with the young girl, but he knew that the feeling would never be the same for her, because of the way he looked. The pain of this heartache gradually made him grow weaker and weaker, until it seemed that he was on the point of dying. Beauty found him on his deathbed, and, so moved by the sight of him, she burst into tears.

One of the girl's tears fell on the Beast's face, and that was enough to work the miracle. Suddenly, the monster changed into a handsome young man. He sprang from the bed, they embraced each other, and from that day on the two lovers lived happily together in perfect harmony.

5 The Crystal Castle

A prince and a princess were very much in love, and had already exchanged betrothal rings, when a jealous magician kidnapped the girl. For many years, the desperate young man wandered about the land in search of his beloved. Finally, he found that she was being kept prisoner in a castle with high crystal walls that were so smooth that even a fly could not climb them.

No matter how hard he tried, the prince could not think of a way in. Then one day, in the woods nearby, he heard some cries for help. There he found three hideous old witches who had wandered into a swamp. 'Good riddance,' thought the prince, but then, because the cries were so pitiful, he relented, and rescued them from the swamp. In gratitude, the witches gave him three gifts; a stick which could open any door, a horse that could fly, and a cloak which would make the wearer invisible. With these gifts, the prince was at last able to release the princess from the crystal castle. Invisible in the cloak, he flew on the horse to the topmost tower, and with the stick opened the door to her prison. And soon after, they were married and the three witches were welcome guests at the feast.

6 The Frog and the Ox

A frog decided that it wanted to become as big as an ox.

So it began to breathe in, and in, and every time it swallowed more air, it did in fact become bigger.

But it soon began to tire of its efforts.

'Am I big enough yet?' it asked hopefully of its many watching companions.

Then they had another look at the ox and shook their heads, 'No, a bit more.'

So the ambitious frog kept on puffing itself up and up. . . . until it burst like a balloon!

7 The Generous Camel

At the beginning of time, in a large Arabian city called Tamul, the earth began to heave and tremble until eventually a huge camel burst forth from it. From the camel's head to its tail was over seven hundred paces, and it was as tall as the nearby hills.

Before the people could get over their surprise, this giant camel gave birth to a baby camel. Then the two of them went off together into the mountains.

Thereafter, the great camel would come down into the city every morning to give its milk to whoever wanted it, so nobody was hungry any

more. But the great camel itself needed a lot of water to drink, and as Tamul did not have enough water for everyone, the inhabitants decided that they themselves could only use the wells on alternate days. Thanks to this, everybody had enough to eat and drink.

But the miraculous camel was not popular with the owners of goats, because nobody would buy goats' milk any more. And the owners of gardens no longer had enough water for their lawns. So these two groups joined forces and chased the giant camel away.

From then on, in Tamul, only a few people had milk and flowers, while all the others suffered hunger and thirst.

8 The Spirit in the Bottle

A young student was walking in the woods, when he heard a small voice calling to him. He looked all around, but could not see anyone. The voice called out again, and appeared to come from the roots of an enormous oak tree. There the student found a bottle, in which there was a tiny man, who begged him, 'Let me out.'

So the student removed the cork, and a cloud of smoke emerged and grew into a frightening giant.

'I am a genie,' said the giant, 'and I was imprisoned in the bottle by a magician. But now that I am freed, prepare to meet your end!'

'Wait a minute,' said the young man. 'I don't believe one word you have said. A giant your size could not have really come out of that little bottle. You could never get into it.'

'Of course I can,' said the genie. 'I'll prove it to you.' But as soon as the genie returned to the bottle, the young man put the cork back in. The next time, in order to get free, the spirit had to make a bargain with the student: not only would it refrain from killing him, but it had also to give him a dagger which turned to gold everything it touched, and healed all wounds. And afterwards, thanks to that magic dagger, the student became a rich and famous doctor.

9 The Story of the Thistle and a Fairy Tale

With so many beautiful flowers growing in the garden, nobody paid any attention to the thistle; but one day a party was held in the house. Each young girl was to offer a flower to the young man of her choice. Amongst those present was a young Scots girl, who particularly noticed the purple flowers of the thistle, because it is the emblem of her country. So she picked one, and placed it in the buttonhole of the young master of the house; and the plant was very proud of the honour which was given to one of its flowers.

Time went by and the young couple were married. More time went by, until just one flower remained on the plant. The young wife saw it, and remembered such a flower had led to her and her husband falling in love, so she picked it and gave it to him. He placed it onto their wedding portrait, right on the buttonhole of the young groom. This made the thistle even happier.

'Now that I know that my children have achieved such greatness,' it sighed, 'I can accept my own future with resignation.'

'Don't worry,' smiled a sunbeam. 'There's still a good thing coming to you.' 'What?' asked the thistle. 'Will I be put in a vase? Will I be framed?'

'No, but you will end up in a fairy tale!' replied the sunbeam.

10 Why Beans Have a Split in the Middle

A woman, who was preparing a pot of soup, dropped on the floor a bean, a piece of red hot coal and a piece of the straw she had used to light the fire. These three things were all glad to have escaped, and they decided to run away, before they were picked up again and thrown in the fire.

As they ran down the path, they found a small stream in their way. The piece of straw generously offered to lie down and make a bridge from one side to the other, so that its companions could cross over.

The bean and the coal were very grateful, but the coal, who went first, reached the middle of the bridge, looked down and became so frightened that it stopped. Then, because the coal was still hot, it set fire to the straw, and both fell into the water and were carried away. All this made the bean laugh so much that it split its sides. Luckily, a passing tailor found it, and sewed it back together again. And from that day on, all the beans in the world still carry the scar down their backs.

11 The Geese Who Kept Guard

In ancient Rome, at one time the people were so complacent that they sent their army to fight far away, and left the city itself without defences. Then an invading army of barbarians, called Gauls, attacked the city and captured it. Only a few young men retreated to the rock of the Capitol, where the treasures of the city had been taken, and there they prepared to defend it, until the return of the Roman army.

Many times, the Gauls tried to climb the steep sides of the rock, but they were always driven back and they had to content themselves with laying siege to the Capitol. But, in the end, they found a secret path up the side of the hill, and decided to attack by night.

It was so dark that the Roman sentries did not see them, but the alarm was raised by the geese on the Capitol, which were kept there for sacrificing to the gods. The geese heard the Gauls and began to honk loudly. The Romans awoke, seized their arms, and repelled the attack.

Later, when Rome was saved by the returning army, it was decided that the geese should never again be sacrificed to the gods, in recognition of their services as sentries on the Capitol.

12 The Gnome and the Little Tortoise

Thunderbolt, the gnome, was the best messenger in the land. He could carry messages, letters or packages from one place to another so quickly that he earned many rewards. But still he was not content, because he had no son to inherit his position.

One day, another gnome gave him a box to take to a witch, but as soon as he set off, Thunderbolt heard a voice from the box, begging him to open the lid. Inside was a tiny prince, made small by an evil spell. Thunderbolt would have really liked to help the prince, but he did not know the magic words which would open the box, so he had no choice but to deliver the box to the witch. Then he picked up the receipt, and took it back to the gnome who was really very angry, because he knew that Thunderbolt had dared to speak with the tiny prince. But he acted as though nothing had happened, and paid Thunderbolt with a pigeon's egg, from which, he said, a child would be born. Thunderbolt was delighted, and persuaded a pigeon to sit on the egg. Then he waited, but when the egg finally hatched, out came, not a child as promised, but a tortoise. Nevertheless, Thunderbolt decided to keep the little creature, and he loved it like a son.

Contrary to appearances, little Tortoise was very fast, so much so that he could travel long distances, in order to pass on a message, and be back in a few minutes. People would come from all over the world to marvel at him. Then, one day, along came a richly dressed man who, to the amazement of Thunderbolt, suddenly struck little Tortoise with a hammer blow so hard that it broke the shell. Out came a handsome young gnome.

Then it was revealed that the rich man was none other than the tiny prince in the box. He had been released from the evil spell, and had come back to reward Thunderbolt by granting him his dearest wish, for a son. So everyone lived happily ever after.

13 The Butcher and the Thieves

Two thieves went into a butcher's shop. While one was waiting to be served, the other one stole some sausages off a plate, and passed them to his companion. The butcher noticed the sausages were missing, and accused the pair of having stolen them. The one who had the sausages swore he had not stolen them, and the one who had stolen them swore he did not have them. Both told the truth, but the butcher beat them anyway.

'Whoever took the sausages can take one of these as well,' the butcher said between blows, 'and whoever has them can have one of these as well.'

14 The Vixen's Wedding

There was once a vixen whose mate had died. She was rich and beautiful, and had a cat as a maidservant. This vixen wanted to get married again, but was very hesitant over her choice.

One day, a wolf came along and asked the cat, 'Is the vixen at home?'

'She is in her room,' replied the cat.

'Go and tell her that I want to marry her.' Off went the maid, but her mistress asked her, 'Does he have red trousers and a pointed muzzle?'

'No', answered the cat.

'Well, then, I don't want him.'

After the wolf came a dog, then a deer, followed by a hare, a bear, and all the other animals of the woods. But none of them had what the vixen was looking for. At last, another fox turned up. 'Does he have red trousers and a pointed muzzle?' asked the vixen of her maid. 'Yes,' said the cat.

'Good,' smiled the vixen, 'then let us prepare for a wedding.'

The cat went into the kitchen and baked the cakes. The other animals from the woods did not get invited to the feast, but the vixen, the fox, and the cat ate, drank, and danced till dawn.

15 The Boastful Athlete

There was once a very loud-mouthed and ambitious athlete who was not, however, very talented. One day, tired of being booed at by the crowd, he decided to leave and seek his fortune abroad.

When he finally returned, he was forever telling stories of his victories.

'In London,' he would say, 'I jumped so high I was out of sight. If you don't believe me, go and ask anyone who was there.'

'There is no need,' said a listener. 'Why don't you pretend you're in London and jump out of sight right now!'

16 The Dog, the Cockerel and the Fox

A dog and a cockerel, who met while on a journey, decided to travel together. Night fell: the cockerel went to sleep up in a tree, and the dog settled down at the base of the trunk. Just before dawn, as was his custom, the cock crowed. He was overheard. by a fox, who rushed up and said, 'What a magnificent voice! Come down, I want to congratulate you.'

'I'm afraid I can't,' replied the cockerel. 'The doorman of this hotel is asleep and I can't come down until he wakes up.' 'I'll wake him up right now,' promised the fox. The dog leapt up, growled and the fox fled.

17 The Shopkeeper in Paradise

One day, there arrived in paradise a shopkeeper who, during his life, had cheated as much as he could on all the prices and weights in his shop.

The angel at the gates knew this and sent him away; but the man begged so hard, that the angel was moved and let him in after all.

From then on, the shopkeeper, while being very tolerant about his own sins, to prove that he had the right to stay in paradise, became the harshest judge of other people's sins.

One day, as often happened, he sneaked off to sit on a throne, from which he could see everything that happened on earth. He spotted a boy stealing an apple from a tree, and immediately grabbed a nearby stool and threw it down at him. An angel saw this and dragged the shopkeeper out of paradise by the ears.

'Imagine what it would be like,' the angel reprimanded him, 'if we were all as severe as you. By now, all the stools would have been thrown out at the sinners, and we would have to stand all the time in paradise!'

18 Catherine and the Golden Coins

Catherine was a very dull young woman. What was worse, like a lot of ignorant people, she thought she was quite clever. Her husband, who knew her, tried to guard against her stupidity as best he could.

One day he had to go away, but before departing he put all the gold coins he had saved into a wooden box, and he buried it in the garden. When his wife asked what he was doing, he said he was burying a box of sunflower seeds.

Some time after, some pot sellers came to the village. They offered their wares to Catherine, but she told them that she did not have any money and could not buy anything.

'Unless you'd like to trade some pots for a few sunflower seeds?' she added. 'Why not? Show us these seeds,' said the pot seller, filled with curiosity.

'I haven't got time to dig them up. You do it yourself,' said Catherine, showing them the exact spot where the box was buried. The merchants, of course, were very pleased to take the 'seeds' in exchange for a few pots. When the husband returned home, Catherine very proudly showed him her new pots. 'Look how much I managed to get for those worthless seeds of yours!'

19 The Thirsty Fairy

A widow loved her own ugly and unpleasant daughter just as much as she disliked her lovely, kind stepdaughter. She made the stepdaughter do all the hardest work in the house, and the girl obeyed her without complaint.

One day, the stepmother sent her out to the well to get water, and there she met an old woman who asked her for a drink. The kind young girl served the old woman as if she were a queen. In truth, that old woman was a fairy in disguise, and she was so moved by the young girl's kindness that she rewarded her with an extraordinary gift: every time she spoke, from her lips, along with the words, fell flowers and diamonds.

The stepmother was furious when she heard what had happened to her stepdaughter. Immediately she sent her own daughter to the well, so that she could come back with the same gift. This time, the fairy appeared in the form of a queen. But when she asked for a drink, the young woman said rudely, 'If you want a drink, get it yourself.' 'You are most unkind,' said the fairy, 'and for that I will give you a very different reward.'

And thereafter, whenever the unkind girl began to speak, her rude words could actually be seen in the snakes and toads that fell from her lips.

20 The Sleep-Fairy and the Painted Lake

The sleep-fairy dusted Henry's eyelids with her magic powder and he fell asleep at once. Then the fairy sprayed her powder on the painting which hung on the wall, and, magically, the beautiful little lake in the woods became real. Henry flew from his bed and landed in the thick grass, which was striped by the sun's rays shining through the tall trees.

Henry reached the lake, and climbed aboard a red boat with silver sails. Then, six swans, with golden collars about their necks and blue stars on their heads, pulled the boat along, while on the banks, butterflies and fairies flew amongst the flowers. In the water splashed fish, with gold and silver scales. Behind the boat stretched a beautiful wake made of little red and blue birds, which flew off into the sky.

Then the little boat passed before a castle with beautiful princesses on the balcony, all of whom were little girls that Henry knew well, and they threw sweets and toys down to him. At the end, though, the alarm clock went off, but little Henry woke up feeling very happy.

21 The Miser and the Thief

A miser was haunted by the fear of being robbed. Neither safes nor banks seemed secure enough to him, so one day he decided that the old ways were still the best ways. He went to a goldsmith and exchanged all his money for a bar of gold. Then he chose a suitable place and, in the middle of the night, he dug a deep hole. In it he buried the bar of gold, then filled in the hole again with earth.

Every now and then, he would return there to make sure everything was well, and also because he was so attached to his gold that it was as if he had buried his heart there.

One day he arrived there to find that the hole had been dug up, and the bar of gold was gone. You can imagine how much he cried and sobbed.

'Why worry so much?' a friend tried to comfort him. 'You didn't really have the bar of gold even before it was stolen from you. What good did it do you buried in the ground? Take a stone, bury it and pretend it is your bar of gold. Everything will be just the same for you as before, because it is no use at all having something if you can't enjoy it.'

22 The Trojan Horse

The most courageous heroes of ancient Greece, with their armies, had been laying siege for ten years to Troy, but the mighty walls of that city still resisted every assault. However, one morning, at sunrise, the Trojan sentries discovered that their enemies had boarded their ships during the night and sailed away.

None of the Trojans gave any thought to what could have caused the Greeks to depart so suddenly. Nor did many of them wonder about the great wooden horse which had been left on the beach. A few of the Trojans suspected that it might be some trick of the cunning Greeks, and proposed that it should be burnt at once. The majority, however, decided to take this strange horse into the city, and there offer it as a thanksgiving to the gods of Troy.

The horse was mounted on wheels, but nevertheless it needed hundreds of men and horses to drag it into the main square. By then it was night again, and while the Trojans slept, from within the wooden horse Greek warriors crept out and opened the city gates to the Greek army, which had returned in the darkness. And, in one night, Troy was conquered, a city which had withstood ten years of attack.

23 Redfeathers the Hen

Redfeathers, the hen, was so-called because all her feathers were red. One day, the fox caught sight of her in the farmyard and his mouth began to water.

He ran home and told his wife to put on water for boiling a chicken, and then he rushed back, and before Redfeathers knew what was happening, she found herself snapped up and inside a sack, not even able to call for help.

Luckily for her, her friend the dove saw what had happened. She fluttered on to the path in the woods, and lay there, pretending to have a broken wing. The fox was delighted to find that he now had a first course as well as a main dish. He put down the sack with the hen in it, and chased off after the dove, who began cleverly to hop further and further away.

Redfeathers slipped out of the sack and put a stone in her place, then she too ran off. When the dove saw that her friend was safe, she flew up into a tree. The fox then went back and picked up the sack, thinking that the hen was still in it. When he got home, the fox tipped the sack into the pot of boiling water, but the stone splashed it all over him, and he burned his greedy paws.

24 The Cricket and the Ants

It was summer and the cricket sat on an ear of wheat happily singing and enjoying the sun.

He felt extremely sorry for the ants, who worked ceaselessly, looking for grains of wheat to take back to their store.

Poor things, they really did not know how to enjoy life.

But soon the winter came, and the thoughtless cricket had no food at all to eat.

He would surely have died of hunger if it had not been for the generous ants who had given him some of their grain.

25 The Ignorant Prince

A powerful king of India had a son, who was not very bright. He wanted him to have the best teachers, so he called them to the palace in order that they could teach the boy everything that they knew. They did their best, and after a few years the prince could answer all their questions. The king was well satisfied, but one old wise man warned him, 'Everything your son knows is about the past, but a truly wise man has also to know the future.'

A fortune teller was then called to the palace and he too taught the prince all about his art. Months later, the wise man tested the boy again. The wise man showed the king and his courtiers something which he held in his hand; then he closed his hand and showed it to the boy, asking him to guess what was inside.

'It is a hard, white object,' the boy said, concentrating hard. 'It is round and has a hole in the middle. . . . It must be a grindstone.'

Everyone burst out laughing, because the object was indeed hard, white, and round, with a hole in the middle, but it was a pearl, not a grindstone.

'True wisdom,' commented the wise man, 'lies not in knowing everything, but in making proper use of whatever knowledge we do have.'

26 The Distracted Astronomer

An astronomer was in the habit of going out every night to observe the stars; but as soon as he was outdoors, he was so totally absorbed in the sights above him, that he did not look where he was putting his feet, so he fell into a hole in the ground.

A passer-by heard his shouts and ran to help him. 'How do you hope to discover what's up in the sky,' he said to the astronomer, 'when you're not even capable of seeing what's under your nose?'

Many men, while following their dreams, show themselves incapable of facing up to reality.

27 The Fox and the Monkey King

All the animals of the forest gathered in assembly to elect their new king. They chose the monkey because they were amused by his antics. The fox was very disappointed at not being chosen and waited for a chance to get his own back.

One day, he found a piece of meat on a path. He realised at once it was the bait for a trap. But off he went to the monkey and offered to show him where it was, as a sign of his loyalty. The monkey king at once fell into the trap, and the fox burst out laughing. 'With so few wits, you cannot even rule yourself, let alone animals.'

28 The Grocer's Elf

One evening, a young student entered a grocer's shop, and asked for bread and some candles. However, he did not have enough money for both, and ended up buying the candles only. The grocer gave them to him, wrapped in a page which he had torn out of a book. The student looked at it and was enchanted to read the poem written on it; in the end, he asked if he could have the rest of the book. The grocer, however, wanted to be paid for it and so the young man gave up the candles as well. He went away happily with the book.

A little elf also lived in the shop and he was curious, so he decided to follow the student to the loft where he lived. Here, the elf saw a very bright light showing under the door. How could that be? The elf looked through the keyhole. It was the book which was giving off the light. It was like a huge tree of light which spread its branches over the student. Every flower on the tree was the smiling face of a young maiden and every fruit was a star.

The elf was so enchanted by this light that he decided to remain in the poor attic, and return no more to the delights of the grocer's shop.

29 The White Snake and the Black Snake

One day, King Solomon was out hunting when he noticed two snakes engaged in a fight.

The larger snake was white and shining. The other was smaller and black with long, poisonous fangs. Just as the black snake was about to give its opponent a fatal bite, the king grabbed up a stone and killed it. Safe at last, the white snake went off into the trees.

Some time later, the king was confronted by a giant who appeared out of the forest. Solomon was very frightened, but the giant reassured him. He told him that he was the white snake that Solomon had helped earlier, and he explained that the black snake was an enemy who had been trying to poison him. In the course of their battle, both had changed into snakes.

'To show my thanks for your help,' the giant went on, 'I would like to offer you a gift. Would your prefer a gift of gold or a gift of healing?'

'I'm already rich enough,' replied the king, 'and the other gift would be more suitable for a doctor.'

'Well, what do you want?' asked the giant. 'Wisdom,' replied the king.

'You shall have it in abundance,' promised the giant. And that was how King Solomon became the wisest man in the world.

30 The Three Little Pigs, the Tomatoes and the Apples

The big bad wolf wanted to get at the three little pigs who lived in the house of bricks.

He had already tried once to capture them by force, so this time he decided to try with cunning.

He knocked on their door, and, smiling politely, said, 'Hello, friends. Do you want some sweet red tomatoes? There's a whole field of them nearby.'

'Oh really, where?'

'Over at Jack's farm. If you like, I'll take you there tomorrow.'

'Thanks. That would be nice. Come by for us at six,' said the pigs. The wolf turned up on time, but discovered that the little pigs had already been to Jack's farm, and returned laden with tomatoes.

He tried again. 'Over at John's farm there is a tree laden with delicious apples. Do you want me to show you where it is?'

'Thanks, why not. We'll meet you at the farm at six.'

But this time the wolf was not to be fooled, so he went to the farm at five. But he found the three little pigs already up in the tree.

'You were right,' they greeted him. 'These apples are really delicious. Why not try some?'

And they bombarded the wolf with apples until he was forced to flee.

31 The Old Sheep and the Young Goats

A shepherd took his sheep out to pasture, but when it was time to return to the sheep pen, he found that some wild goats had become mixed up with his flock. Nonetheless, he was very pleased that the flock had grown by itself, and he closed the goats into the pen along with the sheep.

The next day was rainy and the shepherd decided not to go out. He gave his sheep only a small handful of food, while he gave much bigger rations to the goats, thinking that if he treated them well, they would stay with him. In spite of this, as soon as the shepherd opened the gate, the goats ran out and he was unable to catch them again.

'Ungrateful beasts,' shouted the shepherd after them. 'To think I treated you better than the others!'

'That's why we're going,' answered one of the goats. 'If you prefer us new animals to your sheep, how will you treat us if you find some more animals in your flock?'

So do not be too happy if someone shows you that they prefer you to their old friends. You too will soon be an old friend and could be replaced just as easily.

Contents

The fairy tale of the month: The Ugly Duckling
Hans Christian Andersen

The fairy tale of the month

Jack
and the Beanstalk

A poor old widow and her son had only one thing left of any value, the milk from their cow, which they sold each day at the market. One day, Daisy the cow became sick, and after that she gave no more milk, so the widow decided to sell her instead. She told Jack, her son, to take the cow to the market.

But nobody there wanted to buy a cow that did not give milk anymore. Jack was just about to give up and go home when an old man approached him, and offered to buy Daisy the cow for a handful of beans. He explained to Jack that they were very special beans, capable of growing, in one night, until they reached the sky. The young boy could not believe his luck. He gave the man the cow and took the beans home.

When his mother found out about Jack's bargain she was furious. She took the beans and threw them out of the window. Poor Jack had to go to bed without his supper.

The next morning, the boy was awakened as usual by the sun shining into his room. But today, only a few rays were reaching him through the thick foliage, which had not been growing outside his window when he went to bed. Full of curiosity, Jack looked out of the window. The beans had taken root, and in a few hours had grown into a beanstalk so tall that its top disappeared into the clouds in the sky.

The thick branches made the bean-stalk easy to climb, so Jack went up and up to the top, where he found himself on a long road which led to a huge castle. Jack made his way fearlessly towards it, hoping to find something to eat there.

The door was opened by a giantess. Jack asked her, 'Kind lady, could you spare me a little something for breakfast?'

'You'll be turned into breakfast yourself,' she exclaimed, 'if you don't escape in time. My husband is on his way home. He is a giant who is especially fond of eating little boys on toast.'

Then the woman felt sorry for Jack and let him in. She set bread and milk before him, but just as he was about to eat, the castle began to tremble with the thundering footsteps of the returning giant.

'Hurry, hurry, hide in the oven,' the woman ordered the boy. 'There'll be all sorts of trouble if he finds you here.'

The giant was huge and terrifying, and as soon as he entered the kitchen he began looking around and sniffing: 'Fee, Fi, Fo, Foy,' he said in a terrible and frightening voice, 'I smell the blood of a little boy.'

'Oh no,' said his wife, trying to distract him. 'It must be the smell of the goose I cooked you for dinner yesterday. It's still lingering in the kitchen.'

The giant was reassured, and he ate a very hearty breakfast. Then he began counting bags of gold coins on the kitchen table until he fell asleep.

Jack crept out of the oven, grabbed one of the bags, and made off as fast as his legs would carry him, down the beanstalk and home.

With the gold coins in the bag, he and his mother were able to live for some time without problems; but then the money was spent and Jack decided to go back to the giant's castle for more.

The giantess failed to recognise him, and everything went as it did the first time. When the giant came home, the boy hid in the oven again, but this time he watched what went on in the room.

The giant grabbed a hen and commanded, 'Lay me an egg.' And the hen immediately laid, not an ordinary egg, but a solid gold one.

When the giant and his wife fell asleep, Jack came out of his hiding place, grabbed the hen that laid the golden egg and made off again, back down the beanstalk.

The golden eggs that the hen laid were enough to cover all their needs. However, one day, Jack felt the desire to go back up to the castle. Once again he climbed up the beanstalk. This time he did not knock on the door, but crept in through a window and immediately hid, not in the oven, but in a bucket hanging above the fireplace.

The giant arrived and sniffed the air: 'Fee, Fi, Fo, Foy, I smell the blood of a little boy!' He looked all around, but did not think of looking into the bucket. Then he had his breakfast, and after that he pulled out a golden harp.

'Play,' he ordered it, and all by itself the harp began playing a lullaby, which soon made the giant fall into a deep sleep.

Then Jack jumped down from the bucket, grabbed the magic harp, and made off. But as soon as he took hold of the harp, the instrument began shouting: 'Master, help, help. I'm being stolen.'

The giant jumped up and chased after the boy, who was already climbing down the beanstalk. The giant followed after Jack, but when the boy reached the ground, he ran into the house and brought out an axe. With it, Jack chopped down the beanstalk, and the giant plunged down, to fall on the ground with a thunderous crash.

Jack was already rich, thanks to the hen's golden eggs, and now he became famous as well. Everyone sought him out, to hear the music of his magic harp. Eventually, he was able to marry a royal princess, and together they all lived happily ever after.

1 The Gardener and the Good King

There was once a man who loved gardening so much, that he cultivated his vegetable patch and lawns with a passion that bordered on the ridiculous: he watched with love over the cabbages and the roses, he gently stroked the tulips and the artichokes, he cuddled the hyacinths and the tomatoes. In return, his garden was a wonder to behold. His vegetables were so tasty that they were famous throughout the kingdom.

But one terrible day, the hare broke into the vegetable garden, and the man despaired when he saw so many of his plants had been eaten. He tried everything he could to drive out the hare. In the end, he turned to the king to ask for help. 'It must never be,' thundered the king, 'that one of my good subjects should suffer such damage from an animal.'

So the king arrived the next day to hunt the hare. He brought his whole army and all his courtiers with him.

He demanded that everyone should be served roast chicken and ham for breakfast. The hunt began only when the meal was finished.

The hare was duly chased away. But the damage, done by the hunters, from their horses plunging through the vegetables and across the lawns, was worse than a hundred hares could have done in a thousand years.

2 Blockhead and the Gnome

A woodsman had two sons. He preferred the older one because he thought that the younger one was too simple. He even called him Blockhead. One day, the older son was going off to cut wood in the forest, and his mother gave him a basket of lunch. When it was time for his meal, the young man was approached by a little man, who asked him for some of his food and wine.

'Get lost,' shouted the older brother. 'Anything I give to you is so much the less for me.'

He finished his lunch and went back to work, but almost at once he cut himself with the axe and had to rush home, not realising that the wound was, in fact, the little man's vengeance on him, for the little man was really a woodland gnome.

The next day, Blockhead had to go to cut the wood, but to him his mother gave only bread and water. Blockhead generously divided his meagre lunch with the little man, when he came to ask him for some food.

'You are not such a blockhead,' said the little man. 'On the contrary, you are much smarter than your brother. He ended up with a nasty cut. But everything you gave to me will be returned to you, only in solid gold.'

3 The Fox and the Geese

A fox jumped into a flock of geese, ready to eat them all. Feeling generous, he thought he would grant them a last desire.

'Please let us say our prayers, so we can die in peace,' they asked. The fox agreed and the first goose began to honk loudly, with great feeling. It had not yet finished, when a second goose began to honk, followed by a third, then a fourth.

As soon as one goose finished, another began: eventually all the honking gave the fox such a bad headache, that he decided to go home without any supper at all.

4 The Four Brothers and the Lost Camel

Four brothers, who were all good at tracking, came upon the footprints of a camel.

Further on, they met an Arab, who asked them if they had seen his missing camel. He was sure it had been stolen.

'Is it blind in one eye and lame in one foot?' asked one of the four brothers. 'Has it lost its tail?' asked a second. 'Is it bearing a sack of grain on one side and a jar of honey on the other?' the third brother wanted to know.

'That's the one,' exclaimed the Arab. 'Do you know who stole it?'

'No,' said the fourth brother. 'We have never seen your camel.'

The Arab was convinced that they must be the thieves, so he brought them before a judge. 'They described my camel so exactly that it must have been them who took it.'

But the explanation was simple.

The first brother began, 'The camel had only grazed on the grass on one side of the path, so it must be blind in the other eye. One of its hoofprints was less marked than the others, and that means it must be lame in one foot.'

'As for me,' said the second brother, 'I noticed that all its droppings were in one heap, instead of being spread around as usually happens. So I thought that this camel must be missing its tail.'

'Yes, all this is possible,' admitted the judge, with little conviction, 'but how could you possibly have guessed what load it was bearing?'

'On one side,' explained the third brother, 'some wheat grains had fallen on the path and the ants were carrying them away. On the other side of the path, the flies were sucking at the drops of honey.'

Thereupon the judge freed the four brothers, and took them into his own service. And thanks to their amazing powers of observation, they helped him to catch many thieves.

5 The Wandering Coin

A little silver coin had journeyed all over the country, passed from one hand to another. Then it was taken abroad, further and further away from its home country. In the money bags, where it stayed for short periods, it met some very interesting other coins. They were French and Spanish, some called Mark and some called Lira. . . . This busy life on the move was just what the coin liked.

One day, however, it was mortally offended: 'This coin is not genuine,' said somebody. False! Accused unjustly only because the coin came from another continent and no-one had ever seen one like it before.

From then on its whole life changed. Nobody wanted it, and if someone managed to pass it off to someone else, it was filled with shame as if it were a thief. Then, one day, it found itself greeted with an exclamation of joy: 'Oh look, a coin from my country!'

The emigrant treated it with great affection, because, for him, the coin was like a piece of his homeland. He guarded it jealously and he even wrapped it up in a piece of cloth so that he would not give it away by mistake.

6 The Mosquito and the Bull

A mosquito landed on a bull's horn and there it settled down comfortably to make itself at home.

Only when it was time to leave did it remember its patient host, and it said to him:

'You'll be happy to know that I won't be disturbing you anymore; I'm going.'

'Me happy!' replied the bull. 'I didn't feel you arrive and I won't even notice that you've gone.'

And that's the way it is.

If someone is worth nothing then nobody cares whether he's there or not.

7 Gianni and Pippo

A long time ago in Florence there lived two merry fellows called Gianni and Pippo. One day, Pippo met Gianni at the market buying fish.

'They are for Bruno,' explained Gianni. 'He's giving a dinner party tonight and was worried that there might not be enough fish for everyone, so he sent me out to buy some more. Why don't you come as well?'

Pippo did not wait to be asked a second time, but when he arrived for dinner he found only dry bread to eat. He realised that he had been tricked and began working out how to get his own back. The next day Pippo sent a boy with a flask to master Giorgio, a wine seller who was well-known for his bad temper and foul moods. 'Tell him,' Pippo said to the boy, 'that Gianni wants him to fill it up with wine from the winecasks, and not from the river as he usually does.'

When Giorgio, the wine seller, heard these words he was furious. He rushed after Gianni and beat him with a stick. And poor Gianni, limping and bruised, not knowing why he had been treated like this, met Pippo on his way home, and heard him say:

'Which was better then, Bruno's fish or Giorgio's wine?'

8 The Horse and the Wolf

A horse was grazing in a field when he saw a wolf approaching. The frightened horse pretended it had a limp. Knowing that horses are strong, the wolf thought it would be cunning.

'Why are you limping?' asked the wolf.

'I've put my hoof on a thorn,' replied the horse. The wolf said, 'That looks like a serious wound. I've studied medicine. Perhaps you'd like me to look at it.' But as the wolf was bending to take hold of its leg, the horse gave it a mighty kick.

'Each to his own trade,' thought the wolf, as he flew through the air.

9 Blockhead and the King's Daughter

Thanks to the gold that the gnome had given him, Blockhead became such a rich man that he was even able to ask for the hand of a princess. The king was not at all pleased that his daughter should marry the son of a woodcutter. But he did not dare refuse openly, knowing that the young man had a powerful friend in the gnome. So the king made a condition that would be impossible to meet.

'I will say yes when someone arrives who is capable of drinking all the wine in my cellars,' the king promised.

Blockhead asked the gnome for help, and, during the night, sure enough, the little man drank all the wine in the cellars, leaving not a drop.

'I will say yes to a marriage,' said the king, imposing another condition, 'when someone manages to eat a mountain of bread.' This time, to take no chances, he had all the flour in the kingdom made into bread. But the next morning all the bread was eaten.

The king made yet a further demand: 'I want a ship that can sail on the sea and on the land.'

In response, the next day Blockhead brought him a sailing ship on wheels, which had been attached during the night by the gnome. This time the king was forced to give Blockhead the princess's hand. The last gift from the gnome to the couple was a happy and peaceful life.

10 The Three Lucky Sons

A father called his three sons to him on his deathbed and left them everything he had: a cockerel, a scythe and a cat. 'They may seem to be worthless,' he said, 'but if you take them to where nobody knows them, then your fortune will be assured.'

The first son set off with his inheritance under his arm, but there seemed to be cockerels everywhere; eventually, he reached a far off island where cockerels were unknown. When the inhabitants heard it sing 'cock-a-doodle-doo', they offered the son as much gold as his donkey could carry in exchange for the bird.

The second son journeyed all around until he reached an island, where the harvest was reaped by shooting cannon balls into the wheat, but this was a very wasteful method. When he showed them his scythe, the people also gave the second son as much gold as his donkey could carry.

The third son, with the cat, ended up in a land plagued by rats; the cat made short work of them. The people decided to keep the cat and gave the owner all the gold a horse could carry.

Do you think those three brothers were very lucky? Well, yes they were, but the fact is that each one of us has fortune in our grasp, but very few of us are capable of taking hold of it.

11 The Sun and the Children

In ancient times, the Sun was a man who lived on the earth. This man gave off light from under his arms, but when he put his arms down, everything became cold and dark again. He was a very lazy man and hardly ever got out of his bed, so only around his hut was there any light and heat, while the rest of the world was always dark and dismal. The wheat that the pigmies grew never dried out properly and it went bad; the hunters could not see what they were hunting and came home empty handed.

This kind of life could not continue. The womenfolk of a great African tribe decided to do something about the situation. But they had a lot of cleaning to do and a lot of cooking, so instead they asked the children to go and see the Sun. So off went the boisterous crowd of children to the Sun's hut. When they arrived, he was sleeping as usual, so they grabbed him by the arms and feet and shook him about. Then they swung him up into the sky and away.

He flew at such a speed that he changed shape and turned into a round ball. Ever since then, the Sun has been spinning round the sky, giving light and heat to every part of the world, afraid to come down again in case it meets those rough children.

12 The Emperor's Thrush

In ancient China, there were many marvellous things, but, according to the unanimous judgement of visitors, one thing was more beautiful than all the others; the song of the thrush in the palace gardens. The emperor came to hear of this marvel and ordered that his men bring the bird to him, for he had never seen nor heard it. He was very disappointed when he saw that it was a common looking brown bird. But when he heard it sing, he burst into tears of ecstasy.

For the thrush, such a response was reward enough, and it was truly happy to be so appreciated.

But some time later, the emperor received, as a gift, another thrush. This one was much more splendid in appearance, with many bright feathers, dotted with precious stones, and although it was mechanical, it sang very beautifully, thanks to a hidden device inside it. Moreover, it had a lot of advantages over the real bird. It was not necessary to watch over a mechanical thrush to prevent it from escaping, and it could sing any song to order, once it had been wound up. In no time at all, the artificial thrush became the idol of the whole court, and the real thrush was thrown out into the garden again.

Several months passed, and the mechanical thrush stopped singing. Its spring had broken and nobody was capable of repairing it. But the emperor was so used to falling asleep to the sound of the bird's song, that he could not sleep anymore. He fell so ill that the doctors said he would be dead before the morning. Immediately, his heirs began to quarrel over their inheritance.

However, during the night, the real thrush returned, because it had not forgotten the tears the emperor had shed the first time he had heard the thrush sing. So it sang once again and the emperor recovered his health at once, so that in the morning his doctors and heirs found him lively and cheerful.

13 The Hare and the Fox

'What are you staring at?' said a fox to a hare which was observing him.

'I was wondering,' said the hare, 'if you really are as cunning as people say, or is it that you just take advantage of the foolishness of the others?'

'That's an interesting question,' replied the fox. 'Why don't you come to my house and we can discuss it over dinner?'

But when he got to the fox's house, the hare realised that, although the table was set, there was no food on it, so he ran off at once.

Can you guess what the fox was planning for dinner?

14 The Young Man and the Golden Mountain

Looking for employment, a young man was hired by another man, who took him aboard a ship, which then sailed off to a distant island. There stood a high mountain made of gold.

'Go to the top of the mountain,' his employer ordered, 'and dig out as much gold as you can, then throw it to the bottom where I can collect it.'

'How do I reach the top?' he asked.

'Drink this magic potion,' came the reply, 'and you will be like a feather.' But it was really a sleeping potion, and as soon as the young man was asleep, his master wrapped him in a cow skin and left him on the beach. Along came some seagulls which took the cow skin and carried it to the top of the mountain, and dropped it. When the young man awakened, he scrambled out of the skin, and chased the seagulls away. Then he set about digging, throwing the gold down to his master. 'How do I get down?' the young man shouted. The master replied, 'You don't. You can just stay up there.' But the golden mountain disliked being dug up and robbed. So it began to shake and rumble, as it was really a volcano. Then it blew its top, and the young man was hurled up into the air. He eventually landed safe and sound back in his own country, but the master was caught in the flow of lava and turned into a golden statue.

15 The Cockerel, the Cat and the Mouse

An inexperienced little mouse set off on a journey. He came across a cockerel. Never having seen one before, the little mouse was so afraid of the cockerel's beak, its feathers and red crest, that he ran off as fast as he could. Further on, the mouse saw a cat: what a handsome animal, he thought; what soft fur, what striking eyes!

When the mouse got back home, he told his mother what he had seen.

'You silly mouse,' his mother said. 'Never go by appearances. The terrible animal that you saw was a harmless cockerel, while the fine-looking one is our enemy, the cat.'

16 The Owl and the Seagull

An owl and a seagull went into business together. The owl did not have any money so he borrowed some. The seagull owned a precious jewel and he put that into the venture as well. The two of them went on board a ship, having decided to start their business in a far off land. But there was a storm and the ship sank. The owl and the seagull managed to get to safety, but they lost all of their possessions. Ever since then, the owl only comes out at night for fear of meeting its creditors, and the seagull flies high over the rocks in the hope that the sea will give him back his precious jewel.

17 The Story of Sumio

In Japan, there once lived an old couple who were very happy, but for the fact that they had no children. One evening, they came across a bright and shining bamboo cane. They cut it down and opened it up. Inside, they found a tiny baby girl.

The couple were filled with joy, and decided at once to keep her. They grew to love her like a daughter, and they called her Sumio.

Sumio grew up and became such a sweet and beautiful girl that all the princes in the land desired to marry her. One day, even the emperor himself came to ask for her hand in marriage.

Sumio refused him, just as she had refused all the others. But she had to reveal her secret to him.

She told the emperor that she was the princess of the moon, and that soon her subjects would be coming to take her back to their kingdom.

The emperor refused to allow this and on the night of the next full moon he ordered his army to surround Sumio's house, but to no avail.

Down a pathway of moonbeams came an awesome procession of magical creatures, and at the sight of them the emperor's soldiers were unable to move. Sumio was carried back up into the sky, and with her she took the old couple, who had found her as a baby and loved her so much.

18 The Boy Born with His Shirt On

A king was out on a tour of inspection of his kingdom, when he heard about a boy who had been born with his shirt on. This boy was lucky in everything he did, and a fortune teller had predicted that one day he would marry the king's daughter.

The king did not know whether to believe these tales. However, as he was not all that keen on having just anybody as a son-in-law, he preferred not to take any risks. So he called the young man before him, and gave him a letter to take to the queen at court.

The young boy ran as fast as he could, but at nightfall he was still on the road. He found a little house in the woods and asked for hospitality.

The house was inhabited by dangerous robbers and, as soon as the young man was asleep, their leader went through his belongings, to see if there was anything worth stealing. He found the king's letter and was outraged to read in it that the queen was commanded by the king to have the carrier of the letter put to death at once. A skilled forger, the robber chief wrote a new letter in the king's handwriting. The letter commanded the queen to let the carrier of the message marry the princess. The boy awoke, went to the palace with the new letter, and when the king returned the fortune teller's prediction had come true.

19 The War Between the Flying Creatures and the Animals

One day, a quarrel broke out between a bear and a woodpecker. Things got so bad that they declared war on each other, with all the animals on the side of the bear, while everything with wings, birds and insects alike, sided with the woodpecker.

The flying creatures sent spies into the animals' camp. A mosquito flew round just as the animals' commander, the fox, was giving the orders for the next day's battle.

'My thick red tail is easily seen from far,' said the fox. 'So I will use it to give signals. If I hold it straight out, it means that everything is going well, and you must continue to advance. If we are being beaten or surrounded, then I will put my tail down, and you must all retreat.' The next day the animals began their attack. The earth shuddered under the weight of their feet. But the noise made by the animals' army was drowned out by the roar of beating wings, from the horde of birds and insects in the sky above.

With advance warning of the animals' signals, the winged creatures sent a hornet to attack the fox, who was stung so many times that he could not keep his tail up. That was the signal for the animals to beat a hasty retreat . . . . defeated by nothing but a mosquito and a hornet.

20 The Guardian of the Pigs

A young man came to the court and asked for the hand of the beautiful princess. The king spoke for a long time with the stranger, then gave his approval. The princess liked the young man at first, but then she discovered that he was not a king, nor even a prince. She was outraged and protested so loudly that the king threatened to disown her if she did not marry the man at once.

After the wedding, the bridegroom said he was taking the princess away to her new home, but the carriage stopped right in front of a pigpen. 'We're here,' he said. 'Sorry if I didn't tell you before, but I am a pigkeeper. From now on, you can help me with my work.'

The princess cried and stamped her feet in a tearful frenzy, but she had to give in. In fact, as she grew to love her husband more and more, she eventually began to enjoy her new life.

One day he went away. After several days, a messenger arrived to fetch the princess and lead her to her husband.

So the pigkeeper was taken to a splendid castle and brought before the emperor on his throne. It was none other than her husband, although she almost failed to recognise him. Now that she was no longer so proud and haughty, she was worthy to be proclaimed as empress and reign at her husband's side.

21 The Enchanted Wood of Narumi

In the enchanted land of Narumi, in Japan, all would have been peaceful and happy, but for the practical jokes that the skunk was always playing on everybody. Eventually the hare decided to teach the skunk a lesson. He took two baskets, one big and one small. He coated the big one with tar, and then he went off to find the skunk.

'Come with me to gather emeralds on the mountains,' he invited him.

The skunk agreed and, as the hare had expected, he grabbed the biggest basket. When the skunk tried to put it down, his paws were stuck to the tar, and in the effort to release the basket, he tore his skin. Then the hare gave the skunk some ointment for sore paws, but when he had rubbed it in the skunk found out to his cost that it was his own practical joke ointment made up of pepper and lemon juice. The skunk decided to run away back to its lair across the river. On the river bank there were two canoes, one old and made of wood, the other shiny and sparkling with precious stones. Obviously the skunk leapt into the expensive looking canoe, which sank under his weight. Soaking wet and with sore, smarting paws, the skunk resolved not to play any more tricks, especially on the hare.

22 The Cat and the Old Mouse

A black cat happened to wander into a warehouse, where mice lived.

'This is the place for me,' thought the cat. 'I'll pretend to be dead.' And the cat lay down on the ground. The younger mice ran towards it shouting, 'There's a dead cat.' But a wise old mouse stopped them and said, 'Don't you know that a cat has nine lives?' Then the old mouse climbed up above the cat and chewed open a huge sack of flour that was resting on a large bin. The flour poured out and covered the cat, which lay still for a moment. Then there came a sneeze and out of the flour came a white cat.

23 The Repentant Skunk

In the woods of Narumi, there was a couple, so old that they were not even able to go shopping in the village. But all the animals, who lived nearby, helped them and looked after them. The beavers gathered wood for them, the squirrels brought them nuts; the hares brought fruit; the bees placed their honey on the window ledge; the goats gave them milk, and the birds brought in flowers for the table. As thanks, the old woman made lovely cakes for everyone.

But the skunk managed to ruin even this perfect harmony. He went to the old woman and demanded a whole cake. Naturally she refused, because she wanted to give everyone a slice, so the skunk threatened her.

When the animals heard about this they decided to punish the skunk. They all ran about the woods, crying and shouting that the old lady had been killed by a robber.

Frightened by the news, the skunk raced to the house, where he found the old woman lying motionless on the bed. The skunk was convinced that she really was dead, and burst into tears because he realised how much he would miss her. Then the old woman suddenly rose from the bed and hugged the tearful skunk, who was now very sorry for what he had done.

24 The Donkey in the Lion's Skin

A donkey disguised itself by dressing up as a lion, and then went around spreading terror amongst the other animals.

Some time later, when it encountered a fox, the donkey roared as fiercely as it could, but the fox just burst out laughing:

'If I hadn't heard you braying, I might also have been scared by that lion's skin.'

There are a lot of stupid people who, like the donkey, would like to dress up in fine clothes and pretend they are important, but they betray themselves.

25 The Crafty Trader

A farmer had to go away for a few days, and before he departed, he told his son what to do. 'If the cattle trader comes along,' he said, 'offer him those three cows. But, beware! Don't let him have them for less than two hundred ducats.'

Sure enough, the trader came the next day. He looked at the cows and asked the price. 'Two hundred ducats is a very fair price,' he commented, 'I'll take them.' He began to untie the animals and lead them away; but the farmer's son barred the way. 'Just a moment, my friend. If you want the cows, first you have to pay.'

'You are absolutely right,' said the trader, still holding onto the three cows. 'The fact is that I don't have the money with me, but I'll bring it to you. Surely you trust me. . . .'

'How can I trust you?' asked the son. 'Yes, I understand, you're right,' agreed the trader. 'I was just about to say that I could leave you something, as a guarantee that I will come back and bring you the money.'

'What will you leave me?' the young man wanted to know first.

'Suppose I leave you a cow, is that good enough?'

'That certainly seems fair enough,' said the son.

So the trader left one cow, and went off with two, and never came back.

26 The Old Woman and the Healer

An old woman whose eyes were inflamed called in a healer, and he told her that her eyesight would become faultless again, provided she would pay a very expensive fee for his services. She agreed and he insisted that she keep her eyes shut during the treatment, at which time the healer stole all the old lady's furniture.

When he asked the woman for his fee, she refused to pay, so the healer took her to court. 'It's not true that he's made my eyes better,' the old lady told the judge. 'They have got worse. Before, I could see everything in my house, now I can't see at all.'

27 The Weasels and the Mice

The weasels and the mice were at war, and the mice kept on losing. They thought that this might be due to the fact that they were not well organised and disciplined, because they had no leaders. So the mice appointed some generals, and to set themselves apart from the soldiers, the generals made themselves helmets decorated with long horns.

The next battle was won by the weasels again and the mice only saved themselves by running into their burrows; but the generals could no get in because of the horned helmets so they were all eaten by the weasels

28 The Twelve Daughters of the Sea-King

Ivan was sunning himself on a beach when he saw twelve seagulls. As soon as they had landed, the birds turned into beautiful young girls. Not noticing Ivan behind some rocks, the twelve girls took off their gowns and dived into the sea.

As a joke Ivan crept out and took away one of their feather gowns. When the young girls emerged from the sea, eleven of them drew on their gowns and, transformed into seagulls again, they flew away. One girl remained weeping on the beach, and Ivan felt sorry for having played a trick on her, so he gave her back the gown

of feathers. The grateful girl insisted that Ivan accompany her back to see her father, the sea-king, who would reward him for returning the gown.

So Ivan followed the girl to a fairy tale castle beneath the ocean waves. The king welcomed Ivan, and, in reward, promised him the hand of his daughter in marriage. The king insisted only that Ivan must be able to recognise her three times from among the other daughters. They looked alike, except that one of them was already in love with Ivan, so each time she gave Ivan a secret sign which enabled him to recognise her. Ivan married the sea-king's daughter, and lived happily for years beneath the waves.

29 The Four Friends and the King's Ring

The king had a magic ring which guaranteed that he would keep the throne as long as he had the ring on his finger. When he lost it, the king was so scared that he promised his daughter's hand in marriage to whoever brought the ring back to him.

Many people tried to find the ring, and eventually it was the turn of a young man with three exceptional friends. The first, Lynx-eyes, had such keen eyesight that he could see through doors. The second friend, Man Mountain, was so large that, when he lay down, he looked like a small mountain. The third friend, Long

John, was so tall that when he lay down he stretched for miles.

Of course, Lynx-eyes spotted the ring at once. It was stuck on a rock a the bottom of the sea.

First, Man Mountain knelt down an drank all the water from the sea. The the young man crossed the muddy bottom on Long John, who lay down to make a bridge. Lastly, all that he had to do was reach out and gathe the ring.

The young man married the princess and, when he became king, he appointed Long John as minister of transport, Lynx-eyes as minister of defence, and Man Mountain as th treasury minister.

30 The Dragon and the Goddess

Once upon a time, the people who lived on the coasts of Japan were terrorised by a terrible dragon, which would leap suddenly out of the sea, and threaten any children that it found playing on the beach. Up in the heavens, Beltana, the goddess of happiness, observed what was happening. She felt pity, not only for the people, but also for the dragon.

'Perhaps,' she thought, 'he is so aggressive because he is condemned to live in solitude in the ocean depths. How can he be kind, if kindness has not been shown to him?'

Beltana climbed onto the back of a swan-shaped cloud that she used to take her down to earth. She set down on the surface of the ocean and summoned the dragon. The sea immediately started bubbling: then it opened and up rose a desolate island, which was the dragon's lair.

A gesture from the goddess and the island became flower covered, with fruit trees and streams. The dragon was overcome at the sight of so many unknown things. Fearlessly, Beltana drew near and smiled at it.

The warmth of the smile from the goddess transformed the dragon from savage beast to gentle giant. From that time on, the children on the beach were no longer afraid, for the dragon from the sea no longer threatened them. Instead, it played with them.

31 The Son of the Tsar and the Witch's Niece

A prince met a beautiful young girl, who had learnt some magic arts from an old aunt, who was a witch. The two young people fell in love, and duly set off on the journey back to the prince's palace. When they were near their destination, the prince said he would go on ahead and give the news of his bride-to-be to his father, the tsar.

'You must not kiss your sister,' warned the girl, 'or a spell will be cast on you, and you will forget me.'

The prince paid no heed to this warning. As soon as he reached the palace, he kissed his sister and immediately forgot his betrothed.

Time passed and the prince became engaged to wed another princess. Throughout the kingdom, preparations began for the wedding feast. Every subject had to contribute something. The witch's niece took a big cake to the palace for the feast. When the prince cut it open, two doves flew out. The she dove picked up a piece of cake and flew off with it.

'Beloved she dove,' said the second dove, 'let me eat a piece of cake.'

'Never,' said the she dove, 'for if you do, you will forget all about me, as the prince has forgotten his first love.'

With the dove's words, the prince's memory returned. He sent his new princess home again, and married the witch's niece amidst general rejoicing.

Contents

The fairy tale of the month: Jack and the Beanstalk
English Fairy Tale

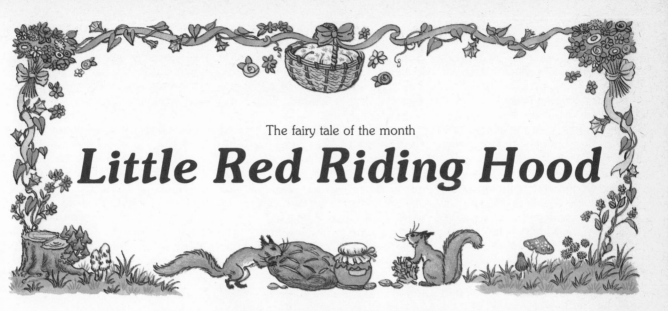

The fairy tale of the month

Little Red Riding Hood

There was once a mother who considered herself truly blessed: her daughter was such a sweet and gracious girl, so well-mannered and lighthearted, that everybody liked her. One day the mother bought a remnant of red cloth, and from this she made her daughter a cloak with a hood. This poor gift pleased the little girl so much that she never took it off. The townspeople, whenever they saw her coming, would smile and say, 'Here comes Little Red Riding Hood!' This nickname became so widely used that soon almost nobody remembered her real name.

Little Red Riding Hood was very obliging and, since she was not yet old enough to go to school, constantly asked her mother if she could help her with anything. Her mother gave her simple jobs to do, and, having observed that her daughter always behaved in a very responsible way, from time to time she asked her to run some small errand or another.

One fine day, she put a cake and a jar of marmalade into a basket, and asked her daughter to take them to her grandmother, who was not feeling well and who lived on the far side of the wood. Little Red Riding Hood went off, skipping down the road with the basket on her arm. She loved her old grandmother very much and it always gave her a great deal of pleasure to go and visit her, all the more so because she felt so useful

taking her good things to eat, and tidying up her little home.

She was also delighted at the notion of enjoying a lovely walk in the woods, gathering flowers and wild fruits, and playing with the little birds and animals, which not only were unafraid of her, but had become her good friends and loved her company.

On this occasion, however, neither the hare nor the little red squirrel ran out to greet her as usual. All the animals had fled, because of the big, bad wolf who was hiding, in the hope that something tasty would come within reach of his great jaws. He had already spied the little girl, and his mouth had watered, thinking about how tender and delicious she would

be. The only reason he had not already leapt out on her was that he had noticed some hunters nearby, and thought it safer to remain well hidden.

Nevertheless, he did have a plan for catching Little Red Riding Hood. He went to get the old clothes worn by a scarecrow and he put them on. Then he stuck balls of cotton wool to his long muzzle until he had a white beard. The wolf was very satisfied when he saw his reflection in the lake: without a doubt, the little girl would believe him to be an old ruffian. And that, in fact, is just what he really was.

The wolf came up to the girl. 'Where are you going to, pretty little girl?' he asked, forcing himself to make his deep gruff voice as soft as possible.

Red Riding Hood told him, and without the slightest suspicion replied to all his questions, explaining precisely where her grandmother's house was to be found. The wolf rubbed his big paws together, thinking how lucky he was that day. With a little patience, he would procure not only a good lunch, but an excellent dinner as well!

The wolf spoke to the little girl for a few moments longer, advising her not to lose time playing in the woods, and, above all, not to talk to strangers. Then he said goodbye to her, and ran off. He knew all the short-cuts through the woods and was much faster than Little Red Riding Hood. He was sure he would arrive at the grandmother's house long before her little grand-daughter.

The wolf found the house at once and knocked on the door. 'Can I come in, grandmother?' he said, imitating the voice of Little Red Riding Hood. 'It's your granddaughter.'

'Come in, darling! The door is open, as usual!' said the old woman. She was lying in bed in almost total darkness because the light made her eyes water. This suited the wolf, since he could come right up to the bed without being recognised. He leapt on the old woman, but he did not have the time to eat her there and then. That would come later! He took off her nightshirt and nightcap, tied her up and gagged her, and shut her up in a trunk. Just in time! Little Red Riding Hood was already knocking at the door! The wolf put on the shirt and nightcap and slipped into the bed, pulling the covers right up to his eyes to hide himself better. All the same, Little Red Riding Hood thought that there was something strange about her grandmother, and she approached the bed with caution.

'Grandmother, what big ears you have!' exclaimed the little girl.

'All the better to hear you with!' said the wolf.

'What big eyes you have!'

'All the better to see you with!'

'And what long arms you have!'

'All the better to hug you with!'

Little Red Riding Hood, it seemed, now had very little chance.

'What big jaws you have, grandmother!' 'All the better to eat you with!' said the wolf, as he leapt out of the bed onto the little girl.

But in that same instant, a rifle shot sounded from the doorway. A little bird had watched every move the wolf had made, and, in order to save her little friend, had attracted the attention of a hunter, and led him to the grandmother's house. The wolf, seeing the rifle being aimed at him again, ran off as fast as he was able. Little Red Riding Hood released her grandmother from the trunk, and they enjoyed a happy supper with the hunter who had so bravely and luckily come to save them.

1 The Three Gifts that the Eagle Gave the Tsar

Out hunting one day, the tsar was about to shoot an eagle, when the bird began to beg for its life: 'Don't kill me! Keep me with you for three years and you will see that sooner or later you will be very glad of me.'

The astonished tsar could not believe what he was hearing and took aim again with his rifle. This time the eagle repeated its plea and the tsar was moved to pity. He spared the eagle's life and took the bird home.

One by one, the eagle devoured every last lamb and calf belonging to the tsar. Despite the fact that he had no more livestock and was that much poorer, the tsar kept the promise he had made to the eagle, and looked after the bird for three years, even though he was obliged to sell everything he owned, in order to feed it.

When the three years were finally over, the eagle bade the tsar to climb on its back and flew off, high over the sea. The tsar was afraid of falling and drowning. The eagle, however, carried him safely. 'I have already taught you,' the eagle said to the tsar, 'to keep promises, be generous, and to fear death, so you no longer need me.'

The eagle flew off, and the tsar, because of the virtues taught him by the eagle, ruled so wisely and well that he became the most powerful monarch in the world.

2 The Seven League Boots

Albert was never happy unless he was sticking his nose into everything; but in this he was not motivated by mere nosiness, so much as by a lively interest in the world around him.

However, as you can imagine, he very often ended up by getting into trouble, like the time he went exploring in the woods, and chanced on a large house. This house happened to belong to an ogre, one of the really horrible types that eat children for breakfast and for lunch.

The ogre smelt the possible meal immediately and shouted his classic hunting cry: 'Fee, Fi, Fo, Foy, I smell the blood of a little boy!' But when Albert heard this, he quickly ran away.

'Hurry up! Give me my seven league boots!' shrieked the ogre to his wife. 'I want to eat that boy!'

In his boots, every step the ogre took crossed a mountain or forded a river, but Albert managed to hide from him. When the tired ogre lay down for a rest and fell asleep, Albert sneaked out, pulled off the seven league boots and put them on his own feet. Since they were magic boots, they fitted perfectly. Now it was Albert who could walk seven leagues with every step and, thanks to this, not only did he easily escape from the ogre, but he also became later the most important royal messenger in the kingdom.

3 The Dog with the Little Bell

There was once a dog which had the bad habit of biting anyone who came within reach.

For this reason, its master hung a little bell on the collar around its neck, so that everybody would be warned of the dog's approach, and could take care not to get too close to its somewhat fearsome teeth and extremely powerful jaws.

The dog was very proud of its little bell and liked to boast that the tinkle of it scared men away. A wise old dog, however, warned it: 'The bell resounds to your shame, not to your glory!'

4 The Hunter and the Fisherman

The king of Japan had two sons and, of these, there was one who loved to hunt and one who loved to fish. One day, they decided to make an exchange, and thus, the older brother, who was the hunter, went fishing and the younger, who was the fisherman, went hunting. Unfortunately, the older brother lost the fishing-hook. The younger brother was so angry at this, that he made his brother promise to scour the sea until he found it.

After many hours, the hunting prince was about to give up the search, when a crocodile offered to carry him to the palace of the sea-king, who would certainly be able to help him find the fish hook.

In the undersea palace, the hunting prince was well received. The sea-king ordered a search to be made and the missing hook was found. Parting, the sea-king presented the prince with a black stone which had the power to make the oceans rise and cover the earth, and a white stone which had the power to make the waters recede.

Upon his return to his kingdom, the hunting prince discovered his father was dead and his brother had ascended the throne. Since the crown was the older brother's by right, the king was furious at the return of his brother, who had been away for so long. He ordered his palace guards to kill him at once. The hunting prince attempted to flee, but realising all was lost, he took up his black stone and squeezed it in his right hand. At once, the sea poured over the land and swept away both the soldiers and the wicked brother with them.

On the point of drowning, the usurper cried out for mercy to his older brother. Hearing his cry, the hunting prince dived into the flood at the risk of his own life. As soon as he had done this, the older brother squeezed the white stone in his right hand, and, in an instant, the waters had retreated.

Touched by the great forbearance of his brother, the fisherman prince resigned the throne, and remained faithful to him for the rest of his life.

5 The Mad Fisherman

It was market day in the city and carts and animals had arrived from all over the countryside. There were pedlars and merchants, breeders and farmers, noblemen and clowns. Even the arrival of the king was expected.

In the stable, a young foal was born. But as soon as it was able to stand, it fled in terror from all the noise and excitement, and hid between two oxen who were pulling a plough.

The owner of the foal wanted his animal back, but the owner of the oxen said: 'The foal is mine, because it has chosen for itself.' They took their dispute to the king, who decided that the foal should remain where it was, as if the two oxen had become its parents from the moment the foal itself had chosen them.

The next day, the king was out in his carriage, when he came across the first owner of the foal standing in the middle of the street with a fishing net. He was casting his net as if he were fishing, to the amusement of everyone around.

'What on earth are you doing?' the king asked him.

'I'm fishing, your majesty,' replied the man. 'If two oxen can be parents to a foal, why shouldn't I be able to catch fish in the middle of the street?'

6 The Fox and the Grapes

There was once a fox with an empty stomach, who went in search of something to eat. He chanced upon a vineyard, where large bunches of golden grapes hung from the vines above his head.

The fox jumped up and down, trying to bite into a bunch of the grapes, but he fell short. He tried again, and again, with all his might, but he still failed to reach the grapes. He was obliged to give up the attempt but consoled himself as well as he could by telling himself: 'It doesn't matter, because they weren't ripe yet anyway.'

7 The Mad King and His Faithful Wife

Once upon a time, there was a king who had been happy with his wife for many years. Unexpectedly, however, either out of jealousy, or because of wicked gossip, or from some madness in his character, he tired of his wife and ordered her to return and live with her parents. The poor queen was desperate but could not change her husband's mind.

'I will allow you,' said the king, making a solitary concession, 'to take with you the dearest and most precious thing you have.'

The next morning, when the king awoke, he was in a bed and room he did not recognise. He blinked his eyes and had a good look round, but the only thing he was certain of was that he was not in the palace.

Angry, and a little alarmed, the king called out, and at once the queen came in. 'Where am I?' he asked her. 'What have you done?'

'You said I could take with me the dearest and most precious thing I have. Nothing is more dear or more precious to me than you are. When you fell asleep last night, I ordered the servants to bring you here to the house of my parents. I could not live without you!' The king realised he had been foolish. He embraced his wife and they returned happily to the royal palace.

8 The New Moon and the Old Moon

We all know that when the moon shines, it brightens the darkness and the darkness retreats.

Then the sun comes and chases the moon, cutting it away with its knife, little by little, until only the backbone remains for us to see.

The moon then goes home in discomfort but, after only a few days, it recovers to become a new moon and feels as though it has been reborn.

The moon again begins to move across the sky, until it becomes round and bright, and the sun arrives to chase it off again.

9 Little Brother, Little Sister

Maltreated by their stepmother, who was a witch, a little brother and sister fled into the woods. After running for a while, the brother said: 'I'm so thirsty. Let's find a spring and have a drink.'

However, as the young boy bent down to drink, his sister heard a voice which said: 'Who drinks from me will turn into a fawn.' It was the witch! Too late, the sister tried to prevent her brother from drinking. The young boy changed at once into a fawn. In tears, the little girl made a lead and collar out of her belt, and led the fawn off into the woods. There they found an abandoned cottage and lived together, far from any danger.

One day, however, the king was hunting in the woods, and he spied the fawn, which could not resist the urge to wander away from the cottage. The king and his hunters chased the fawn all the way back home. There, the king followed it into the cottage, where he found a young girl stroking the frightened animal. She was so beautiful and gentle that the king fell in love with her at once. He asked her to be his wife, and his words caused the maiden to cry for joy. When one of her tears fell on the fawn, it changed back to her brother once more. Their goodness and love had overcome the witch's evil spell, and they lived safely and happily with the king for ever after.

10 The Knight and the Beautiful Witch

A young and valiant knight had succeeded in freeing a beautiful princess held prisoner by an evil magician. They rode away as fast as they could to escape pursuit. but the magician's servants gave chase.

The princess knew a little magic herself, and she transformed herself at once into a jug, the horse into a well, and the young knight into an old man. Not suspecting anything, the magician and his men asked the old man if he had seen the princess and he sent them off in the wrong direction. In a short while, the magician realised that he had been deceived and set off once more. Then the princess changed herself into a church, the horse into a bell, and her knight into a priest.

Once again, the magician and his servants were deceived. The magician turned back by himself and followed the trace of the fugitives. The lovely princess saw him and changed herself into a duck, the young man into a poppy, and the horse into a river of chocolate which flowed between banks of marzipan. Now the magician was greedy and could not resist chocolate. He sat down and ate and drank so much that he finally burst.

So both the young people were saved, and they became their true selves again, embraced and swore that they would never be parted.

11 The King's Field and the Golden Mortar Bowl

A peasant was so poor that the king gave him a small piece of land, so that he could grow enough food to feed him and his family. One day, while he was ploughing, the farmer unearthed a heavy, golden mortar bowl. Since he was an honest man, he decided to take the golden bowl to the king, who, as owner of the field, also owned whatever was found in it.

'No, don't do that!' his daughter begged him. 'The king will demand that you also hand over the pestle, and then it will be the worse for us!'

'The king can't expect us to give him something which we do not have,' the farmer said, paying no attention to his daughter's warning.

He went off to the royal court, but, unfortunately, everything happened as his daughter had predicted. The king decided that the farmer had hidden the pestle, which should have accompanied the mortar bowl, in order to keep it for himself. He had the farmer thrown in prison. For days, the poor man had nothing to eat and chided himself bitterly, 'Oh, if only I had listened to my daughter!'

The king asked why he said this, and so heard the whole story. He so admired the wisdom of the maiden, that she was brought to court and appointed minister of the treasury, after he had liberated her father.

12 Tom's Crumbs

A woodsman had seven children and was so poor that he just could not even feed them. He worked from dawn to dusk each day, but what he brought home was not even enough to give everyone a spoonful of soup.

'Rather than watch them all die slowly of hunger,' he said to his wife, 'it would be better to leave them in the woods, where there is at least a chance they will survive!' However cruel this appeared to be, there was no alternative. Although the poor mother was in tears, she agreed. 'We'll take them into the woods tomorrow,' the woodsman decided.

This whole conversation was overheard by Tom, the youngest of their seven children. The next morning, just as they were all leaving for the woods, Tom filled his pockets with little white stones. He dropped one of these every so often on the path. And so, after the children had been left by their parents in the heart of the forest, they were still able to find their way home again.

Two days later, their parents took them into the woods again, but this time Tom did not have enough time to collect little white stones. Instead he dropped crumbs of the bread they were supposed to eat for lunch. Unfortunately, little birds ate all the crumbs, and so by nightfall the seven children found themselves well and truly lost in the woods. Fearful and weary, they thought there was no hope for them. But suddenly, they heard in the distance the desperate cries of their parents, searching for them.

It had happened that another woodcutter had come to their father's house to repay an old debt, and thanks to this money, there was enough food for the whole family to eat well, at least for a while. The woodsman and his wife had suffered so much after abandoning the children, they swore they would stay together as a family in future. And so, the parents embraced their children, and that night there was more joy and gladness than at any royal wedding.

13 The Fisherman and His Flute

There was once a fisherman who was also an excellent flute player. One day he took his flute and a fish-basket, jumped up on a rock and began to play his flute, convinced the fish would be enchanted by his music and leap into the basket willingly. Unfortunately, he did not catch a single fish, so went home, collected his net, and threw it into the water. He caught so many fish his basket overflowed.

'Stupid creatures!' he exclaimed, as he watched the fish twist and jump in his net. 'You would not dance when I played my flute, but when I'm not playing, you can't stop dancing!'

14 Yvette's Daydreams

Beautiful little Yvette was on her way to the market, balancing on her head the jug of fresh milk which she intended to sell there. While she walked, she made a lot of plans as to how she would spend the money she was going to earn.

'With the money I will get from selling the milk,' she thought, 'I will buy a hen. The hen will lay a lot of eggs and I will sell them. I will save that money and buy a goose, which will lay even bigger eggs, which I will be able to sell at a higher price. Then I will buy myself a sheep. . . .'

Since Yvette was also more than a little vain, her thoughts began to change direction at this point.

'With the wool from the sheep, I will make myself a lovely dress; with the milk, I will make lots of little cheeses, and I will take them to the market, and sell them as well, and that way I will have the money to buy myself a fine, fine hat and a pair of dancing shoes. I will be so elegant that the king will notice me, and will invite me to a royal ball, believing me to be a great lady. I shall dance all evening with the prince, who will be sure to fall in love with me, and ask me to marry him. . . .' At that moment, her daydreams came to an end. The jug fell from her head, all the milk was spilt on the ground, and Yvette was left with nothing.

15 The Brother, the Sister and the Witch

A witch found two children playing beside a river and stole them away. They succeeded in escaping one day, but the witch set off to bring them back. A good fairy, who was passing by, saw the children and took pity on them. She set a great ring of fire around them to keep them safe; but the witch managed to blow out the flames. So the fairy built round them a high wall of glass so smooth it could not be climbed. The witch returned to her house to find a hammer to break it with but when she returned the fairy had spirited the children away, and they were safe at home.

16 The Fox and the Woodcutter

Long ago, a fox which was being chased by hunters took refuge in the house of a woodcutter, and asked him to conceal her. The astonished man agreed, but when the hunters arrived, although he said that he had not seen the fox, he tried to point out with dramatic gestures, the place where she was hiding. The hunters paid no heed and went on their way. Afterwards, the fox came out of hiding and prepared to leave. 'Are you not even going to thank me?' complained the woodcutter. 'And should I thank you for what you said?' retorted the fox. 'Or for what you did?'

17 The Wooden Calf

Everyone in the village was rich, except for one man who possessed nothing. He wanted at least to own a calf, so carved himself one out of wood. The wooden calf's head moved, the tail swung, and it almost seemed real! 'It is small now,' the man said, 'but one day it will become a cow!' The next morning, he entrusted his calf to the shepherd.

'You'll have to carry him to pasture,' the poor man informed the shepherd, 'because he is young and has not yet learnt to walk.' So the shepherd carried the calf to the meadow and left it there, convinced that it was browsing and nibbling. 'From its weight, it must eat a lot,' he thought. 'It will soon grow really big.'

When evening came, he called the calf to return to the stall, but it did not move. 'Well, if you can eat by yourself,' the shepherd said, 'then you can also walk back by yourself.'

The poor man was angry when the shepherd came home without his animal. They went back to the meadow, but the calf was no longer to be found. 'It's your fault if it is lost,' said the poor man. 'You did not look after it properly!' The judge decided in favour of the poor man, and the shepherd was made to give him a cow as compensation. So the little wooden calf actually did become a real cow.

18 The Language Student

A rich man wanted the very best education for his son, and so he sent him abroad, with no expense spared, to learn other languages.

A few years later, when the young man returned home, the only language he had learnt was the language of dogs. The father was so indignant that he drove his son out of the house, and said he wished to have nothing further to do with him.

After a great deal of wandering, the young man arrived in a village which was terrorised by a pack of ferocious dogs. Despite the fact that everybody advised him against it, the young man insisted on going into the woods where the dogs lived, and, to much amazement, returned without even a scratch. He said that the dogs had spoken to him, explaining they were ferocious because they were compelled by a spell to keep guard all the time over a rich treasure chest buried in the woods. The young man solved all the problems by digging up the chest for himself, so the dogs were free to wander off and troubled the villagers no further.

The rich man, too, never insulted his son again, after he saw him come home in a luxurious carriage, followed by a long line of carts, loaded with all the riches he had accumulated as a result of his ability to talk with dogs!

19 The Old House on the Street

In the elegant street, there now remained only one old house, in which there lived a very rich old man who was always alone. He had only memories and thoughts to keep him company. Directly in front of his house, however, there lived a little boy, and the two of them had begun to say hello to each other from their windows. Then, after the little boy had actually visited the old man for the first time, he returned there often to drink the hot chocolate with cream, and eat the little cakes which the old man always made for him. On one occasion, the little boy presented the old man with one of his tin soldiers as a sign of his sincere affection. He was not to know that this was to be the last time he would see the old man, who died a very short while later.

The old house was knocked down and in its place a gracious villa was built. It was the little boy himself from the house opposite who went to live there, when he had grown up and married.

One day, he and his wife were working in the garden, when, digging with his hand in the earth, he pricked his finger. It was his little tin soldier with the sharp bayonet attached to the rifle. He cleaned it and placed it in the living-room, where it always provided him with happy memories of his childhood and his friend, the old man.

20 The Lion and the Ass

The lion had decided to go hunting and had chosen the ass as his companion, for he had thought of a way to make use of its distinctive braying.

The silly ass was extremely proud at being chosen as the lion's companion, and with complete docility he allowed the lion to dress him up in a cloak of leaves, thinking that this must be the correct hunting costume, whereas it was really only to be a disguise.

Following the lion's instructions, the ass went and stood in the middle of a meadow. At the agreed moment, the ass began to bray loudly, and the deer were so terrified by the din that they fled every which way. And not a few of them finished in the great paws of the lion, or rushed straight into his huge jaws.

When the hunt was finished, the ass was quick to claim the credit for the great success of their joint venture. The lion, however, interrupted him at once: 'Be careful!' he growled. 'I might find that I have a taste for asses!'

The ass was wise enough not to press the point, and left with his tail between his legs, and nothing at all to show for his work.

21 The Stonebreaker and the Mountain

Once upon a time, there was a stone-breaker in Japan who was very weary of his exhausting work, and wished more than anything to live the luxurious and lazy life of a fat merchant. Who knows how, but his wish came true. After a time, however, from his shop window he saw a mandarin passing by, being carried in a comfortable seat by his many servants. 'Oh, how lovely it would be if I were a mandarin!' he sighed, and soon after that, he too became a mandarin.

However, since he was still obliged to obey the emperor, the mandarin really wished he was in his place. Time passed and his wish came true: he became the Son of the Sun, as the emperor was known. But the sun still burnt him. 'Oh how lovely it would be if I were the sun!' he exclaimed.

At once, he was the sun; but when a cloud obscured him, he became a cloud, only to find that the wind was stronger than a cloud, and so he had to become the wind. He went to blow against a mountain, and discovered that it was stronger than the wind: so he became a mountain. At this point, he heard the hammer blows of the men who were digging out the mountain, and at last he realised that the stonebreaker was the strongest of all, and then he became, once again, what he had been at the beginning.

22 The Cup Winners

That year, like every other, a cup was awarded to the two fastest animals in the meadow. The first prize was given to the hare, and the second to the snail. It was this decision which stimulated endless discussion.

'We have taken both strength and perseverance into account,' explained the sunflower, who was on the panel of judges, 'and although it is true that the snail required six months to cross the meadow, it got there in the end and even carried its house the whole way.'

'I deserved the first prize!' the snail protested. 'I spend my whole life racing about, while the hare only runs when he is afraid!'

'What are you getting so upset about?' interrupted the lamppost, who, on account of his elevated position, was president of the judges' panel. 'The prizes are awarded every year in alphabetical order, according to the Latin name of each animal, just so that nobody ever feels cheated. This is the twelfth year that the cups have been presented, and therefore the letter L took the prizes, Lepus the hare and Lumachus the snail.

There was no doubt at all that the first prize should go to the hare; and since the snail is always behind the hare, it was only right that it received the second prize. Next year, it will be the turn of the letter M. . . .'

'Unfortunately I will never qualify for a prize, because I'm one of the most important judges,' the donkey stated. 'But I can tell you that this year, before I voted, I took into account all the many fine qualities of the hare; his speed, agility, intelligence, and even beauty. After all, who could fail to admire the hare's lovely long ears? They are so similar to my own fine ones!'

'If you ask me,' the rose concluded, 'the sunbeam should have been given the first prize. Only she couldn't care less! When we are long gone and forgotten, she will still be here, sparkling in the meadow!'

23 The Dog and the Donkey

The dog was awakened by a noise, but went back to sleep at once.

'Why don't you bark?' asked the amazed donkey. 'It could be thieves!'

'You would be better advised to mind your own business,' he told the donkey. The indignant donkey began to bray as loudly as he could. He frightened off the thieves and caused the master to come running. The master was so furious at being woken up, that he began to beat the donkey.

'I warned you,' said the experienced old dog afterwards. 'With a master like that, it is better to think only of yourself, first and foremost.'

24 The Stallion and Its Master

Dimitri was a very strong and courageous prince. More than anything else, the prince wanted a brave and fiery stallion of his own. He decided to ask his cavalry captain for advice.

'How can I tell which horse would be most suitable for you, my lord,' said the captain, 'if I do not know first how strong you are? Try to uproot this oak tree, so I can judge your strength.'

In Dimitri's hands, the tree came up like a mere blade of grass. Beneath the roots, he found buried a set of richly decorated reins, a carved saddle, and an ornate battle axe.

Dimitri then took the most fiery stallion in the land, and, on a strong rope, made it walk round and round the pasture. At the end, the animal was drooping, exhausted. Dimitri slipped the saddle onto its broad back and tied it there tightly, put the reins over its head, leapt onto its back, and struck it with the axe handle. Furious, the stallion galloped off and carried Dimitri through valleys and over mountains, but could not throw its intrepid rider. At last the horse accepted it had been mastered. 'Give me three more days of freedom; after that I will serve you faithfully forever,' it said.

Dimitri agreed, and in three days the stallion returned. From that day on, the two of them became inseparable.

25 The Key in the Flax

A very rich young man was looking for a wife. He wanted one who was not only beautiful and good, but also skilled at domestic work. He went to the house of some friends, who had a daughter of an age to be married and, without letting it be known why he was there, he had a good look round. He noticed a spinning-wheel with the spinner stuck into a huge bundle of flax, and he was amazed.

'Is it your daughter alone who spins and weaves all this flax? Surely so much flax will take her a month!'

'On the contrary,' said the mother, with studied indifference, 'it will take her a good deal less than that!' For the mother had guessed the purpose of the young man's visit, and wished to make a good impression.

The young man said nothing, but, later, when nobody was watching him, he took the key of their storeroom, hid it well beneath the flax, and left.

A month later, the family told him a strange tale: the key to the storeroom had disappeared and no-one had been able to find it anywhere. The young man went immediately to the pile of flax and found the key exactly where he had left it. 'Perhaps it is true that your daughter can spin and weave very quickly when she works,' he said, 'but she certainly doesn't seem to want to work very often!'

26 The Fox and Wolf in Court

The wolf accused the fox of having cheated him; the fox, in turn, accused the wolf of having robbed him. They took their dispute to court, and it fell to the monkey to judge the issue. Unfortunately, the whole case was so full of contradictions that no-one could make head nor tail of it. Finally the monkey lost his patience.

'The wolf is guilty because he falsely accused the fox,' he decided, 'and the fox is guilty because we all know he is a thief by nature. And since the right place for both liars and robbers is prison, it is to prison that I will send them both!'

27 The Generous Prince

Alexander was the son of the tsar and the heir to the throne. When, however, his father died, his wicked stepmother immediately plotted to kill Alexander. However, by his own kindness, the prince was saved.

One day, the prince was walking beneath the high towers of the castle, when he thought he heard strange voices calling out to him, 'Free us! Your stepmother is holding us prisoner unjustly!' With a sledgehammer, Alexander breached the wall and out crept a lion, crow, and snake.

'We thank you for having saved us,' they told him. 'And in return, we can save your life. Tomorrow morning, your stepmother will try to kill you by giving you poisoned buns for breakfast.' Then the three animals disappeared, and the prince thought little of their warning. But he remembered it the next morning when his stepmother brought him buns for breakfast. He pretended to eat them, but stuffed them in his pocket instead.

A few hours later, when he was about to put his hand in his pocket for the buns, he found they had crumbled to pieces, and he pulled his hand away quickly when he found a viper, a scorpion, and a toad crawling about there. When this became known to the people, the wicked stepmother was driven out of the land forever.

28 The Mouse Princess

A daughter was born to the king and a great feast was prepared for the baptism. Unfortunately, through a terrible oversight, the witch was not invited. To avenge herself for this insult, the witch put an evil spell on the baby girl and turned her into a mouse. 'She will only become herself again on the day my sister laughs!'

All the clowns and comedians in the kingdom were called, but they did not succeed in getting even a smile from the sister of the witch. The king had no alternative in the end but to banish all cats from his kingdom so that the royal mouse would not be eaten.

One day, a prince in the next kingdom held a ball at his castle. The other three daughters of the king all attended, dressed magnificently, of course. The little mouse, on the other hand, was left at home as usual, but decided she, too, would go to the ball.

She jumped on the back of a cockerel, and tied some red ribbon through its beak as reins, and set off. When she got to the ball, the sight of the ribboned cockerel, with a white mouse on its back, was so comical, that the witch's sister at last burst out laughing. Then, the little white mouse was changed back into a young lady, so beautiful that the prince fell in love with her at once, and asked for her hand in marriage.

29 Little Tuk

Tuk was a little Danish boy, and one afternoon he was studying geography. Unfortunately, he also had to look after his little sister, Wenche, and it is very difficult indeed to study when a little girl wants to play with you instead. Tuk, however, forced himself to concentrate . . . .but the geography of Denmark is even more complicated than our own. When it was time to go to bed, Tuk put his geography book under his pillow, because he had heard that this was an excellent way to learn lessons. 'I just hope it works!' he thought.

Tuk went to bed and fell asleep . . . . or rather, did he fall asleep? The book seemed to be moving about under the pillow, scratching him. Tuk, too, was moving. He was no longer in bed, but on the back of a horse. A splendidly dressed knight, with flying plumes on his helmet, held Tuk in front of him, on the back of a great white horse. They galloped, and galloped. All the cities of Denmark appeared beneath him, and the knight recounted the history of each, and informed Tuk of the number of inhabitants.

With the sunrise, little Tuk woke. He jumped out of bed at once and began to read his book again. Suddenly, he realised that he knew it all, from the first to the last word. He immediately thought of the splendid knight. 'Thank you, my friend,' he said, with a smile.

30 The Tsar and the Mugik

There was once a mugik (a Russian peasant), who saw the great tsar himself enter his field. The tsar watched the mugik hoe the earth for a while, and then asked him how much he managed to earn.

'Eighty roubles,' the mugik replied.

'And how do you spend them?'

'A quarter of it goes on paying taxes,' the mugik explained. 'With a quarter of it, I pay my debts; a quarter of it, I lend, and what is left, I throw out of the window.'

'I understand that a quarter of your money goes to pay taxes,' said the curious tsar, 'but the rest?'

'I keep and maintain my father, and, in this way, I pay the debt I owe him for having brought me up,' the peasant replied. 'I loan money to my son, so that he can study, and he will repay me by looking after me, when I am old. The money I throw out of the window I spend on my daughter, who will marry and leave me one day.'

This story so pleased the tsar that he used it later as a riddle. He would wager with his courtiers that they could not solve it; and since nobody ever did manage to solve the riddle, the tsar always won the wagers. However, in view of the fact that he was honest and wealthy enough already, he always sent all the money he won in this way to the clever mugik.

Contents

The fairy tale of the month: Little Red Riding Hood
The Brothers Grimm

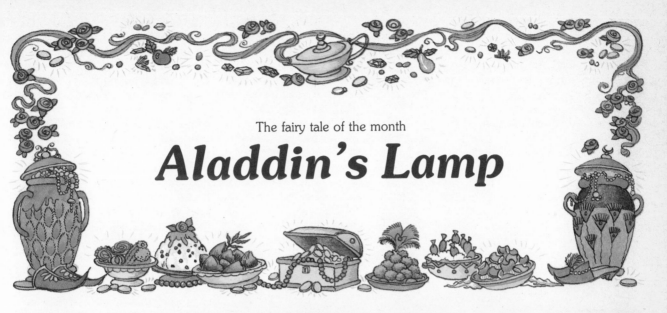

The fairy tale of the month

Aladdin's Lamp

It was market day in a big city in Ancient Arabia, and, as usual, the bazaar was full of strangers. Among them, there was a man who was dressed much more richly than all the others. He was taller and rode about on a camel, and, instead of buying things, he was closely observing all the boys there, and asking questions about them. He seemed taken particularly with Aladdin, the son of a poor widow. Aladdin had an intelligent and trustworthy air. So the man asked him if he would like to enter his service. As the mother gave her agreement, the rich stranger left with the boy.

After a long journey, they reached a remote village, where they found a cave that the man was looking for.

'Enter the cave,' the man commanded Aladdin. 'Go down the stairs which lead to an underground garden. I want you to find for me a lamp that I left there some time ago. Bring it back to me.'

The young man obeyed, and before he set off, his master gave him a magic ring to protect him from any dangers.

Aladdin found his way down to the garden, and there, sure enough, was the lamp, which he promptly lit. In its weak light, he could see that the trees in the garden bore flowers and fruits of precious stones. He could not resist filling his pockets with them. Then he began climbing back up the stairs. But the cave was bewitched, and the more Aladdin climbed, the longer the stairway became. Soon he was overcome by a strange weariness, though he was not even halfway up. He sat down on a step and fell fast asleep.

Up above, the master waited for a long time, then decided that Aladdin had tricked him, and left in a rage.

In the cave, Aladdin slept for three whole days. When he finally awoke, he realised that he was a prisoner of the magic cave, and he became desperate. As he was wringing his hands, by good fortune he rubbed the magic ring that had been given him. A spirit appeared out of nowhere.

'I am the genie of the ring,' it said. 'Command me and three times I will obey you.'

'I want to go home,' said Aladdin.

In a flash, he was back at home with his mother. She began shouting at him for having left his master, and for being away so long. The poor woman could not stop crying, even when Aladdin pulled from his pockets the rubies and emeralds he had taken from the cave. 'What will I do,' she cried, 'with these pieces of glass?'

But it was time to think of dinner, and as there was no money in the house, the woman thought of going and selling the lamp that her son had brought back. She decided first of all to clean it, so it would look better. When she rubbed it, out came an even bigger spirit than the one that had

appeared to Aladdin in the cave.

'I am the genie of the lamp,' it said. 'Command me and three times I will obey you.'

'Serve us a good dinner then,' said Aladdin, on the spur of the moment, taken by surprise and unable to think of anything else to ask for. In a flash, a table appeared, set with all the most exquisite foods on plates of solid silver.

As a consequence, Aladdin and his mother were able to eat not only that evening, but every day thereafter, because whenever they ran out of money, they sold one of the plates.

The years passed, and Aladdin became a very handsome young man, so that all the young girls in the city smiled at him; but he had fallen in love with none other than Badur, the daughter of the sultan. When he told his mother he was going to ask for the princess's hand, the poor woman thought her son had gone mad. 'How can you think that the sultan would give you his daughter?' she asked him.

'The bits of glass I found in the cave are truly valuable precious stones,' Aladdin said. 'Take them to the sultan, and perhaps he will agree to my marriage with Badur.'

And so it was. The sultan accepted the proposal. But, in exchange for the hand of his daughter, he asked for ten chests full of jewels, and he insisted that after her wedding the princess should live in a palace at least as luxurious as his.

Thanks to the genie of the lamp, Aladdin was able overnight to satisfy these two conditions, so that the splendid wedding could be celebrated the next day.

Badur and Aladdin lived happily for many years, until one day the stranger returned to the city. In reality, he was a magician, and having looked into his crystal ball he had managed to find out where his former servant was hiding. He thought still that Aladdin had deliberately betrayed him, stealing the lamp, and he had returned to take revenge.

The magician waited patiently till Aladdin was away on a journey, and he went to the palace.

He persuaded the servants to give him the old magic lamp, and then he summoned the genie. 'Carry Badur and this whole palace to my kingdom,' he ordered it.

When Aladdin returned and realised what had happened, he remembered that he still had the magic ring. He rubbed it and ordered its genie to take him to his wife. With the help of Badur, Aladdin caused the magician to fall asleep which enabled him to take back the magic lamp. Then the genie, who appeared when summoned, fulfilled Aladdin's third wish, by taking the young couple back to their own city, where they lived happily ever after.

1 Tom Thumb

A poor woodsman's wife sighed one day and said, 'If only we could have a son, even if he was only as tall as a thumb.' Time went by, and in the end a child was born to her, a little boy who was exactly as tall as a thumb; so they called him Tom Thumb.

As the years went by, he remained small, but he became a kind and intelligent boy. One day, it was necessary to take the cart and go and fetch his father, but his mother was unable to go. 'I'll go,' said Tom Thumb. It seemed impossible that someone so small could hold the reins; but then he climbed into the horse's ear, so that

he could speak and tell it where to go. When this happened, all the passers-by thought that the horse must be very intelligent, to be able to go places by itself. A circus master wanted to buy it, only then he learned that the horse was really not so clever, but was guided by Tom Thumb. So he wanted to buy the tiny boy instead. His father would not have sold him for all the gold in the world, but Tom Thumb convinced him, by saying: 'You need the money, don't you? Sell me to the circus and leave everything up to me.'

In fact, as soon as he was able Tom Thumb ran away from the circus, and since he was so small, he was able to avoid being recaptured and make his way back home.

2 The Misadventures of Tom Thumb

When he ran away from the circus, Tom Thumb hid in a stable and fell asleep in the hay. While sleeping, the farmer's wife came to feed the cows. Without realising it, she lifted Tom Thumb as well as the hay on her fork. He only woke when he was in a cow's stomach. There was a door inside which opened from time to time to let more hay in. Tom Thumb found that he was running out of space inside, so he began to yell: 'That's enough! You're crushing me!'

The farmer's wife heard the noise. She was terrified and ran off to tell her husband: 'The cow spoke to me!'

The farmer also heard the strange voice and, thinking that the animal was possessed by an evil spirit, he killed it. The stomach, with Tom Thumb still inside it, ended up on the rubbish heap, where a wolf swallowed it. The voice persuaded the wolf to go to a cottage where there were sausages to be had for the asking.

The greedy wolf followed the directions given to it. But Tom Thumb directed it to his own house, where he started yelling until his father came outside, found the wolf and killed it. As he could still hear the voice, he cut open the body and found Tom Thumb. 'I'll never sell you again, not even for all the gold in the world,' the man promised. And he never did.

3 The Madonna's Cup

A long, long time ago, a heavy wagon became stuck in the mud, and the wagon driver was unable to free it. Just then, by sheer chance, the Madonna passed by.

'I am thirsty,' she said. 'Give me a drink and I will set your wagon free.'

'Willingly,' said the man, offering her the bottle, 'but I don't have a cup.'

'I can provide the cup,' said the Madonna. And she broke off a white flower, with red stripes, in the shape of a chalice, and she used it to drink from. Ever since then, people have called the flower of the convolvulus, 'The Madonna's Cup'.

4 Prince Ivan and the Firebird

The tsar was furious: every night a bird with feathers as red as fire was stealing his golden apples. The tsar ordered his son, Ivan, to catch the firebird.

That night the bird returned, but Ivan could not catch it, though he did chase it away. While he was following it, he came across a great wolf, which was really a bewitched animal. 'I'll carry you on my back,' said the wolf. After a while, they came to a castle. 'Enter,' said the great wolf. 'You will find the firebird within. Take the bird, but do not touch the cage.' But when Ivan saw the golden cage, he tried to take it. Immediately, the king's guards

came running. The king was the powerful Dolmat.

'Who are you?' Dolmat asked him. 'And how dare you steal the firebird?'

Ivan told Dolmat his story, whereupon the king said: 'I will give you the firebird, if first you bring here to me the beautiful princess, Helen the Fair.'

So Ivan and the great wolf made their way to the castle, where Helen the Fair was imprisoned, and after many battles they set her free. But the princess and Ivan fell in love with each other at first sight, and Ivan's heart cried out at the thought of taking her back to King Dolmat. The great wolf said, 'Princess, hide in the woods. Ivan and I will go to Dolmat.' Then the wolf rolled about on the ground, until it

assumed the shape of the princess.

'Well done,' said Dolmat when he saw Ivan returning with the false Helen. 'Take your firebird.' So Ivan went away with the firebird. When safely beyond the reach of Dolmat, the great wolf turned back into a wolf, and fled from the king's castle to rejoin Ivan. Then Helen the Fair and Ivan were carried back to the tsar. On reaching the palace gates, the wolf bade farewell to Ivan: 'My task is finished, now you must find your own happiness,' and disappeared as mysteriously as it had come. The two lovers married, the tsar had the magnificent firebird with its golden cage, and the apple tree continued abundant harvests of golden apples.

5 The Two Friends and the Bear

John and James were two friends who were crossing a forest, when, suddenly, they stumbled across a huge, black bear. Imagine how terrified they were. They attempted to flee and the bear chased them. John managed to climb up into a tree. James, just as he was about to be caught, fell to the ground and pretended to be dead. He knew that a bear will only attack something if it is alive.

The bear sniffed him all over, while the man tried to hold his breath as best he could, hoping that the animal would not discover the pretence. In

the end, after sniffing thoroughly, the bear must have thought that the man really was dead, because it ambled off on its huge paws.

With the danger over, John came down from the tree, and as often happens after a big fright, he felt like making jokes. So he asked his friend, 'Well, what did the bear whisper into your ear?' But James was not in the same mood for jokes, and he did not appreciate the question at all.

'The bear said,' he answered, looking John straight in the eye, 'that it would be advisable for me not to travel again with a friend, who runs off and abandons me when danger threatens!'

6 The Hare and the Frogs

A hare was berating itself for being so afraid all the time and running away from everything. He was just promising himself that he would behave more courageously in future, when a sudden noise made him run away again as fast as he could.

He came to a pool, where, as soon as they heard his approach, all the frogs dived into the water and hid in the mud.

'Thank goodness,' thought the hare. 'That just proves that no matter how scared you are, there is always someone else who is even more scared!'

7 The Cow and the Princess

The king's wife died and, since he had a beautiful daughter to look after, the king married again, this time to a queen from a nearby land who had three ugly daughters. Now the new queen was very jealous of the king's daughter, and she made the princess work as a farmhand, and take her cow, Brindle, out to pasture herself.

The princess did as she was told, but each day, as soon as she was far enough away, she climbed up into one of the cow's ears. When she came out of the other one, she was well fed and clothed. When it was time to go back to the palace barns, the princess climbed into one of Brindle's ears again, and when she emerged from the other one, she was dressed in rags.

As time went by, the stepmother began to suspect something, and so she sent her oldest daughter out to the pasture with the princess. But the princess sang her a lullaby, and she fell asleep, so she did not see anything. The same thing happened to the second daughter. When it was the turn of the last, she kept her eyes open and saw everything. But she kept the knowledge to herself and the next day she too went into the cow's ear. But she took the wrong turning inside, and when she came out, she had changed from a girl into a calf, and she is now an old cow.

8 Indecisive Elsa

Elsa went out to help harvest the grain. Because she had always been taught to think hard before doing anything, she asked herself: 'What should I do first? Harvest the grain or eat my lunch?' She decided to eat her lunch, and afterwards she asked herself: 'Now what should I do first? Harvest the grain or have a nap?' She decided to have a nap, and she slept so much that when her husband arrived he found her slumbering still, without having done anything yet. Her husband was angry, and in order to teach her a lesson, he stretched a net for catching birds all over her.

When Elsa woke up, she could not understand how it was that she had been caught in a net. She thought she must be going mad.

'Am I really me, or am I not me,' she wondered worriedly. She went home to ask her family: they would be able to tell her if she was Elsa or not.

The front door was closed. 'Is Elsa in?' she called out. 'Yes, she's here,' answered her husband. 'Well, if Elsa is here, then I can't be me!' thought Elsa. The poor girl was very confused and started going round all the houses asking if Elsa was there; but everybody answered, 'No, Elsa is not here. . . .' And some people say that she is still wandering around, looking for herself.

9 The Monkey and the Crocodile

The crocodile was very greedy for the bananas, which grew on the palm trees around its pool, but no matter how hard it tried, it could not manage to pick them. A generous monkey noticed this, and threw him down a bunch. The crocodile ate its fill and also left some of the bananas for its wife. But the wife turned the crocodile against the monkey: 'If that monkey lives on bananas, then its liver must be big and sweet,' she said.

She went on so much that the crocodile began to think like her. He went back to the monkey the next day, and asked it to pay a visit to his wife, as she was sick and needed advice on the proper medicine to take.

The monkey jumped onto the crocodile and was ferried to its island.

As soon as she saw it, the female crocodile cornered the monkey, and said, 'Foolish one, your liver is the only medicine I need.'

'You should have told me that before you brought me here,' replied the monkey, without batting an eyelid. 'My liver is so valuable to me that whenever I go out, I leave it in a safe place up in the tree. You'll have to take me back to fetch it.'

So the monkey was ferried back across the pool, where it climbed quickly up its banana tree. . . . and the story goes that the crocodile is still waiting for it to come back.

10 The Miser Woman and the Woodpecker

On one of his tours round the world to see how things were going on, the Lord stopped off at the house of a baker woman, and asked her for some bread. The woman, who was wearing a red hat, did not dare to refuse the Lord, but she wanted to. So she began to knead a lump of dough, but she rolled it so much, that it became such a large thin leaf of dough that it blew away.

Then she took a smaller piece of dough, but by rolling it and rolling it, she made it so thin that it was almost transparent.

The third time she began with a crumb of dough, but she rolled it into such a large, thin slice for baking, that it would not fit into any of the trays.

'It's no good,' she said. 'I'm afraid you can't have any bread here. You'll have to go somewhere else.'

'As a punishment for being so mean,' the Lord said to her, 'you will become a bird with a red cap. You'll have to look for your food in the bark of trees, and you will only be able to drink when it rains.'

With its red hat on, the bird flew up the chimney and the soot made its body black: that was how the first woodpecker came into being.

11 The Gnome and the Farmer

A farmer came across a gnome sitting in his field. At once the farmer thought that there must be a treasure buried there.

'That's right,' confirmed the bad gnome. 'There is more gold and silver down here than you have ever seen in your whole life.'

'Well then, it's mine,' exclaimed the man. 'It's in my field.'

'It will only be yours,' said the gnome, 'if you give me half of what your field produces over the next two years.'

'I'll agree to that,' said the farmer. 'What is on the top is yours and what is down at the roots can be mine.' The gnome thought of the abundant grain crop that had just been harvested and he accepted the proposal. But the crafty farmer planted potatoes for the next two years, so that what was on the top was useless to the gnome. Tricked and furious, the gnome went back home, and the farmer was free to go and get the treasure, which was just where the gnome had said it would be.

12 Goldilocks and the Three Bears

Father Bear, Mother Bear and Little Bear lived in a house in the woods. One day, after they had prepared their porridge, they went out for a little walk, in order to give it time to cool down. While they were out, a little girl came to their house. Her name was Goldilocks, and if she had been a good little girl, she would not have gone in without being invited; but she was curious and a bit cheeky. She saw the porridge on the table, so she sat down and helped herself.

First of all, she tried the big plate, but the porridge was too hot. So then she went on to the middle-sized plate, which belonged to Mother Bear, but the porridge was too cold. Finally, she tasted the plate belonging to Little Bear, and there the porridge was just right, so she ate it all up.

'Now I feel like a rest,' she thought, looking at the three chairs. But Father Bear's chair was too hard, and Mother Bear's chair was too soft. Little Bear's chair was just right for her, but she sat down on it so hard, that she broke it into pieces.

Then Goldilocks went upstairs for a sleep. The big bed was too high off the ground and the middle-sized bed was too low down. The little bed was just right, so Goldilocks lay down on top, and fell fast asleep.

When the three bears came home and saw all the mess, they were very angry. 'Who's been eating my porridge?' said Father Bear and Mother Bear. 'Mine has all been eaten,' cried Little Bear. 'Who's been sitting in my chair?' said Father Bear and Mother Bear. 'My chair is broken,' snivelled Little Bear. 'Who's been sleeping in my bed?' said Father Bear and Mother Bear. 'Someone is still in my bed,' howled Little Bear.

All the noise woke up Goldilocks, who got such a fright to see the three bears that she jumped out of the window and ran away home, and never went near the three bears' house again.

13 The Silly Wolf and the Billy Goat

An old wolf was no longer as strong or as cunning as it used to be, and the other wolves thought it was just plain silly sometimes. One of these times it was chasing a billy goat, which jumped to safety up on a high rock.

'Why do you waste time chasing me?' the goat asked the silly wolf. 'If you want to catch me, just open your mouth wide and I'll jump into it.' The wolf obliged and the goat jumped, not into the wolf's mouth, but onto its head, landing so hard that the wolf was knocked out. When the wolf woke up with its mouth open, it could not recall if it had eaten the goat or not.

14 A Poor Man in Paradise

A poor man arrived at the gates of paradise at exactly the same time as a very wealthy one.

Saint Peter looked out through the peephole, then he took out his huge bunch of keys and opened the gate, and let the rich man in right away. He did not even seem to notice the poor man.

As soon as the gate was shut, heavenly songs and music began to issue from within; obviously, a big party was going on. The poor man was a bit upset at this, but he waited patiently until Saint Peter came out again and opened up for him at last. The poor man had imagined that his arrival would also be greeted with singing and dancing. Instead everything was quiet, even if the angels were very friendly when they came to show him to his assigned place.

'So,' moaned the poor man bitterly. 'Even in paradise, the rich are treated better than the rest.'

'Not at all, my friend,' the angels reassured him. 'You will have the same eternal joy as the rich man; it's just that dozens of poor people come up here every day, but we only get a rich man about once every hundred years!'

15 The Lantern on the Oak

In ancient times on Earth, nights were completely dark; so you can imagine the surprise of four men who, on a journey, came across a village which was illuminated by a silvery light.

The light came from a big round globe, which appeared to be hanging from the branches of an oak tree in the village square.

'What is it?' they wondered.

A man from the village explained: 'It's the moon. Our mayor bought it and hung it out there on the oak tree; he has to keep it clean and fill it up with oil regularly, so we give him a ducat each week.'

The four friends decided that a sum of money like that would be very acceptable to them as well; so they stole the moon, and took it back to their own town, where they stuck it on another large oak tree. But the real owners soon discovered its whereabouts, and to get their moon back they caused so much trouble that the noise could even be heard up in the sky.

The Lord was very annoyed at being disturbed like this. To put an end to all the fighting, he sent an angel down to take the moon away, and he had it stuck up in the sky, so that it could shine freely for everyone.

16 The Poppy's Riddle

A beautiful woman had been transformed by a witch into a poppy in a field. Each evening, she returned to normal, and was allowed to pass the night at home. One morning, before she went back to the field to become a poppy again, she said to her husband: 'If you succeed in picking me, the spell will be broken.'

This was true: but how could the man recognise his wife amongst all the other thousands of poppies? The answer was simple: since the woman had spent the night at home, she was the only poppy in the field that was not wet with dew.

17 The Lion and the Badger

A lion and a badger had adjacent dens and they had become friends. One day, the lion caught a sheep, and he shouted at his friend to come on over, and eat it with him; but the rude answer came back: 'You eat it. I've got better things to do.'

The next day, the badger received the same reply, when it called out for the lion to come over, and eat some honey it had found. However, on the day after that, when they met in the woods, they overlooked each other's rudeness and began to talk together. Then they both realised that neither had heard the invitation from the other, and that neither of them had, therefore, answered back rudely.

'Someone is trying to cause trouble between us', decided the king of the jungle. 'Let's find out who it is.'

They hunted around in the bushes and discovered a fox. Once it had confessed, they decided to punish it.

'Oh please,' begged the cunning fox, 'don't throw me into that pile of ashes. I would rather be put to death than thrown onto a pile of ashes.'

'You don't have any choice,' roared the lion. 'If it's ashes you're frightened of, then into the ashes you go.'

But when the lion and the badger threw the fox onto the ashes, the crafty animal kicked up such a cloud of dust that it was able to get away.

18 The Friendly Bird

A farmer came across a bird with a broken wing. He picked it up, took it home and looked after it lovingly, even though his wife complained bitterly about his wasting too much time on the creature.

After some time, the wing mended and, because the bird did not want the farmer to have to keep on arguing with his wife all the time, it decided to go back to its nest.

When the farmer discovered that the bird was gone, he was so upset that he went out to look for it. Eventually, he found it again, and was greeted happily by the whole family of birds. As a sign of their thanks for his care and attention, the birds gave him a little box, and told him not to open it until he got home.

The box was full of precious stones. When she saw them, the wife decided that she too deserved a reward, and she went to see the birds. They gave her a little casket; but this one was full of devils, who jumped on her as soon as she released them, and chased her away.

Left alone, the farmer went to live near his friend, the bird. There he built a hut from perfumed wood; and the birds decorated it with flowers of every kind.

19 A Rain of Stars

One cold day, a little girl was wandering along, eating a slice of bread. An old woman came up to her and asked her for something to eat. Without hesitation, the little girl gave her all that remained of her bread. 'Please take it,' she said, and went on.

A short time later, the girl came across a little boy, who was holding his head and crying. 'What's the matter?' she asked him. 'I'm cold. So very cold,' cried the boy. 'I haven't a cover for my head.' So the girl gave him her scarf to wrap round his head.

A bit further on, she saw another little girl who wasn't even dressed in a jacket, and so she gave her the one she was wearing. Then she gave her dress to another little girl who didn't have one, and she went on without one. Bit by bit, she was left in just her petticoat. But then another poor girl came up to her and said: 'You can always go home to a warm house. I have nothing to keep me warm. As it's dark now, and no-one can see you, please give me your petticoat.' And the little girl did.

Just then, all the stars came down from heaven, and they wrapped the little girl round in a shining, sparkling cloak; the moon came to rest on her head like a crown, and two rays of sunshine came from the red sunset, and wrapped themselves around her hands like gloves of the finest wool.

20 The Three Brothers and the Three Sisters

As soon as word got out, about the mysterious kidnapping of the three daughters of the king, three young brothers came to the court to ask for permission to search for the princesses. They were all skilled trackers and they found the footprints of a gnome in the woods, leading to a chasm. They lowered themselves down the edge to the bottom, where they found an incredible kingdom.

The younger brother found a castle made of copper. He went in and there, imprisoned in it, he found the youngest of the three princesses. He was about to free her, when a three-headed dragon attacked him. The young man cut off all three heads with a single blow of his sword.

The second brother won a similar battle, having found the second princess locked inside a silver castle, guarded by a six-headed dragon.

The dragon which was guarding the third princess, in a castle of gold, had twelve heads but met the same fate from the oldest of the brave brothers.

Before hauling themselves out of the chasm, the young men demolished the castles and put the rubble into sacks they had brought with them. Back up on the ground again, they emptied the sacks and rebuilt the three castles, and lived in them with their princesses happily ever after.

21 Buttered Lamb

There was once a little boy who was so fat that everyone called him Buttered Lamb. His reputation spread far and wide, and one day along came a witch who wanted to eat him.

The boy's mother, who saw the witch approaching, told her son to hide in the cupboard, and then said that he was not at home.

'That's a shame,' said the witch. 'I have brought him a lovely present.'

When he heard the word 'present,' the boy jumped out of his hiding place, and the witch quickly put him in her sack and ran away with him. Except that there was a knife in the sack, and when the witch stopped to have a nap, Buttered Lamb managed to cut the sack open and get away.

The next day, the witch returned to the house for Buttered Lamb. She used a different trick, but she managed to get him in the sack again. This time she was careful not to stop for anything, until she got home. Then she lit the fire, and put the pot on it to cook the little boy. But she had forgotten a heavy spoon in the sack, and as soon as she undid the knot, the boy leapt out and banged her on the head with it. Then he popped the old witch into the pot, and went home to his mother.

22 The Right Bride

A young shepherd knew three girls, who were each so beautiful that he did not know which one to marry. So he asked his mother for advice.

'Invite them to dinner,' she said, 'and watch how they cut the cheese.'

So he did.

The first girl ate the cheese with the rind still on; the second girl cut the rind, but she also cut off a good deal of edible cheese with it; the third girl took off exactly the right amount of rind, and left all the edible cheese.

'Marry her,' said the mother, with certainty.

23 Jack and the Comet

Jack was a rather poor student, but to make up for it he was full of good intentions and always interested in everything. When the teacher in school spoke about comets, Jack asked a lot of questions.

'When will the comet come?' he asked.

'It came already. Didn't you see it?' replied the teacher.

'No, sir, but I would like to. How can I see it?'

'You could see it tonight. All you have to do is go out into the vegetable garden after dark.'

The next day, the teacher asked the boy if he had seen the comet, but Jack shook his head. 'No. I went out into the garden, but I didn't see it.'

'Maybe you didn't look properly,' said the teacher with surprise.

'No, sir', protested Jack. 'I looked very hard and for at least half an hour.'

'How can that be? Where did you look?' asked the puzzled teacher.

'Everywhere,' Jack answered. 'Under the trees, in the cabbage patch, in between the rows of beans. If the comet was there, I'm sure I would have seen it, especially since I took the lantern with me. Only. . . .'

'Only what, Jack?'

'I think I might have forgotten to light the lamp. Probably that's why I didn't see the comet.'

24 The Donkey and the Grasshopper

A poor donkey was not happy with his voice. One summer's day, while grazing in a field, he was captivated by the delightful music of the grasshopper. 'What is it that you eat that allows you to give off a sound like that?' he asked one of them.

'Dew,' answered the grasshopper, joking.

'That's what I need,' thought the donkey. So he went on eating grass with great enthusiasm for the rest of his life, especially at dawn, when it was covered with dew. His voice never changed, but, luckily, nature had bestowed on him a healthy appetite.

25 The Wise Shepherd

A shepherd became famous for being a wise man. The king heard of him, and tested his wisdom with three questions. 'The first question is this,' said the king. 'How many drops of water are there in the sea?'

'Your majesty,' replied the shepherd. 'Dam up all the rivers in the world, so that they no longer run into the sea. Then I'll be able to tell you exactly how many drops of water there are in the sea.'

'Well, then, tell me how many stars there are in the sky?'

The shepherd had an enormous sheet of paper brought to him, and he drew dots on it with a pen, until the paper was completely covered. 'I can assure you that there are as many stars in the sky as there are dots on this paper,' he said. 'So all you have to do is count the dots.'

'How many seconds are there in eternity?' asked the king, finally.

'There is a mountain as wide as the sea which reaches up to the stars,' said the wise man. 'Once every hundred years, an eagle goes to the mountain and pecks it with its beak. When the eagle has worn down the whole mountain, then one second of eternity will have passed.'

'You have answered like a true wise man,' approved the king. 'From now on, you will be my counsellor.'

26 Bondo the Wolf and the Stray Dog

Poor old Bondo the wolf was always getting into trouble; but when he met a stray dog, chased away from home and reduced to skin and bones from hunger, Bondo yelped for joy.

'Now I'm going to make a meal of you,' he said.

'Skinny as I am?' answered the dog. 'You'd be better off fattening me up a bit first.'

Bondo the wolf thought this was a good idea; but by the time that the dog had become fat enough to eat, he had also become strong enough to frighten the wolf away, just by baring his teeth.

27 The Two Friends and the Plane Tree

It was noon on a hot summer's day. Two friends, Jack and John, had been walking since early morning, when they came across a big tree in the middle of a vast meadow.

The men were hot and tired, and only too pleased to sit down and rest in the shade of the great tree. Their destination was still some hours ahead of them.

They took off their backpacks, and took out their lunch boxes, and settled down to rest and satisfy their hunger and thirst.

'What kind of tree is this?' Jack asked his friend.

'A plane tree,' replied John. 'Ah, a plane tree!' mused Jack. 'Big leaves, a strong trunk. It is a pity it's a useless tree; it doesn't give edible fruits, it's really no use for anything.'

The plane tree was listening to this conversation, and it was outraged. 'What an ungrateful pair,' it fumed. 'Here I am giving shade to the two of them, giving them shelter from the sun, which they can't find anywhere else around here, and, apart from forgetting to thank me, they don't even appreciate how useful I am to them.'

28 Snow-White and Rose-Red

In the woods, lived a widow, whose two daughters, Snow-White and Rose-Red, were so beautiful and gentle that they resembled wild roses. Everyone loved them, even the trees, and the animals were their friends.

One day, someone knocked on the door of their hut. It was a big, black bear. They were fearful, but the animal reassured them: 'Don't be afraid. I am cold. I want only to warm myself by your fire.'

The two girls brought him into the house, sat him down and wiped the snow off his fur. All three soon became good friends, and played together happily, until the bear went away. The bear returned every evening, until the spring, when it bade them farewell. 'Goodbye, little friends. I must go now to defend my treasure from the gnomes. I don't know if I'll be back.'

It was a sad parting. Time passed, and one day Snow-White and Rose-Red were out in the forest, gathering wood. They came across a dark cave and wandered into it. The cave held the most unbelievable treasure. The girls were staring in amazement, when suddenly there appeared a gnome with a pointed beard, who screamed at them: 'You've been spying on me. Now you will be punished.' Just as he raised his arm to strike them, a black bear sprang into the cave. With one blow from its paw, it knocked the gnome lifeless to the ground.

The bear said, 'Snow-White, Rose-Red, don't be afraid.' Then the girls recognised the voice of the bear that had become their friend so long ago. The black, furry bearskin fell away, and out came a handsome young man, dressed in gold. 'I am the son of a king,' he said, 'and I was put under a spell by the gnome, who stole all my treasure. Now, thanks to you, I have found my treasure, and the gnome is dead.' And so Snow-White married the prince, and Rose-Red was wed to his equally handsome brother.

And when their old mother died, the princesses planted two rose bushes over her grave.

29 The Jealous Sole

Once upon a time in the sea, there was a loud argument about which fish was the fastest swimmer. The dispute grew so bad tempered that at last some of the senior fish demanded that a race should take place to determine the matter once and for all. Amongst the competitors was the sole, a very arrogant fish, always sneering at the others. When the race was over, on this occasion it turned out that the winner was the herring. The sole said, 'The herring. That common little fish!' with its mouth twisted in jealousy. And ever since then, the sole's mouth has remained twisted.

30 The Song Fairy

Many, many centuries ago, the Song Fairy decided to teach the peoples of Central Asia to sing, and she called them all together one evening, in an oasis.

The Kalmuks, who arrived first, listened to the fairy all night long and learned thousands of songs. On the other hand, the Kergers and the Turcomans, because they lived a long way away, only arrived at the oasis just in time to hear the last songs.

The Tartars, who lived even further away, arrived when the songs were finished. All they heard was some dogs howling at the moon, but they thought that it was the voice of the Song Fairy.

As a consequence, the Kalmuks are still extraordinary singers: they know thousands of songs, all full of emotion. The Kergers and the Turcomans, on the other hand, have a more monotonous and uniform way of singing, with little variation.

Last of all, the Tartars, poor things, sing like dogs, because, in the belief that they are imitating the Song Fairy, they actually imitate the howling of the dogs that their ancestors listened to that night in the oasis. And it is the only song they know.

31 Boiled Eggs and Boiled Potatoes

Amir set off to look for his fortune, and when he returned, years later, he was a very rich man.

A shopkeeper decided to take advantage of this and delivered a dozen eggs to Amir's house, then sent him a bill for a thousand ducats. Amir refused to pay such a high price for the eggs, so the shopkeeper took him to court.

On the day of the hearing, Amir arrived very late. The trial had already begun and the shopkeeper was stating his case: 'I asked Amir for a thousand ducats, because from these dozen eggs, a dozen chicks would have hatched, which would have become hens and multiplied, giving birth to at least twenty-four chicks, and so on, from year to year, so that, by now, I would have had a huge hen house.'

The judge turned to Amir and wanted to know why he was so late in arriving.

'I boiled the potatoes and then sowed them in my field,' explained Amir. 'So that, next year, I will get a good harvest.'

'Since when have boiled potatoes given a harvest?' asked the judge.

'Since boiled eggs have been hatching chicks!' Amir replied.

Contents

The fairy tale of the month: Aladdin's Lamp
Arabian Fable

The fairy tale of the month

Hansel and Gretel

Peter, the woodcutter, had been made a widower, but remarried, so that there would be somebody to take care of his children if the need arose. He made a bad choice, however, for his new wife was both wicked and selfish.

One year, the woodcutting business went very badly, and there was almost nothing for the family to eat. 'If only we didn't have your children to look after. . . .' the wife would often moan. Finally, the stepmother insisted so much that she convinced poor Peter, that he had no choice but to abandon the children in the woods, leaving them to whatever fate befell them. Thus, one morning, the four of them went out together as usual to gather firewood. After working very hard, both Hansel and Gretel were overcome by tiredness and fell fast asleep on the grass. When they awoke, they found themselves alone. Gretel, the little girl, at once burst out crying in fear, but Hansel, her big brother, reassured her: 'Don't worry. We'll find our way home, you'll see.'

They went further into the woods, but no matter how far they walked, they only succeeded in getting themselves even more lost. They were tired, afraid and hungry. Even Hansel, now, had lost heart. Finally, deep, deep in the forest, they spied a little house. The children ran towards it, and, as they drew nearer, they realised that the house was made of gingerbread, and the roof was made of shortbread. What is more, the windows were made of icing sugar.

'Eat up!' shouted Hansel, biting off a piece of the roof, and Gretel followed his example by tasting one of the windows. Their feast was interrupted by a wicked laugh: the door of the house opened and a decrepit, old woman appeared, leaning heavily on a stick. She had a nose like a beak and fingers like claws. 'Come in, my dear children. Come in and stay with me, no harm will come to you,' said the old woman, who was really an evil witch, who had built the gingerbread house with the sole purpose of attracting children. Whenever she succeeded in luring children into her power, she would kill them, cook them and eat them for her supper. She was especially delighted to find two chil-dren outside the house on this occasion.

Hansel and Gretel attempted to run away, but, perhaps because of an evil spell, or perhaps just out of tiredness, they found they could not take even a single step. The witch took each of them by the hand and led them into the house. She closed the door and bolted it. Then she pinched Hansel with her cold, hard fingers and said, 'You are too lean. When you are nice and plump, I will eat you. I will put you in this little cage and fatten you up. Then I will do the same thing with your little sister.' Then she turned to Gretel, and added, 'Move yourself, you lazy girl. Go and boil the water to cook something nice for your brother.'

Gretel began to cry, but to no avail: she had to do as she was ordered by the witch.

The most tasty food was prepared for poor Hansel. Every morning, the witch hobbled over to his cage and cackled: 'Hansel, put out a finger, so that I can feel how fat you have become.' Hansel, however, always put out a small bone from the meat he had eaten, and the witch, who had very bad eyesight, never realised she was being tricked, although she was astonished the child remained so thin.

After four weeks, during which Hansel had shown no signs whatsoever of putting on any weight, the witch finally lost her patience. 'Fat, or thin, it doesn't matter. Tomorrow, I will cook Hansel,' she said to poor Gretel, and she secretly intended to eat the little girl at the same time.

The following morning Gretel lit the fire in the oven. The witch then said to her: 'Jump in and see if it is hot enough.' Gretel, however, guessed what the witch had in mind, and said: 'It's too small. I can't get in.'

'Stupid girl,' replied the witch. 'Of course, it's big enough. Even I could get into it.' And saying that, she went to the oven to show Gretel, and stuck her head inside. At once Gretel gave her a mighty shove, and pushed her completely into the oven, and closed and bolted the iron door.

Horrible screams issued from the oven because it was so hot inside.

Gretel ran to Hansel, unlocked the cage and shouted: 'Hansel, we are free. The wicked old witch is dead.' With nothing to fear any longer, the two children looked around the witch's house, and found a hoard of pearls and precious stones. Hansel stuffed as many as he could into his pockets, and Gretel filled her apron. Then they set off to try and find their way out of the forest. They came to a river, but had no idea how to cross it.

'There is not even a little boat,' Gretel sighed. 'But, look, there's a white duck. If I ask politely, it will surely help us across.' And Gretel asked very politely, 'Little duck, please hurry. Little duck, don't worry. Carry us over on your white down, for there is no bridge and we may drown.' The little duck approached them and it ferried, first Gretel, and then Hansel, over to the other side.

After a long, long walk, they finally saw their father's house in the distance. From the moment he had left his beloved children in the woods, the father had not slept, and he had sent away the horrible stepmother, who had persuaded him to do such a wicked thing. When Hansel and Gretel appeared, safe and sound, on the doorstep, he wept tears of joy and threw his arms around the pair of them. Gretel emptied her apron. Hansel emptied his pockets, and the pearls and precious stones sparkled before them on the ground. Thus, their hardship ended and they lived happily ever after.

1 The Faithful Mongoose

Indi and Lavea were a young Indian couple and they had a beautiful baby boy. One day, Lavea said to her husband: 'You must look after the baby, while I go down to the river.' Indi sat down beside the pram, and the baby fell asleep at once. A short time later, a messenger arrived from the royal palace and ordered Indi to follow him there to speak on behalf of a friend. Indi had to entrust the baby to the pet mongoose, which the young couple kept in the house. In India, they keep mongooses rather like we keep cats; but where cats hunt mice, a mongoose does not hesitate to confront a snake. What is more, mongooses are more loyal than cats. Indi's mongoose at once sat down to guard the baby. When a huge python entered by the window and approached the pram, the mongoose was ready for it, and killed the python.

When Indi came home and found the mongoose, mouth and paws dripping with blood, he immediately thought the worst and beat the faithful animal. How surprised he was when he went into the house and found the baby sleeping peacefully, and a huge python dead on the floor by the pram.

From that day on, the young couple loved the courageous mongoose even more, and Indi learnt that he should never doubt a faithful friend.

2 The Improvident Girl

Bianca was as beautiful and rich as she was lazy and disorganised. She would throw away her dresses when she had only worn them a few times, as soon as they no longer pleased her, and when she was weaving, she wasted more flax than she used.

The serving girl, Rosa, was much more careful, and was quick to gather up and put in her bag all the clothes that were cast off, and every thread that her mistress threw away.

One day, a young man asked for Bianca's hand in marriage. Since he was handsome, kind and in a great hurry, the wedding was quickly arranged. A huge celebration was organised, all of Bianca's friends were invited. Even Rosa went along. She wore a beautiful dress she had made herself out of Bianca's rejects.

When Bianca noticed the beautiful dress, she sang out: 'That serving girl, who looks so stunning, actually wears my cast-offs to my wedding.' The bridegroom asked what she meant.

When, however, Bianca had explained it to him, the young man thought for a moment, then laughed and said, 'Well, while Bianca is improvident and throws away so much that is good, Rosa is the exact opposite. Rosa shall be my wife.'

Wasteful Bianca lost her fiancé, and the provident Rosa found a husband.

3 The Farmer and His Sons

A farmer, who realised that he was on his deathbed, called his sons to him.

'I am about to leave you,' he murmured, 'but I have provided for you. Dig up the vineyard and share everything you find there.'

The sons thought that the father had meant a hidden treasure, and, thus, the moment he died, they began to hoe and dig at a furious pace. They did not find any treasure, for there was none to find, but the earth in the vineyard, hoed and dug so thoroughly, produced that year an enormous quantity of excellent grapes.

4 John and the Little Cat

An old miller called his three sons together and announced: 'I will leave my mill to whichever of you brings me the most beautiful horse.' The three of them set off on this quest, but John, the youngest, got lost in the woods.

While he was wandering about, he met a little black and white cat, which said to him, in a friendly fashion, 'If you serve me faithfully for seven years, I promise to give you the horse that you seek.'

'What a strange cat,' thought John, but he decided to accept the offer. The cat took him to her little enchanted castle, where she was served only by other cats. John worked there for seven years, and at the end of this period, the cat said to him: 'And now build me a house of silver.' John built the house, and, when the cat opened the front door, out trotted seven superb horses.

'I will not give you your horse at this moment,' said the cat. 'But return to your home now, and I will arrive with the horse in three days' time.'

When John got home, his brothers asked what he had done with his horse. He replied: 'It will be here in three days.'

Three days later, however, a coach arrived at the mill, pulled by six extraordinarily beautiful horses. A beautiful princess alighted from the coach, and John recognised her as the black and white cat he had served for seven years. The princess asked the miller to show her the two horses brought back by the other sons. It was obvious that one was blind, and the other lame. She then ordered one of her servants to bring in the seventh horse, which now belonged to John. When the miller saw the splendid beast, he declared: 'John, the mill is yours.'

But it was the princess who replied: 'Keep the horse. Keep the mill as well. I will take John as my faithful husband, for it was he who helped me to become a princess once again.' And John and the princess returned to the woods and their silver house, where they lived happily ever after.

5 The Legend of Seraphina

Long ago, the Lord appeared to King Solomon in a dream and ordered him to build a Temple of Peace, but not to use any iron in the work, for iron was used to make weapons of war. Solomon was baffled, because the picks, which were indispensable for hacking the stone from the mountains, were made of iron.

Then, one of the king's wisest counsellors had an idea. 'Moses,' he said, 'wrote the Ten Commandments in stone by using seraphina. You, my lord, should use the same.'

Nobody, however, even knew what seraphina was, much less where to find it. So Solomon, who also ruled over the animal kingdom, called all the birds and the beasts to him and found that they, too, knew nothing. Only the eagle failed to answer his summons, and so Solomon took the eaglets from their nest and placed them under a glass bell. When the eagle attempted to free its young, its beak was not strong enough to break the crystal. The eagle flew off and returned with a fiery stone. It was seraphina, and with it the eagle cut the glass easily.

'Where did you find it?' asked Solomon. 'On the Sunset Mountain,' replied the eagle. And there Solomon found the seraphina he sought and was able to build the Temple of Peace without using iron.

6 The Two Cockerels and the Eagle

There were once two cockerels. Both wanted to rule the roost in the farmyard, and they decided to resolve the question, once and for all, by fighting a duel. They both fought bravely, but, in the end, one had to give up and run away. The winner flew up onto a little wall and launched its triumphant, 'Cock-a-doodle-doo.'

Unfortunately, the noise attracted the attention of an eagle, which swept down and raked the cockerel with its claws. From this, we see that God gives grace to the humble, while he does not hesitate to punish those who are too proud.

7 Peter the Braggart and the Giant

Peter the braggart had grown tired of being laughed at by his friends, and he decided to set off and see the world.

He soon caught sight of a mountain, upon which there stood a tower that seemed to disappear up in the sky. Filled with curiosity, he walked towards it and was greatly surprised and extremely frightened when he discovered that the tower was, in fact, a giant. By now, it was too late to run away: the giant captured him and kept him as a servant.

'Go and get a jug of water,' the giant ordered him one day.

'Why not the whole stream?' Peter replied, in such a casual way that the giant almost believed that he could do it, and began to feel a little fear.

'Go and chop up that bit of wood,' he ordered the day after.

'Why not the whole forest?' Peter asked.

'Go and kill two or three boars for dinner,' he was ordered the next day.

'Why not a thousand with a single blow, and then all the rest?' boasted Peter shrewdly.

The giant was now so afraid of his servant that he could not sleep a wink all night. The next morning, all he wanted was to be rid of Peter as quickly as possible, so he gave him a bag of gold coins and sent him home.

8 The Monkeys and the Bell

A thief, who was escaping with a stolen bell, was killed and eaten by a tiger. The bell was found by the monkeys, who began to ring it. The noise frightened the people of the nearby villages, who thought it was the sound of a giant. Only one woman was not afraid, and she went out with a basket of fruit. Near where she heard the bell, she left the basket on the ground and hid. No sooner had the monkeys thrown themselves on the fruit, the woman picked up the bell, and ran back to the village. She was praised for her heroic courage. . . . in stealing the bell from the giant!

9 The King of the Birds

Many long years ago, Zeus, the king of the gods, of men and of animals, fixed a date on which all the birds of the world had to appear before him. It was his intention to choose the most beautiful of all the birds, and appoint it king to rule over the others. As soon as they heard the news, all the birds gathered on the banks of the river to wash and preen themselves, and to make themselves look beautiful.

There were starlings and pheasants, peacocks and eagles, nightingales and herons. The crow was also there, and, amongst all the other birds, he soon realised how ugly he looked.

'There's a way around every problem,' he thought. He gathered up all the feathers the other birds had dropped, and he stuck them all over his back and wings. He now looked like a fabulously beautiful bird.

The appointed day arrived and all the birds appeared before Zeus. The crow, too, decorated with feathers every shape and hue, was there. Zeus was about to declare the crow king when there was a great noise.

All of the other birds, in their rage and indignation, had thrown themselves on the crow to tear their feathers off his back.

'There is a way round every problem. . . . except unfortunately the problem of getting caught when you are cheating,' thought the crow.

10 The Princess with Long Sight

A young and beautiful princess lived in a castle, which had a tower with twelve magic windows. It was so high that from it she could see everything that happened in the world. The princess had many suitors, but did not wish to marry, because she liked to rule by herself. Moreover, she had made it known that she would only marry the man who could hide himself so well that she would not be able to see him.

Already, many had tried and failed, but the last suitor asked to be allowed to undergo the test three times. The princess agreed. The young man, who was a brilliant hunter, called for help from a crow, a toad and a fox, for in the past he had saved their lives.

The crow put him inside her egg and hid him in the nest; the princess discovered him almost immediately. The toad swallowed him and settled on the bottom of the pond, but she still spied him there. The fox, however, transformed him into a golden crown, encrusted with precious stones. When the princess put it on her head she could not, of course, see her suitor anywhere. 'He is even more clever than me,' she thought. And when the young man returned to his natural form, the princess accepted him as her husband.

11 The Friend's Pot

A woman asked to borrow a pot from her friend and handed it back the next morning, together with a much smaller pot.

'It is the son of your pot, and was born during the night,' she explained. The friend was delighted to accept this. A few days later, the woman borrowed the pot again, but this time she did not give it back. When the friend asked if she could have her pot back, the woman replied: 'It's dead.'

'A pot can't die,' her friend insisted.

'And why not?' the woman went on. 'If it can have a son, then it can surely die.'

12 All the Fault of a Drop of Milk

There were once two peasants, husband and wife, who talked constantly of work, but never actually managed to get anything done. And yet, when it came to making plans, they were never short of grandiose ideas.

'You know,' the wife said to her husband one day, 'I really would like to buy a cow.'

'I'd like that, too, but how could we afford it?' he asked.

'All I need to do is find fifty coins in the street,' said the wife.

'Yes,' replied her husband. 'But it still would not be enough.'

'My relatives could give us another fifty; I could borrow fifty more; but you would have to find fifty coins as well.'

'You know, you really have a good idea there,' said her husband approvingly. 'The cow could have a calf, and then I would have milk every day.'

'No, you would not,' interrupted his wife, getting angry. 'We will sell every last drop of milk. Do you really think that I'm going to work myself to death, so that you can drink all the profits?'

'Well then. Why should I give you my fifty coins?'

If those two do not own a cow by now, it is only because they still have not stopped arguing, and have therefore not had the time to earn any coins at all.

13 Felix the Terrible and the Fox

A fox met a cat in the forest. 'Who are you?' she asked the cat. 'I am Felix the Terrible,' came the reply, 'and I am the king's new governor.'

The fox believed him, and thought that to be seen with such a great personage would add considerably to her own prestige. In the end, the two of them got married and went to live behind the woodcutter's hut.

The fox began to spread the word that the new governor, her husband, was a ferocious and fearsome animal, and that it would be better to have him as a friend by taking him some kind of gift. Thus the bear brought an ox, and the wolf brought a sheep, but they were both so afraid of the reputation of the new governor that they sent a hare to announce their arrival and their friendly intentions. Even then, to be on the safe side, the bear hid in a tree and the wolf hid in a hole.

The cat appeared and threw itself on the meat, making noises which the bear interpreted as 'I want more, more, more.'

The wolf shifted beneath the leaves and the rustle startled the cat, who leapt into the air and landed right on the wolf's nose. The wolf was completely terrified and fled as fast as he could.

From that time on, all the animals of the forest have been afraid of cats.

14 The Summer of St. Martin

Long ago, on a November day, when the rain was falling heavily and incessantly, a young soldier named Martin was riding along on a country road. At a crossroads, his attention was caught by a man wearing dirty rags, crouching in the mud and completely soaked and numb with cold. Martin was filled with pity and he did not hesitate for an instant: he took out his sword and sliced in two his heavy cloak, so that he could give half to the poor man.

A little further on, the young soldier came across another old man, who was dressed in rags as well, and he, too, was trembling beneath the rain which was pouring down without a moment's break. Martin gave the old man the other half of his cloak.

Now Martin, too, was exposed to the cold and the rain, and he had nothing left to offer, except his sincere commiseration, to the other poor people he met on the road. But his genuine expression of pity caused an amazing thing to happen: the rain stopped, the clouds vanished, and the sun shone in a clear blue sky, as warmly as in the summer.

From then on, whenever the sun shines in the first fortnight of November, and there are a few warm days, everyone who knows this story says, 'This is the summer of St. Martin.'

15 The Selfish Giant

Every afternoon, the children went to play in the giant's garden; it was the most beautiful garden that anybody had ever seen, with flowers like pearls and precious stones, and many little birds.

One terrible day, however, when the giant returned from a visit to another ogre, he found the children in his garden and shouted: 'What do you think you are doing here? This is my garden, and nobody can play in it except for me.'

Afterwards he built a high wall around his garden, and on top of it he placed a sign which said, 'Private Garden. No Entry To Strangers.' In truth, he was a very selfish giant.

The children now no longer had a place to go and play; they would walk round the high wall and say, 'Oh, how happy we were when we could play in that lovely garden.'

The spring came and the whole countryside was alive with buds and baby birds. Only in the garden of the giant did it remain winter. 'I cannot understand why the spring is so late this year,' the giant thought to himself. Still spring did not come, neither did the summer nor the autumn. 'He is too selfish,' said the flowers and the little birds.

One morning the giant was lying in bed, numb with cold, when he heard the twittering of little birds in his garden. 'It must be spring,' he laughed. He jumped out of his bed and looked out of the window. And what did he see? The children had got into his garden again, and it was so happy to have them back that it had filled itself with flowers and birds once more.

'How selfish I have been,' exclaimed the giant. 'Now I know why spring did not want to come.' He ran down to the garden, picked up a big hammer and knocked down the wall. 'This garden is yours, children,' the giant shouted, and suddenly, like a miracle, a tree behind him burst into leaf and a little bird went and perched on his shoulder.

16 The Amazing Feats of Shiro

In a small village in Japan, there once lived an old and impoverished peasant. One day, he came across a completely white, stray dog. He gave the animal what he had to eat and took it home. There, he and his wife treated the dog with love and named him 'Shiro' which means 'White' in Japanese.

One night, Shiro began to bark and paw at the ground. The peasant came running and, to his amazement, he heard the dog shout, 'Dig here. Dig here.' The old man dug and discovered a treasure trove.

A neighbour heard of this and asked to borrow the dog in the hope that it would lead him, too, to a treasure. To force the animal to search, he whipped it and maltreated it. When, however, he dug where the dog had indicated, he found only a pile of worthless broken tiles.

From that day on, Shiro worked many feats of magic, rewarding the good actions of men and punishing the wicked ones. When he died, a pine shoot sprang up on his grave, and in the space of a few weeks grew into a tree, so big that three men could not circle it with their arms, and the many branches held precious stones as flowers.

17 Prince Igor and the Beautiful Irina

When the king had to go away, he left to his son the keys to every door in the palace, telling him he could go into any room he pleased, except the one opened by the golden key.

Yet it was that very room that Prince Igor entered first. There he found only a telescope, which he took to the window. At once he saw a beautiful girl, who was smiling from a castle tower. She was a distant dream, yet that smile was enough for Prince Igor to fall head over heels in love with her.

When the king returned, he realised at once what had happened. 'Why did you disobey me?' he asked his son.

'Father, please forgive me,' begged Prince Igor. 'You must help me to find the maiden of whom I dream so much.'

'The dangers of the journey are many,' said the king. 'Do you think you are steadfast enough to confront them?'

Prince Igor gave his father every assurance, so the king consented and, as protection for his son from the dangers he would meet, gave him his magic ring. Thus Igor arrived unharmed at the castle he had dreamt about.

The next day, Irina, for this was the name of the princess with the beautiful smile, was walking in the park. Suddenly, she found herself face to face with the handsome young man she had seen in a dream, and with whom she had fallen completely in love. Igor was amazed by her joy, and asked:

'Do you know me?'

'I have seen you in a dream,' Irina replied sweetly.

'I too have seen you in my dreams,' said Igor, in turn. 'But now I have found you, and, if you will accept me, we shall live together in my father's palace.'

When Igor's father saw the young couple arriving, he rushed out to meet them. 'You are welcome, beautiful Irina,' he addressed the princess. Then he gave orders to prepare a great feast and there were long and joyful celebrations in the castle.

18 How Deserts Are Formed

On the day of creation, the whole world was one huge garden of flowers. The Lord, however, called man to him and gave him this warning:

'Beware, every time you do something wrong a grain of sand will fall on the earth.'

But mankind paid no attention at all to this warning.

What harm could a few grains of sand do?

They continued to do wicked things, and thus, little by little, the world has been invaded by the rivers and the seas of sand, which form the great deserts.

19 The Thanksgiving Gift

In order to get to the market with a cow and two hens that he wanted to sell, a farmer had to go through a wood that was full of brigands. He was very afraid. 'Oh Lord,' he began to pray, 'if you bring me through this forest safe and sound, then I will give to the church everything I receive from the sale of the cow.'

Nothing happened to him at all in the wood, and he rebuked himself for having been too rash with his promises while he was praying. However, he soon thought of a way of not sacrificing too much. At the market, he offered the cow for sale at the price of a pair of hens and, naturally, there were many people who wanted to take advantage of such an offer.

'But,' the farmer went on, 'whoever buys the cow must also buy the hens.'

'Agreed. How much do you want for them?'

For the two hens the farmer asked the price of a cow. Given that the total price was still reasonable, the deal was done. The farmer gave to the church the small amount of money he had received for the cow, and so kept his promise.

When he got home, however, he could no longer find the larger sum of money which he had pocketed for the pair of hens: he had lost it coming back through the woods.

20 The Lazy Servants

Several servants were boasting about their laziness, as if it was something to be proud of.

'When the master calls me, I pretend not to have heard,' said the first, 'and I wait until he has called me at least three times before I get up.'

Then the groom spoke: 'When I have to brush a horse, I lie down in the trough, stretch out my leg, and pass my boot along the flank of the horse. It's not easy!'

'I always sleep fully dressed,' interjected a third, 'so I don't have to put my clothes on in the morning, or take them off at night.'

'Listen to this, then,' the fourth interrupted. 'I was at table and because I couldn't be bothered lifting the jug and pouring myself a glass of water, I nearly died of thirst.'

'That's nothing,' yet another chimed in. 'If I see a stone in the middle of the street, I find it too tiring to raise my foot. I just bang into it.'

'Yesterday,' began the last of them, 'I lay down and fell asleep in the grass. Then it began to rain, but I wasn't going to go to the trouble of getting up just for that. Finally, I was deluged by a torrent of water so strong that it tore the hair from my head. Have a look.' And thus saying, the foolish servant took off his cap and showed them all his shiny, bald head.

21 The Ox and the Horse

The ox and the horse realised that their master was preparing to depart for the war. The horse was very worried when it thought about the dangers it would have to face up to in battle. The ox, on the other hand, was extremely cheerful in the belief that, in the absence of the master, he would have less work to do.

All this changed a short while later, when the news arrived that the enemy had already surrendered. To celebrate the great victory, the cavalryman held an enormous banquet with plenty of roast meat: who was the loser then, do you think?

22 The Fox Becomes a Shepherd

A woman once was looking to hire a shepherd, and a bear volunteered to do the work. 'Can you call the flock?' the woman asked the bear.

The bear had a go. It gave a loud grunt, and all the sheep ran away. Exactly the same thing happened when the wolf said it could do the job and gave its howl. The fox, on the other hand, showed itself able to call the sheep, and was hired at once as shepherd. The woman entrusted her animals to the fox and left contentedly.

One by one, the fox ate all the animals. It so happened, however, that the woman came back earlier than expected and the fox was taken unawares.

The woman looked all around for her sheep and could not find them, so she asked the fox for an explanation.

'Ah, well, you see, half the sheep are pasturing near the woods, and the other half are feeding near the lake,' replied the crafty fox.

The woman went off to see for herself. The fox decided to profit by her absence again. It slipped its nose into the milk urn and licked up the cream. The woman, once again, surprised the fox, and beat it.

The fox managed to escape, but during the struggle a drop of cream fell on the point of its tail, which from then on has always had a white tip.

23 The Street Sweeper and the Judge

A street sweeper was doing his job when he came across some money lying on the ground. He decided to use it to buy a surprise present for his little daughter. He bought a jar of honey, rushed home and left it on the table, so that his daughter would find it as soon as she came home from school. But, alas, it was the flies who ate the honey.

The sweeper was so angry that he went to ask the judge to give orders for the flies to be arrested and condemned to death.

'You are absolutely right,' smiled the judge. 'But, as you will well understand, we cannot mobilise the army against these rascals. We shall see justice done in another way. Every time you see a fly, strike it down. I authorise you to execute them yourself. Furthermore, I demand personally that you do not allow even a single one of these thieving flies to escape.'

'Yes, your honour. You can count on me,' the sweeper assured him.

At that very moment, a fly decided to settle on the judge's head and the sweeper did not hesitate: he raised his brush and brought it crashing down on the judge's head. The guards were about to arrest him, when the judge recovered and intervened. 'Leave him be,' he ordered. 'He has taught me not to say foolish things to simpletons.'

24 The Nightingale and the Rose

A young student once wept in a garden. 'Tomorrow my beloved will only dance with me if I take her a red rose. But there are none to be found in the entire garden and my heart must break in two.'

A nightingale heard him and thought: 'Now I understand the mystery of love.' She flapped her brown wings and flew off. 'Give me a red rose and I will sing you my most beautiful song,' she said to a rose bush. 'I cannot, for my roses are as white as the foam on the sea,' was the reply.

As fast as she could, the nightingale flew to another bush. 'My roses are more golden than the rays of the sun,' came the reply.

The nightingale flew on. 'My roses are as red as the coral in the oceans,' came the reply at last.

'But they have been killed by the frost. If you truly want a red rose, then you must sing for me all night long, as you press your breast against a thorn.'

'Death is the highest possible price to pay,' thought the nightingale, 'but love is better than life.' So all through the night, the nightingale sang, while she pressed her breast against a thorn. And, on the highest branch of the bush, there grew a splendid rose, as red as the fire of love which had given it life.

25 The Eagle and the Badger

The eagle and the badger lived in the same oak tree, the eagle in a high nest in the branches, the badger in his set, down amongst the roots. Although they had never become great friends, they had both successfully avoided any kind of disagreement.

Then, one day, a cat climbed up as far as the eagle's nest. 'Don't you realise,' she said to the eagle, 'that the badger is digging through more and more of the roots? He is trying to uproot the tree, so that your little eaglets will fall to the ground and he can eat them.'

Having spread this fear and distrust in the house of the eagle, the cat went down to the set of the badger. 'Make sure you never leave the safety of your home,' she said to him. 'Haven't you noticed that the eagle is standing guard on a branch and is just waiting for you or your children to step outside, so that it can attack you?'

The result of all this was that the eagle no longer left her nest even for an instant, for fear that, in her absence, the tree would fall; and the badger, too, was afraid to leave his set. They could no longer go hunting for food, and their children came close to starving to death. In the end, they both decided to eat the perfidious cat, who had caused them so much unnecessary hardship.

26 The Miser and the Beggar

A poor man, who was reduced to rags, begged a rich Arab for a suit of clothes; and, since he had been asked in the name of Allah, the rich man could not refuse, but made sure he gave the beggar his oldest suit. The beggar put it on, and, according to custom, hung a sign on the collar stating, 'There is no god but Allah.'

'Are you not going to add, "And Mohammed is his Prophet"?' asked the rich man, because they were the traditional words.

'No,' the beggar replied, 'because when they made this suit, the prophet hadn't even been born yet.'

27 The Good Manners of the Ignorant Man

A rich but ignorant man decided to learn good manners, to make a better impression in society. He was invited to the celebration of a friend's birthday, and he asked what he should say to be well mannered. 'You must say "I wish you a hundred such days as this" ', he was told.

However, on the way to the celebration, he came across a funeral and he repeated his new phrase to the relatives of the deceased: they beat him black and blue. When the misunderstanding had been cleared up, they taught him what he should have said.

He then came across a wedding procession. 'Heartfelt condolences,' he said to the bride and groom, and the wedding party lost their temper with him. Finally, he learnt from them what he should say the next time.

He then encountered a group of monks. 'Good health, and many children,' he wished them. Here again, he was lucky to escape unharmed.

After a farmer had punched him for one of his inappropriate phrases, he learnt another beautiful phrase: 'That the most tiny grain beneath your eyes should grow as large as a pomegranate tree.' He learnt this phrase by heart, but said it to the daughter of the king, whose face was covered in spots. He was arrested, and people say he is still in prison.

28 The Monkey and the Fishermen

Two fishermen were throwing their nets into the river, and a monkey in the branches of a tree watched their actions with interest. At midday, the men went off to eat and left their nets on the river-bank, intending to use them again after lunch.

The monkey came down from the tree, picked up one of the nets, and tried to throw it as he had seen the men do. The only thing it succeeded in doing, however, was to imprison itself completely in the tight netting.

'Now,' said the monkey, 'I have learnt that it is better to leave every task to those who know how to do it.'

29 The Magical Club

A young and hardworking man had been in the service of a magician. He had worked so well that when he left, he was rewarded with a magical club: it was enough for him to say 'Play' and the club would begin to bash people until he said 'Enough'.

During the whole of his long journey home, the magical club showed itself to be very useful in keeping away those with wicked intentions, or for teaching lessons to anyone who tried to take advantage of the young man. One evening, the inn at which he was staying was attacked by brigands, and the club put them all to flight in a few minutes. Instead of being grateful, the innkeeper plotted to steal the club when night fell. However, the young man only pretended to be asleep. 'Play,' he ordered, and it was the innkeeper's turn to feel the magical club.

When the young man finally got back to his own country, he discovered that the capital city was being besieged by an enemy army, and was about to fall into their hands. So the young man climbed a hill which overlooked the field of battle, and set his club to work.

He won a crushing victory, in the literal sense; and his reward was the hand of the beautiful princess in marriage.

30 The Dragon's Nest

There was once a young king who was a brave hunter and had already killed every sort of ferocious beast. In order to put his skill to the supreme test, he decided to go on a dragon hunt. He was lucky: after many days of fruitless searching, he heard the unmistakable thunder of a dragon's wings. It was colossal, with a serpent's body and wings as big as sails. Like lightning, the king had an arrow in his bow, fired at once, and the dragon fell dead . . . . Almost at once, however, he was attacked by another, smaller dragon, the female of the pair. With certain aim, the king killed her as well.

At that very moment, however, he saw the heads of four new-born dragons sticking out of a cave. They were almost as small as lizards.

The king felt guilty that he had deprived them of their parents, and, to make amends, he gathered up the baby dragons, and carried them to his palace, where he himself undertook to bring them up.

The four little dragons became very affectionate, and obeyed the king like trained puppies. When he went out, they would walk behind him, even if the very sight of the dragons would terrify his subjects. Little by little, the king trained them to accept reins and a saddle and to be ridden: when he went visiting, hunting, or to war, the four dragons were the king's steeds.

One day the king's mother suggested to her son that he should look for a wife. The king agreed, on the sole condition that the new queen should show herself worthy of him, by going for a ride on a dragon.

Messengers were sent to the royal palaces all over the world, but almost all of them were told: 'Your king must be mad.'

Only one princess, more courageous than the others, agreed to undergo the test, and experience the exhilaration of a flight on a dragon, in the arms of her future husband.

They married when the dragon returned to earth and, as far as we know, they lived happily ever after.

Contents

The fairy tale of the month: Hansel and Gretel
The Brothers Grimm

The fairy tale of the month

The Christmas Tree

Once upon a time in the woods, there was a young fir tree, whose one desire was to grow to be big and tall like the other trees. He did grow, little by little, year by year, but he was very impatient and it never seemed to be fast enough.

From time to time, men would come to the woods, armed with heavy axes, and they would chop at the very trees which had grown most tall and majestic, and then they would fall to the ground with a fearful crash. The men would saw up the branches and the trunk, and all the wood was then loaded onto long carts.

'Where do they take them?' the young fir tree asked.

Nobody in the wood knew the answer, but, from time to time, one of the swallows, who were great wanderers and went all over the world, would bring back news of a fir tree that had become a telegraph pole, or the mast of a ship.

'Oh, that such a destiny could also be mine!' sighed the little tree, dreaming of the moment when he would tower above the waves, and bear great white sails.

Other fir trees, on the other hand, were pulled up from the ground with their roots intact, and loaded with great care onto the waiting carts, without damage to a single branch. The sparrows, who often went to peek through the windows of the houses, would return saying that these trees were replanted in beautiful living-rooms, illuminated and decorated with silver ribbon, candles, sparkling balls, sweets and toys. The children, said the sparrows, were never happier than when playing around these fabulous trees.

'Oh, that such a great destiny could also be mine,' sighed the little tree. And it did not occur either to him or the other trees to ask the sparrows what happened afterwards to these lucky fir trees.

Another year passed and the young fir tree grew a little bit taller. The woodcutters came and once again cut down the highest, strongest trees, but, once again, the young fir was left in the forest. Then the villagers came to look at all the young, well-formed trees, and this time he was chosen. He almost died with joy when he heard the leader of the villagers give the order, pointing to him: 'Take this one, too!'

He suffered terrible pain, however, when their iron tools bit into the ground and struck his roots; and when their ropes and chains bound him and pulled him by force out of his home earth, he could resist no longer and fainted in agony.

He came back to his senses when he felt himself being prodded and touched on all sides. He opened his eyes to find that he was in the corner of a large square, along with dozens

of other fir trees like himself, piled up against the wall of a building. He heard a female voice say: 'Yes, that is a lovely tree! We shall take it.'

Two uniformed servants picked him up and carried him into a splendid salon, where everything was of the very best. They replanted him in a large earthenware vase, which was covered in white cloth and decorated with roses of red ribbon.

They watered him and looked after him with great care, and the young fir tree frequently repeated how lucky he had been to be brought to that house amongst those people, who admired him so much and had given him such an important place.

One morning, an extraordinary amount of activity took place around the tree. The servants and the lady of the house herself all carried in large boxes, and pulled out, one after the other, glittering glass balls of every shape and hue, ribbons and silver string, and a star which was attached to the very top of the tree. . . . and the little tree, who could see his reflection in the mirror opposite, was over the moon with pride and joy. He realised that the famous feast of Christmas must be approaching, for he had heard much about it from the sparrows.

But there was more to come: that evening, the mistress of the house placed all the presents under the tree, and the governess lit all the candles. Then the children, full of excitement and curiosity, rushed into the room. What a wonderful evening that was for the young fir tree!

He could never forget such a moment, even though his glory, in reality, lasted only a few minutes. Hardly had the children finished unwrapping their presents, than the young tree was left alone in his corner, forgotten by one and all.

Some days later, the gardeners remembered him and they took him and carried him to the park, where he was planted by the wall. In his strange, new home, the young fir observed the enormous cedars, the colossal oaks and the many other majestic trees which surrounded him. Once again, he began to dream of becoming big and beautiful like them.

From time to time, a sparrow or a couple of mice would come to keep him company in his solitude. To each of these he would recount the fantastic story of his life, and the magical night of Christmas. But the mice preferred stories about larders, where they entered thin and came out fat, and the sparrows had seen many greater marvels as they flew around the world.

Eventually, the young fir tree began to realise that it would have been better to have remained in his native forest, rather than to have had the joyful experiences of one, single evening.

1 The Magic Cloak

There was once a poor, young Norwegian boy named Aldar, and the only two things he owned in the world were an old, lame horse and a cloak with seventy patches and ninety holes.

One day in December, when there was snow on the ground and the air was very cold, Aldar was riding sadly along on his half-frozen horse. In the distance, he spotted a well-dressed gentleman with a fox fur, on a splendid horse. Aldar sat up straight in the saddle, opened his cloak and began to sing. When the stranger rode up, he was amazed and asked, 'Don't you feel the cold?'

'Not at all,' replied Aldar. 'The wind blows in one hole and out another, so I stay warm. I am more concerned for you. I can only imagine how cold you must feel wearing that fox fur!'

'You know, you're absolutely right!' the stranger observed. 'Couldn't you sell me your cloak?' 'No, I'm sorry. I can't sell, for then I would have nothing to cover me.' 'I will give you my fox fur in return,' the other insisted. 'It's not worth my while,' said Aldar, 'unless, of course, we decided to exchange horses as well. . . .' 'It's a deal!' said the gentleman. Aldar quickly slipped on the fox fur and galloped away before the stranger discovered what a bad exchange he had made.

2 The Bluebird and the Coyote

Long, long ago, the bluebird had feathers which were dull. It lived on the banks of the lake and dreamed of becoming as bright as the beautiful blue water. It wanted this so badly, that it would dive into the lake every day, praying that the water would dye his feathers blue. One day, however, the poor bird came out of the lake after its daily bath, and it did not have a single feather left; they had all fallen off and the bird was completely naked.

Still it did not lose faith, and continued to dive into the water and pray every day. When its feathers did grow back, they were of the dazzling blue which its species has today.

When the coyote saw the bluebird, he wondered greatly at the transformation, and thought that he too would like to become blue. The bluebird explained how it had happened to him, so the coyote began the daily baths and prayers until he turned blue.

He was so proud that he began to run around the world, so that everyone could admire him, only turning round every so often to see if his shadow had become blue as well. While doing this, he crashed into a tree, and fell unconscious. When he revived, he discovered that he had changed yet again. His coat had become as dull as slate, and he has remained like that to the present day.

3 The Stolen Ass

An Arabian farmer realised that his ass, which he had put out to pasture in a meadow, had been stolen. He immediately grabbed a stick and ran into the town. 'You miserable thieves!' he yelled, waving his club about in a menacing way. 'Give me back my ass, or I shall do what my father did!'

It was so frightening to see and hear him, that even the thief was terrified, and came and handed back the stolen animal. While he was doing so, he asked the farmer: 'What did your father do?'

'He bought another ass!' was the reply.

4 The Happy Prince

On top of a tall stone column stood the statue of the Happy Prince. He was covered in gold leaf, and his eyes were twin sapphires, and a little ruby shone on his sword. Everybody loved him. One evening, a swallow, which was heading for Egypt, settled between his feet for a rest and noticed that the statue was crying. 'What's the matter?' the surprised swallow asked. 'When I was alive, I was happy,' the prince replied. 'But now that I am dead, and have been placed up here, even though my heart is made of lead, I can no longer hold back my tears for the suffering I see all around me. I am

unable to move. Dear swallow, please be my messenger. Take my ruby to that poor mother down there.'

'Alas, prince,' said the swallow, 'I do not have time. I must fly to Egypt for it is already too cold here for me.'

But the prince was so unhappy that the swallow finally agreed to do what he asked. Then he had to take the sapphires, and then one by one, all of the leaves of gold which covered the prince, until the day came when the statue was without decoration.

The poor of the city, on the other hand, were less poor, and their children less pale. The snow arrived. The little swallow was growing colder and colder, but he could not bring himself to leave his beloved prince. The day

arrived when the swallow realised he was dying and he bade farewell to the prince. The next morning the mayor walked out into the square. He noticed the dead bird and ordered that it be taken away. Next, he looked at the no longer splendid statue of the prince and ordered that it also be removed and melted down.

In the huge town furnace, only the heart of lead would not melt. It, too, was thrown away, and landed in the rubbish tip right next to the swallow it loved. A passing angel saw these two precious beings and took them to paradise. From that day on, in the beautiful gardens of heaven, the swallow has sung contentedly on the shoulders of the Happy Prince.

5 The Little Goat and the Wolf

A starving, ragged wolf was walking up the mountain.

'How hungry I am!' he thought. 'And how very difficult it is to find some prey!' If it had not been contrary to his most basic instincts, he might even have become a vegetarian!

All of a sudden, he spied a little goat that was contentedly munching the grass on the rocky summit. It was one of those outcrops of stone which only the most determined of goats ever succeed in reaching.

'Come down, you beautiful little goat!' the wolf called in a sugar-sweet voice. 'Watch where you put your

feet! Be careful not to slip! I don't want you to hurt yourself!'

'I am quite happy here!' replied the little goat, who had learned from her mother to be distrustful of wolves. Moreover, since her mother had also taught her good manners, the little goat added: 'Thank you all the same, but you must not worry about me.'

The wolf, however, insisted: 'Come here! The grass is greener and much more tasty down here!'

The goat gave him a stern look, and said, 'My friend, it is not for my good that you are inviting me down to the meadow, I suspect, but for your own!' And with a spring, the goat leapt up onto a more inaccessible rock.

6 The Fearful Hunter and the Woodcutter

Did you know that many men are very brave while they are talking, and very scared when the time comes to act?

There was once a hunter who was going through the woods in search of a bear. He met a woodcutter and asked: 'My good man, do you happen to have seen the footprints of a bear?'

'Yes, I have seen them,' said the woodcutter, setting down his axe, 'and I will take you to its den.'

The hunter went white with fear and started to shake. 'Thank you, but that won't be necessary,' he stammered. 'I am looking for tracks, not for the bears themselves!'

7 The Demon at the Bridge

In a lonely valley, there once lived a demon who tried to convince the people of the valley of the pleasures of hell. He was extremely active, but unfortunately for him, his work was all rendered next to useless by the prayers and goodness of a saintly hermit who lived nearby.

One day, the hermit went to visit his enemy, and proposed that a bridge be built over the river, so that the inhabitants of the valley could pass more easily from one side to the other.

'And since I am well aware that you demons never do anything for nothing,' the hermit concluded, 'I promise you that the first to cross the bridge will be given over, body and soul, into your power.'

'I know that you holy people are in the ridiculous habit of keeping your promises,' replied the nasty little devil, 'therefore I accept.'

The bridge was built in no time at all, and the next night the demon waited eagerly in the middle for what he was promised. He was furious when he saw that the first being to cross the bridge was an ass!

The little demon was so enraged at how he had been tricked, that he threw himself, with much hissing and smoking, into the river, and, to this day, he has not resurfaced.

8 Man and the Wolf

The wolf boasted that he was the strongest animal. The fox disagreed. 'Man in his prime is stronger!' 'Introduce me to one and we'll soon see,' retorted the angry wolf.

An old man went by. 'Is that a man?' asked the wolf. 'No, he is no longer in his prime,' replied the fox. A boy ran past. 'Is that one?' asked the wolf. 'No, he has not reached his prime,' the fox replied. Then a hunter appeared. 'That's him! That's a man!' exclaimed the fox. The wolf leapt out, and was beaten by the hunter. 'Do you see?' asked the fox. 'Man has strengths which not even you possess!'

9 Thumbelina

A woman who had no children would often sigh and say, 'How I would love to have even a tiny little girl!'

A good fairy heard her and gave her a little seed to plant in a flower pot. The seed grew into a tulip, and when the flower opened, there was a beautiful little girl, no bigger than a thumb amongst the petals. For this reason, she was known as Thumbelina. A nut shell became her bed, and she used a petal as her blanket.

One night, she was asleep in her little bed, when an ugly toad saw her, and carried her off to his pond, where Thumbelina was forced to stay until a swallow rescued her: 'Come with me south to the warmer lands!'

'Yes, oh yes!' agreed Thumbelina, as she made herself comfortable on the swallow's back. The two of them flew across the seas, until the swallow said at last: 'There is my home. You can live in one of these lovely flowers.'

The swallow put Thumbelina inside the biggest of the flowers. How great was her astonishment when she found in the heart of the flower, a handsome young man the same size as herself! He was the son of the King of the Flowers, and he fell at once in love with Thumbelina and asked her to marry him. She accepted and became the Queen of the Flowers. Her mother was the happiest person in the world when she heard the news.

10 The Farmer and the Clever Thieves

Three thieves wanted to find out who was the cleverest of them. Just then, a farmer passed by, riding on an ass, to which was tied a goat, wearing a collar with a bell on it.

'I will steal his goat without him knowing it!' said the first thief.

'I will steal his ass!' said the second.

'And I will get his clothes!' declared the third thief.

The first thief crept up beside the goat, removed the bell and attached it to the ass's tail. Then he untied the goat, and led it away quietly and quickly.

The farmer, reassured by the sound of the bell, went on a good distance before he realised that he was no longer being followed by the goat. At once he began to yell, 'Somebody has stolen my goat!'

'I saw who did it!' volunteered the second thief. 'He ran down that narrow lane!' The lane was so narrow that the farmer had to leave the ass behind, and the second thief walked off with it. The farmer came to a well, where the third thief was waiting for him, yelling, 'Help! Help! My purse has fallen down the well! I will give ten pieces of gold to the man who retrieves it!' The farmer undressed quickly, and climbed into the well. . . . and, of course, lost all his clothes to the third of the clever thieves.

11 The Woodcutter's Three Axes

Ivan was so poor that he owned nothing except the axe he needed to earn his living as a woodcutter. One day, by a stroke of ill fortune, while he was working on the bank of a river, the blade of his axe flew off the handle and sank in the river. Poor Ivan was desperately unhappy; now how could he cut the wood which had always earned him the little food that he ate?

His heartfelt sighs were overheard by a strange, old man. As soon as he was told what happened, the old man dived into the river and re-emerged a few moments later, holding up a golden hatchet.

'Is this the one you lost?' he asked. 'No, that's not my hatchet,' Ivan replied.

The old man dived into the water again and came up holding a silver hatchet. 'No, that's not mine either,' the woodcutter confirmed. On the third occasion, the old man came out holding Ivan's blade. 'Yes, that's mine!' laughed the happy woodcutter.

'Take it. You owe me nothing for the help I have given you. Rather, since you have shown yourself to be neither greedy nor dishonest, you deserve to be rewarded. You can also keep both the golden and the silver axes!'

12 Vassilia the Beautiful Weaver

Left alone in the world, a young girl, named Vassilia, was hired in the household of an old woman. Vassilia was not only very beautiful, she was also a very good worker; she was best of all at weaving and she did this with great skill.

She wanted to repay the old woman, who had been so good to her, and so she took some flax and set to work. She produced a thread that was so fine that she needed a special frame to weave it on. The result, however, was a cloth so soft and fine that it would enhance the finest of wardrobes.

Vassilia gave the cloth to the old lady so that she might sell it, and thus be repaid for her kindness. The old lady looked at the fabulous cloth and admired it. 'No, my dear,' she said to Vassilia, 'I will not sell it. Only the tsar is worthy of cloth such as this. I will take it to court.'

The good old lady then left for the royal palace, and she stood for a long time beneath the windows, until the tsar saw her and sent a servant to bring her in. The old woman showed him the cloth, and the tsar said he would buy it at any price.

'No, my tsar, this cloth is not for sale,' replied the old woman. 'I have brought it to you as a gift.'

The tsar accepted it gratefully, and sent the old woman home laden with gifts. When, however, the tsar requested that a shirt be made from the cloth, there was not one tailor willing to assume the responsibility and cut such beautiful material. The tsar, therefore, had the old woman sent for and she suggested that Vassilia should do the work. The young maid cut and sewed a perfect shirt from the cloth, and she herself was asked to hand it over to the tsar. When the tsar saw how beautiful she was, he fell so in love with her that he led Vassilia to his throne, and asked her to marry him that very day.

13 The Rose and the Amaranth

An amaranth, which was growing beside a rose, said one day: 'How beautiful you are, rose! You are the delight of the gods and of men. I rejoice with you for your shapeliness and your perfume!'

'Oh, amaranth,' the rose replied, 'I live only for a few days and, even if no-one picks me, I still wither and die. You, on the other hand, are always in flower and you live forever!'

Even today, the amaranth is not sure if it is better or worse off than the rose. Is it better to live for a long time, or to be beautiful and glorious and live but briefly?

14 Winter and Spring

The winter was very proud of the fact that but a mention of his name could inspire a vague sense of fear in people, and he was very critical of the spring.

'When you arrive,' winter said, 'it's almost as if people go mad. Nobody can keep still anymore. Some go for walks in the country or at the seaside, some go and pick flowers in the woods and meadows: everybody dresses in bright clothes as though life were an eternal carnival!'

'However,' interrupted autumn, who was listening, 'even in spring it rains and the wind blows.' 'Yes, that's true,' winter appeared to agree for a moment, 'but nobody is worried by that. You ought to follow my example! I make men tremble and, should I choose, I can imprison them all day in their homes. To them, I am a king, a tyrant, and I make them obey my orders. You ought to learn how to win respect like me!'

'That does not interest me in the slightest,' replied spring. 'Mankind would gladly do without you, whereas I am loved and awaited. When I arrive they are glad, and when I leave they are sorry. You, on the other hand, are tolerated with difficulty every day you are with them! And it is precisely because you are glad to be like that, that you are so ugly!'

15 The Wolf and the Goat

The goat went to pasture with the rest of his flock, but it had snowed a short time before and what little grass that remained had been completely covered. The weather was very cold and the wind was blowing. The little goat found a protected hollow and nestled in, and the comfortable warmth made him fall asleep almost immediately.

When he awoke, the flock had already departed for the fold, and the little goat had to try and make his way home alone. On his way, he met the wolf, who attempted to engage him in conversation; but the little goat tried to avoid him and walk on.

'If you wish,' the wolf offered, 'I will walk you home.'

'No, thank you, there is really no need,' the little goat insisted.

'But I am worried that you might come across some wicked beast, who will eat you up in a single mouthful.'

'If you do not eat me,' sighed the goat, 'I don't see who else will.'

'There is no shortage of hunters, on two legs or four,' replied the shrewd wolf. 'And rather than let you end up in somebody else's tummy, I would rather that you finished up in mine!'

Then the wolf jumped on the little goat and devoured him in a single mouthful, as was inevitable from the very beginning.

16 The Peacock and the Crane

The peacock would often laugh at the crane, which, according to the peacock, had very drab plumage indeed. 'I am dressed in gold and purple,' the vain bird would say to the crane, 'while you have absolutely nothing of any beauty on your wings at all.'

'On the other hand,' the crane replied, 'I can sing to the stars while I fly high in the heavens, while you must drag yourself along the ground like the chickens in the farmyard!'

Perhaps, then, it is better to be illustrious in poor clothes, rather than live without glory in but a show of wealth.

17 The Queen of the Meadow

One day, a long time ago, the wind came across a large and empty meadow. Not a single flower grew in the grass. The wind thought that this was a great pity, and went to look for help to put things right.

'Who would like to brighten up an empty meadow?' he asked.

Not a single flower volunteered; they all had some excuse. Some suffered from the cold, they said; some were afraid of heights; some were afraid of ruining their petals; some were fine in their beds. . . .

'You are not, I hope, suggesting that I, the queen of the flowers, should go and live in a mere meadow?' said the indignant rose. Only the shy, little daisy agreed to help the wind, for she lived a hard life amongst the stones.

The wind looked at her very closely, and saw that she had white petals, fringed with pink and lilac. She was very gracious, he decided; exactly what he was looking for.

'But will you not suffer from loneliness?' the wind asked.

'Not at all!' the daisy assured him. 'Anyway, I am sure that my friends, the buttercups, will soon come and join me in the meadow.' The wind took her and blew her gently to her new home, and there the humble daisy was loved and treasured as the Queen of the Meadow.

18 The Sick Lion

The lion had very bad indigestion, and all the doctors in the forest visited him.

'What bad breath you have, your majesty!' exclaimed the zebra.

'How dare you!' said the indignant lion and knocked down the zebra.

'What a pleasant smell!' said the hyena, who had seen what had happened to the zebra.

'Do you think I'm stupid?' roared the angry lion, and killed the hyena as well. 'And what do you think?' the lion asked the fox. 'Unfortunately, your majesty,' replied that shrewd animal, 'my nose is completely blocked with a cold, and I can smell nothing!'

19 The Sick Wolf and the Sheep

There was once a starving wolf in a sorry state. He had been obliged to flee from a pack of dogs, and for many days he had found nothing to eat. He spied a little white sheep and thought: 'At last! Here is a meal for me!'

'Little white sheep,' he said to her, 'could you please bring me a drop of water from the river? As you can see, I am very unwell. If you can bring me something to drink, I will be able to find something to eat.' 'But if I bring you something to drink,' said the little sheep, 'then you will already have found yourself something to eat!' and skipped off in the opposite direction.

20 The Young King

On the eve of his coronation, the young king was alone in his beautiful room. He was thinking about what he was to wear the next day; the clothes woven with gold, the pearl sceptre, the crown encrusted with rubies. In the garden, a nightingale was singing and the scent of jasmine floated in through the window: the young king fell asleep and he had a remarkable dream.

Pale children, with trembling hands, were working the looms.

'What are you weaving?' he asked. 'The clothes for the young king's coronation,' they replied. He sighed with pain, but his dream continued.

Out of a boat which was pushed through the water by the oars of a hundred slaves, the divers plunged into the sea and came up each time with a pearl. The captain placed each of the pearls in a little leather bag. 'What pearls are these?' he asked the captain. 'They are for the sceptre at the coronation,' came the reply.

Once again, the young king moaned in his sleep, but the dream continued. Men were mining in a dry river bed; their clothes were ragged and they dug and sifted through mountains of sand. 'What are you looking for?' the young king asked them. 'Rubies for the young king's crown,' they replied. The king cried out again, but this time he woke up.

The pages came in and they brought him the clothes woven with gold, the pearl sceptre, and the rubied crown. The young king, however, refused to put them on. From an old trunk, he pulled out a white shirt; from the garden he took a stick and held it in his fist like a sceptre, and with some twigs he made a crown.

He walked into the cathedral and his astonished people stared at him.

Then, from the great stained glass windows, the light of heaven burst into the cathedral and dressed the young prince in the most beautiful cloth of gold; lilies, whiter than pearls, bloomed on the stick, and, from the twigs on his head, there sprang roses which were redder than rubies.

21 The Grocer's Shop

Charles could not keep count of the times he would stop and look in the window of the grocer's shop. That attractive sight looked even more enchanting now that it was Christmas time. What delicious foods there were on the great wooden table! An enormous turkey took pride of place in the middle, and it was circled by roast geese, hams, and strings of sausages. Over the rest of the table there were cake stands of multi-hued marzipan fruits, huge sweet chestnuts, toffee apples and sugared pears. In the air, there was a faint aroma of punch which warmed the little boy's heart.

22 The Little Match-Girl

It was snowing heavily and the air was very cold. There was a poor little girl dressed in rags wandering in the street. In her hand, she held a box of matches. She did not dare to go home for she had not sold a single match. Her hands were frozen in the cold; a match might have warmed them up, if only she dared to light it! Finally, she took out a match and struck it against the wall. The little flame was very hot and she held her hands over it. Then, as if looking through a magic lantern, the poor girl saw the most beautiful Christmas tree in the world, with hundreds of little candles glowing on the green branches. The light from the match died and so did the candles. The little girl pulled out another and struck it against the wall: the match lit and, suddenly, there was bright light everywhere. The little match-girl found herself face to face with her dear old grandmother, who was as kind and as loving as ever, but somehow more radiant and more happy than the little girl had ever seen her before. 'Oh, Granny, take me with you!' the little girl said.

Her grandmother gathered her into her arms, and together they stepped through a splendid, shining gate and into a place where it was never cold, and hunger and suffering no longer existed. They had gone to heaven.

23 Father Christmas's Workshop

At his workshop at the North Pole, Father Christmas works all year round to make the toys that children all over the world receive at Christmas. It is an important task, and it requires not only imagination, but also skill and organisation. Fortunately, the gnomes of the North give him a hand. They are the most trustworthy of all gnomes, even if they do have some of the mischievous habits of their kind.

When everything is ready, Father Christmas loads up his sled, harnesses his reindeer, and then, with a crack of his whip, and his merriest laughter, he flies out into the night!

24 The Gifts from Father Christmas

It is the night before Christmas: the big house is completely silent. The children are in a deep sleep in their little beds.

Suddenly, the loud ringing of bells breaks the silence.

At once, a little pair of bare feet jump out of bed and run to the window; a small face, topped with curly hair, squashes its nose against the freezing glass. Two big eyes look out and, lo and behold, there is a long sleigh, pulled by reindeer and driven by a corpulent and capable Father Christmas. (Yes, it really is Father Christmas!). He jumps down from his sleigh.

With surprising agility for his size, Father Christmas lets himself down the chimney, into the large and silent living-room. His bright red suit has large soot stains here and there, but his face, framed in his great white beard, still beams.

Without delay, he sets to work and soon fills the long bright socks which hang from the fireplace. Then he pulls out all the bigger presents and, in a few moments, they are in position beside the tree.

Hurry! The night is short! Father Christmas disappears quickly back up the chimney.

Once again the bells are heard, and the sleigh vanishes into the dark sky above.

25 The Christmas Lunch

On the first day of Christmas week, the father brought home a huge turkey that he had bought in the market square. On the second day, he brought home two partridges to the mother. On the third day of Christmas week, he brought home three smoked salmon. On the fourth day, the mother received four pounds of butter, and, on the fifth, five bags of flour. On the sixth day of Christmas week, the father brought home six sacks of walnuts, and, on the seventh, he handed the mother seven baskets of mandarins. On Christmas morning, the mother took the huge turkey, the two partridges, the three smoked salmon, the four pounds of butter, the five bags of flour, the six sacks of walnuts, and the seven baskets of mandarins, and prepared a mouth-watering Christmas lunch.

She then set the table with her best plates and decorated it with the little twigs of holly. . . . and, at last, all the family and their friends finally sat down to eat their traditional Christmas lunch.

26 The Patched-Up Boot

Castles, palaces, villas, houses, huts. . . . how many different types of buildings we live in. Yet I, who have been all over the world, can assure you that I have never seen a stranger dwelling-place than the patched-up boot, in which I found a mother living with her children. All the conversion work to make the boot comfortable and homely had been done by a master builder, who was a friend of the family. He had opened up thirteen windows, and built a large balcony.

The children were noisy and a little wild: but in a house like that, how could they be expected to be good?

27 Mr. Seguin's Little Goat

Mr. Seguin had had no luck at all with his goats. He would buy them, rear them with love, but, without fail, one fine day they would run away up the hill, and there meet the wolf.

Now, his latest and much loved little goat had been showing definite signs of unrest for a number of days. Finally, the little goat spoke up: 'Master, please listen to me. You must let me out now, for I will die if I stay tethered in this yard!'

Mr. Seguin did his best to dissuade her: the wolf lived on the hill and all the little goats who had gone there before had perished in his jaws. Even Rinalda, the previous goat, had died in the same way.

'I don't care about Rinalda!' the little goat replied. 'I want to be free!'

And thus it was. That very night the little goat ran away.

How lovely it was to be loose on the hill without a rope round her neck! The day passed and night came. For a moment, the little goat even considered returning to her yard, but the thought of the rope and the enclosure made her feel ill. 'Better to die than live as a prisoner.'

The leaves rustled and the wicked laugh of the wolf was heard. All through the night, the courageous little goat tried to escape. Then, when the dawn finally came, the wolf ate her!

28 The Cobbler and the Watchmaker

Two old friends from school had chosen very different professions. One had become a cobbler and remained poor, although he was happy. The other had become a watchmaker and grown very rich. They remained good friends, however, and often went for walks together in the woods.

On one such walk together, they came across a crowd of gnomes, who were dancing around a pile of coal. The oldest gnome, who was the leader, ordered the two men to fill their pockets with coal. The men were so astonished that they obeyed at once. How surprised they were, when they discovered that the lumps of coal had changed into nuggets of gold. Whereas the cobbler leapt for joy, the watchmaker grew very sad because, if only he had known, he could have carried away a lot more coal.

Thinking about the wasted opportunity, the watchmaker decided to return to the same spot with two large sacks. The gnomes were still there. The scene was repeated. When however, the greedy watchmaker returned home, sacks bulging this time, he found they were full of mere coal. Also, the gold he already possessed had all turned into coal.

He would have been ruined, if his generous friend, the cobbler, had not given him half of his own gold.

29 The Miser and the Stars

There was once a very rich miser. One of his friends, who needed money, asked him for a loan. As they were old friends, the miser could not refuse outright, so he set one condition: 'You can have every ducat you wish to borrow, if you spend the night on top of the tower, completely naked, with nothing whatever to warm you.'

It was the middle of winter, and an icy wind was blowing; yet, because of his great need, the other accepted the condition. He risked freezing to death, but he survived the night.

'Did you see anything?' asked the miser the next morning.

'No, nothing. It was a dark night, and the stars gave very little light.'

'Ah, there were stars?' said the miser. 'Then you used their light to warm yourself and therefore you did not satisfy the condition of the loan!' And he refused to lend the money.

A few days later, the man invited the miser to lunch, but there was nothing on the table.

'Let's go and check,' the host suggested,' if the meat is roasted yet.'

The pot was hanging from the ceiling. 'Idiot!' exclaimed the miser. 'How do you expect the meat to cook up there, so far from the fire?'

'How is it,' replied his friend, 'that you expected the stars to warm me up, when they are much further away?'

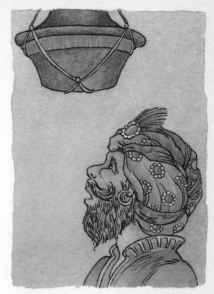

30 The Little Red Shoes

Karen was a little girl who had many good qualities and one serious defect: she was very vain. She would throw a tantrum in order to have things she could see in a shop window; dresses, skirts, shoes, and her poor mother had to buy them for her to get her to stop crying, even though she never had very much money.

The most recent occasion when this occurred had been when Karen had seen a pair of red dancing shoes. Her mother had been obliged to buy them for her, even though it left her without a penny in her pocket. She had come out of the shop with a very worried look on her face, whereas Karen was jumping up and down in delight.

A man with a beard which was half red and half white (he was a devil who had come to the city in search of souls) saw Karen, and cast a spell on her. From that moment, she began to dance and could not stop; the little red shoes moved of their own accord and carried Karen wherever they wished.

The little girl ended up in a deep wood and went on dancing, until the little shoes had worn themselves out completely. She then had to walk home, through the stinging nettles, in her bare feet. Suddenly, Karen woke up: it had all been a horrible dream, but it was sufficient to cure Karen of her selfish vanity.

31 New Year, New Life

This is not a fairy tale, because it really is the last day of the year, and there is, and never will be, a fairy tale as beautiful as our memories of the last year, or as beautiful as our dreams and hopes for the year that is about to begin.

This is the time to bring all the fairy tales to life: frogs that become princes, paupers who become wealthy, greedy and jealous people who, unexpectedly, become generous and kind, wicked men punished, and good men rewarded . . . . New Year, new life! This is the fairy tale that comes to life now, for a whole year!

Contents

The fairy tale of the month: The Christmas Tree
Hans Christian Andersen